THE AUTHORS

Romilly John was born in 1906 in Normandy and grew up at Alderney Manor, near Bournemouth. His family were far from conventional and Romilly received little formal education – he left school at the age of twelve – though he was to go on to study at Cambridge. Shortly after war broke out, he enlisted in the RAF, and later worked briefly as a civil servant. A keen amateur physicist, he has also published a volume of autobiography, *The Seventh Child* 1932, and a collection of poems.

Katherine Tower was born in Dalbeattie, Scotland, and also studied at Cambridge, where she met Romilly; they were married before either had graduated. Her literary career included a long spell as a reviewer for the *Illustrated London News*, but she is best known as a translator of Scandinavian books, notably Odd Nansen's *Day by Day*.

Katherine John died at their home in Hampshire in 1984.

Surreptitious slaughter, and the reasons behind it, have never lost their power to enthrall. Old ladies' wills and wilful old ladies, the sleuth in evening dress, the eccentric village squire and the portly butler (who either saw, or did it) continue to exert their fascination. Some detective stories have worn rather better than others – as a rule, those in which playfulness, assurance and ingenuity are well to the fore.

The Hogarth Crime series, in reviving novels unjustly neglected as well as those by the justly famous, offers a new generation the cream of classic detective fiction from the Golden Age.

DEATH
BY REQUEST

Romilly and
Katherine John

*New Introduction by Patricia Craig
and Mary Cadogan*

THE HOGARTH PRESS
LONDON

Published in 1984 by
The Hogarth Press
40 William IV Street, London WC2N 4DF

First published in Great Britain by Faber and Faber 1933
Hogarth edition offset from original Faber edition
Copyright © Romilly and Katherine John 1933
Introduction copyright © Patricia Craig and Mary Cadogan 1984

ISBN 0 7012 0572 5
ISBN 0 7012 1913 0 Pbk

Printed in Great Britain by
Redwood Burn Ltd,
Trowbridge, Wiltshire

INTRODUCTION

By the early 1930s the conventions governing English detective fiction were well established, and Romilly and Katherine John's solitary detective novel, *Death by Request*, merrily incorporates one after another, in headlong fashion. Here you have a house called Friars Cross, in the village of Wampish, where the night air is dampish, though not damp enough to discourage the son of the house, an ardent lepidopterist, from launching an attack on the moths of Missle Bottom, while another attack, equally murderous, is taking place in the bedroom next to his own.

The corpse, impeccably got up in evening dress in accordance with the usual practice, is soon shown to have had unacknowledged connections with other members of the party. Among the suspects are a socialist manservant and would-be blackmailer, an enigmatic young woman, a potty old woman, the ex-mistress of the dead man's uncle, an inane colonel and a silly girl. A local police inspector, characteristically uninspired, is soon rivalled in his investigations by a debonair young amateur detective who comes whizzing up the drive in 'a fashionable looking two-seater'. Actually, the novel's most noticeable idiosyncrasy is in the lack of an omniscient investigator; it isn't exactly sleuthing that uncovers the solution to the Wampish crime. There is no cheating, however. Readers anxious to work it out for themselves are provided with a suitable array of clues: an exploding geyser, some missing pills, a significant bit of string.

A fair amount of hanky-panky is brought to light in the course of the story, and for maximum impact the authors give us a dry-as-dust narrator, an elderly vicar who recounts the diverting events at Friars Cross in a staid, old-fashioned manner. 'His words struck a curious chill into my heart';

'What new horror was to meet us on the threshold?' – these, and other observations of the sort, recall the artless Edwardian novel in which every step is fateful and every emotion underscored. There is, however, nothing artless about *Death by Request*; among the authors' assets is a notable facility in plot-making, as well as the ability to surprise. The book's ending, it's true, brings to mind an earlier, celebrated work in the genre; but it's only in form that it follows a prototype. As far as style and content are concerned, the John novel is uniquely engaging.

The first thing to go by the board at Friars Cross, as a consequence of the murder, is the cheery atmosphere at the breakfast table; the next is the sedate vicar's tolerance for levity: ' "My dear Matthew!" I remonstrated.' The unfortunate clergyman is then accosted by a succession of more-or-less distraught young women who oblige him to shoulder to the fullest extent his responsibilities as 'a Christian priest' ('. . . to my horror, Miss Grant flung herself at my feet . . .': so it goes on). A highly effective build-up of hilarity and solemnity ensues. The use of a clerical narrator has many advantages for this particular piece of fiction, not least among which is the way it enables the authors to turn out a celebration of hocus-pocus – locked rooms, sinister actions, striking disclosures and all – while remaining essentially poker-faced. *Death by Request* is a splendid example of literary puzzle-setting.

Patricia Craig and Mary Cadogan, London 1983

CHAPTER ONE

Malvern on Murder

It is not without a feeling of horror and reluctance that I take up my pen. The story I have to tell is a painful one; and moreover, I cannot help asking myself if the telling of it is really consistent with my duty as a Christian priest. Is it really serviceable to perpetuate the memory of so much guilt and wretchedness? I am shocked at the thought that my tale may be read by some as a diversion. Yet there is another side to the question, which I cannot bring myself to ignore. The dreadful facts were as I am about to state them; and there is a warning in them, which I alone am fully competent to give. This was the thought in my mind when I undertook the task before me: a task which, as I have said, would appear to me otherwise neither prudent nor holy.

It will be best, perhaps, to begin with that fateful Saturday evening in September, now more than three years ago. On that evening I dined with my old friend Matthew Barry, at his house in the village of Wampish, of which I have been vicar for the past twenty-six years. My acquaintance with Matthew, whom I used sometimes jestingly to call the Squire, is even older than such neighbourhood implies, for we were friends at Oxford, where I knew him as a very fine classical scholar, but inclined to scepticism in religious matters. Had he been without fortune he would, I doubt not, have remained in residence; but at twenty-two he inherited the house at Wampish, together with a small estate. He married young; I knew his wife, a charming young woman, most unaffectedly devout, but unfortunately rather sickly. She died after only four years of marriage, leaving one child, a boy named Edward, wonderfully like her, with the same religious and affectionate heart, and, I am sorry to add, the same delicate constitution. This boy early showed himself attached to me; I am a lonely man, and I was touched by his childish preference. As he grew older, he learnt to count on my interest in all that concerned him, and for some years before the date I have mentioned my visits to Friars Cross had been almost as much on his account as Matthew's.

This particular call was, as it happened, my first outing after a slight attack of rheumatism which had lately confined me to the Vicarage.

There were, I knew, a number of guests in the house. One of them aroused in me a somewhat painful interest; this was Miss Judith Grant, a young woman to whom Edward had lately become engaged. I had seen her before, though never for very long, nor in circumstances which could enable me to form any personal judgment of her character. What I had heard of her was by no means to her credit, and I well knew Edward to be unhappy upon her account: indeed he had almost owned as much to me some days before. As for Matthew, though he felt that interference would be useless, he strongly disapproved the match, and had never disguised his attitude towards it.

About the whole party assembled in the drawing-room before dinner there was, it appeared to me, a certain air of languor. True, they were not long returned from an expedition on horseback, and the weather had been very close. On the other hand, a glance informed me that Edward was in peculiarly depressed spirits, and he seemed to avoid the eye of his betrothed. Miss Grant was, as usual, very elegantly dressed, and her appearance was unquestionably attractive, though I was inclined to think it owed a good deal to cosmetics. She was talking with another of the guests, young Lord Malvern, a recent acquaintance of the family. Rumour asserted that Miss Grant's friendship with him had not always been innocent: but my old friend presumably disbelieved the story, or he would scarcely have asked Lord Malvern to the house when the young lady was already a guest in it.

The other visitors were Phyllis Winter, a pretty and very shy girl of seventeen; Colonel Lawrence, a school friend of Matthew's; and a young woman called Mrs. Fairfax, a widow, as I understood. The two first I had frequently met before, but Mrs. Fairfax was quite a stranger to me. She might have been about twenty-five years of age, and was rather well-looking, but with a somewhat abrupt and reserved manner. I had heard Matthew speak of her intelligence with warm admiration, and felt some curiosity to form my own judgment on this point.

Matthew presently claimed my attention for a new wireless set, which had arrived, as he told me, only the day before. It looked very handsome and efficient, but of course I am no judge of such things.

"We'll give it a hearing after dinner," said Matthew.

"What we *do* need", rejoined old Miss Barry rather acidly—I have forgotten to mention that she was his half-sister and kept house for him—"is a machine for making ice. The heat is distracting. It is most unseasonable. No food can be expected to keep in such weather. I have no objection to wireless machines, or any other harmless pleasure, but necessity should be served first."

Most of us, I think, felt a little embarrassed at this peevish outburst. Miss Barry was a truly devout woman, but a little soured in temper; and she could not well be expected to show great enthusiasm for the purchase, as she was extremely hard of hearing.

"It is, indeed," said I, "uncommonly warm. But we ought not to grumble—it is pleasanter, at any rate, than a wet September."

"Eh?" said Miss Barry. "What do you say?"

I was about to repeat my remark, though feeling rather foolish, when Lord Malvern spared me the necessity by exclaiming:

"Thank God it wasn't to-day I had to go—London must be like hell to-night. Though I dare say it'll be as bad to-morrow."

I felt all the uneasiness at this speech which Lord Malvern might be supposed to feel at having uttered it before one of my calling. Matthew glanced at me, I am afraid satirically, and then said:

"*Must* you go, then? What can you do in town on Sunday?"

"Oh, it's not business—but Jane's expecting me."

Jane was the Hon. Jane Elliston, Lord Elliston's daughter, to whom he was engaged.

At this moment the gong sounded for dinner.

"What about wine?" said Matthew. "Edward, will you bring up the last lot of burgundy—half a dozen bottles? You know the lot I mean?"

"Yes, I think so," said Edward.

"My dear Matthew," I remonstrated, "surely that is rather a large number?"

"We needn't drink it all, but I like to be well on the safe side. Bring them into the dining-room, Edward—we won't wait for you."

We were obliged, however, to wait a few minutes; Edward did not return until some time after we had taken our places, and Matthew said to him, rather sharply, I was sorry to notice:

"Did you bring it up a bottle at a time?"

"No—I'm sorry to have been so long, but I thought I had put the key back last night, and in the end I found it was still in my pocket—and then I couldn't find the wine for a minute or two; I was looking for it on the wrong shelf."

Matthew did not pursue the subject, but I could see he was exasperated. He was not a patient man, and could not make allowance for a little innocent clumsiness, of which poor Edward was sometimes guilty.

I pass over the conversation during dinner, and indeed I did not hear very much of it, for I was placed on one side of Miss Barry, and Lord Malvern, who was her neighbour on the other, rather selfishly and

inconsiderately confined his attentions to Mrs. Fairfax. But the young should not be judged harshly; if
I, an old friend of Miss Barry's, was unkind enough to
find her conversation somewhat irksome, what had I
a right to expect from a spoilt and thoughtless young
man, who was almost a stranger to her? Edward, on
my left, very naturally preferred to talk to Miss Grant
or perhaps was engrossed by her in spite of himself; I
could not hear what they were saying, but Edward
did not appear to have improved in cheerfulness.

After dinner Matthew turned on the wireless; the
first thing we heard was a Schubert symphony, and I
must confess I should have liked very much to listen
to the whole of it; but it was almost immediately
switched off by Lord Malvern, whose chief interest
appeared to be in "getting", as it is called, the greatest
possible number of stations in succession, and who
seemed quite indifferent to what was being broadcast
from them. This amusement is a little tedious to those
not actually absorbed in it; I was not pleased, however, to see it interrupted by the pertinacity of Miss
Grant, who after a number of ineffectual overtures at
last succeeded in attracting Lord Malvern's attention
to herself. Edward made no attempt to join in their
conversation; he sat down by the machine, looking
greatly depressed. The *tête-à-tête*, however, was soon
broken by Colonel Lawrence, who joined himself to
the little group; and presently Miss Grant turned to
Edward, exclaiming with a show of artlessness:

"Just think, Edward—Charles has been to a murder trial! I've always thought it must be terribly
thrilling. Shall we go and see one some day?"

Edward made no reply, but looked at her reproachfully.

"Have you?" said Matthew to Lord Malvern. "What was it like?"

"Made me feel sick—it was a foul cold-blooded sort of business. I left pretty soon. I'd rather be murdered any day."

"Why? Hadn't the fellow done it, do you think?" asked Colonel Lawrence.

"Oh, I dare say he did it; it sounded pretty black. But in any case it struck me as too much of a good thing. If anyone ever murders me I give them leave to let him off."

I was greatly affected by this proof of the young man's really good heart.

"That's all very well," said Mrs. Fairfax, "but they wouldn't really be hanging him for love of you. They hang people to save the lives of potential victims in the future."

"Yes," said the Colonel heartily, "must have a firm hand. Preventive measures. Scares them out of it."

"Not all of them," retorted Matthew.

"Not all of them, of course, but a good many, you may be pretty sure."

"Well, I don't know," said Lord Malvern. "Rather grim to believe England's full of people who would murder you if they weren't afraid of being hanged."

Mrs. Fairfax turned to me with a serious expression.

"What do *you* think of it, Mr. Colchester? Do you approve of hanging people?"

I was taken by surprise; indeed, I could not immediately say anything.

"What I mean is," she went on, "is it consistent, is it Christian? Doesn't it strike you as odd?"

She was wrinkling her forehead, and seemed really anxious. I still hesitated, feeling sadly unequal to my position of spiritual guide.

"Of course," said Miss Grant, "we're supposed to love our enemies." She gave a little giggle.

"Yes," rejoined Colonel Lawrence, "but it's a question of other people's enemies. It's not moral to love them, is it?"

"Oh!" cried Mrs. Fairfax, "if we're all allowed to take our revenge vicariously——"

I could not but see the force of this exclamation.

"Well, Joseph," said Matthew rather drily, "you won't pronounce?"

"The articles of the Church of England——" I was beginning.

"Come, Joseph, as man to man!"

"I confess", I replied, "it is not a question on which I feel at ease. I pray to be spared the necessity of judging."

"After all," said Lord Malvern, "if we're allowed to get rid of other people's enemies, why should the law have all the fun? A fellow's blackmailing a friend of yours—you knock him quietly on the head and bury him in the garden. You'd call that a sound move, Colonel?"

"Very sound morally, perhaps," said Matthew. "Heroic, in fact, considering that you would be hanged. The law at any rate defines what are to be sufficient grounds for murder."

"Yes, but what I mean is, if you did it and got

away with it you needn't let your conscience trouble you."

I disliked the conversation more and more.

"My dear young man," I said, "remember this is a serious question. Remember your own feelings when you saw an unhappy man about to lose his life."

"Yes, but what I mean is, that was disgusting. A decent murder wouldn't be half so bad."

"We're beginning to repeat ourselves," said Mrs. Fairfax. "The fact is, there *is* no answer. Twenty years' imprisonment is disgusting too, and so horribly silly. We'd better turn the wireless on again."

Matthew had been fiddling with it for some time; he now remarked:

"I want to get on to Vienna, but I don't seem to have caught the system quite. See if you can work it, Charles."

Lord Malvern readily joined him at the machine. He succeeded at once in doing what was wanted, and we all listened to the end of a string quartet. When it was finished, Matthew observed:

"I find it impossible to cope with machinery. My inadequacy in that field is almost feminine."

"Come," said Mrs. Fairfax, "don't be so sweeping. There *are* women who understand machines."

"Are there?"

"I do, you know—though I says it as shouldn't. I took an engineering degree at Cambridge."

"*Did* you?" said Lord Malvern. "You never told me that."

"No," replied Mrs. Fairfax, with a look of cold surprise, "why should I?"

"I don't know," said the young man, somewhat abashed. "I thought you might have mentioned it."

"It's unfeminine, as Matthew implied," resumed Mrs. Fairfax less severely, "and so I keep it dark in my more guarded moments."

Colonel Lawrence, who had been chatting in an undertone with Phyllis, now gave a great yawn.

"Never felt so sleepy in my life," he remarked, by way, I imagine, of apology. "Only ten o'clock, too. It's the exercise that does it. 'Pon my soul, I think I must turn in."

"Have a drink first," said Matthew.

Whisky and soda-water, with a trayful of glasses, stood ready upon a side-table.

"Let me see—you're out of it, Joseph—and so am I, thanks to that blasted doctor. Doctors is all swabs. Anne, does your unfeminine streak extend to whisky?"

Mrs. Fairfax replied by a grimace.

"Oh, very well." He poured out three glasses. Edward, after drinking a mouthful, poured most of his away, and filled up his glass with soda-water.

"Dear me," said Matthew, in the slightly ironical tone he was perhaps too apt to assume, "I forgot about you, Edward."

Edward reddened a little and said, "It's all right."

"You ought to take a stiffer glass to-night," said Mrs. Fairfax more kindly. "Remember your dreary midnight stroll."

"What!" I exclaimed. "Are you going mothing to-night, Edward?"

I have not, I think, mentioned that Edward was

passionately fond of mothing. These nocturnal excursions of his were not infrequent; but I had understood from Matthew that Miss Grant disliked his exposing himself to the evening damps, and earlier in the week he had given up an outing of the kind to please her.

"Yes," said he, looking rather confused. "I thought I told you. I promised to take Billy Spinks; he's calling about half-past ten."

Billy Spinks was the butcher's eldest son. There could, I thought, be no doubt that Edward had had a decided quarrel with his betrothed, and that this evening's ramble was a result of it. We conversed a little on the projected expedition; he told me he was going to Missle Bottom, a wooded valley rather more than a mile away, which is apparently—my knowledge of the subject is superficial—a favourite haunt of the creatures.

"Well," I said in conclusion, "I wish you luck, Edward; but be careful not to tire yourself. Remember Dr. Williams advised you to keep early hours."

"Oh, that's all right," he replied. "In any case I shouldn't like to keep Billy out too late."

I respected his scrupulous conscience too much to make any reply to this, though I could not help thinking that Billy, a well-grown, hearty lad of fifteen, was far less likely to be injured by late hours than his companion.

By this time all the younger members of the party, professing, like the Colonel, unusual sleepiness, were beginning to drop off to bed. Miss Barry left us to attend to some household matter, and when Edward, in his turn, went off to collect the implements for his moth-hunt, I found myself alone with my old friend.

"Well," said Matthew, "you're not sleepy, I hope, Joseph? You're staying the night, of course?"

"Yes," I replied, "Miss Barry was so kind as to ask me, and I told her I should stay."

"Good—we can have a game of chess, then, if you feel up to it."

I assured him that I had had the same idea. We are both, as I used jestingly to remark, creatures of nocturnal habits; indeed we both suffer a little from insomnia; and we have had many an absorbing game together in the small hours.

At this moment Edward looked in to announce his departure.

"We'll come as far as the gate with you," said Matthew. "It's very warm—I feel like a breath of air."

It was indeed a lovely night. On parting from Edward we prolonged our stroll in the garden for a little while, and as we walked, Matthew said to me:

"Well, what do you think of Judith now you've seen her again?"

"My dear Matthew," I replied hesitatingly, "a priest is peculiarly bound to the exercise of Christian charity——"

"Quite so," interrupted Matthew with a laugh, "you make yourself perfectly clear. However, I begin to think it may come to nothing after all."

"Indeed!"

"They've had a row, at any rate. Lawrence and I interrupted it in the breakfast-room this morning—

Judith was in tears and Edward's hair standing on end. That's why he's gone off mothing. But of course he may forgive her—he's fool enough for anything."

I was distressed by this language, but I knew from experience that remonstrance would be in vain. We re-entered the house, and settled down in the library for our game of chess.

"I was forgetting about your milk," said Matthew. "Just ring the bell for it, will you? and then Frampton can go to bed."

It is my custom to take a glass of milk and a couple of water biscuits before retiring for the night; and if I sip the milk very gradually while playing, I find that it is of the greatest advantage to my game. I rang, as Matthew had desired me to, and was presently supplied by the man-servant, whom Matthew then dismissed for the night.

A game of chess, carefully thought out on each side, is apt to take a considerable time. Edward came in about twelve o'clock, exchanged a few words with us, and then went off to bed, leaving us still playing. And as Matthew, who at last found himself checkmated, was eager for an immediate revenge, it was at a very late hour indeed that we retired to rest.

CHAPTER TWO

The House Awakened

My friend Matthew, though, as I have said, a
late bird, was habitually an early riser. My
bedroom was next to his; and I heard him moving
about the next morning when the appearance of the
light—for, as usual, I had drawn back the curtains
before getting into bed—informed me that the day
was still in its freshest youth. I glanced at my watch,
which lay on the table beside me; it was a few minutes
after seven. The tree-tops, which I could see from my
recumbent position, looked heavy and quiet, and the
slight haze filming the sky augured a continuance of
the fine weather. A beautiful Sunday morning.

Matthew, whom I supposed to be dressing, was
audible for some time longer in the next room. Then
there came a pause in his moving to and fro; there was
a short silence; and I heard him begin to speak aloud,
with subdued rhythmical intonations, as of one engaged in early morning prayer. Unfortunately, my
knowledge of my old friend's habits forbade this inter-
pretation. It was his unvarying custom to repeat or
read aloud to himself a passage of Homer, or a chorus
from one of the Greek dramatists, before entering on

the duties of the day. The practice had begun as a little piece of undergraduate affectation; but I am convinced that he had long derived sincere comfort from it.

Matthew's devotions, if I may so describe them, being terminated, his door opened, and I heard his footsteps receding along the corridor. I began to think of rising in my turn. I got out of bed, and, approaching the window, leaned out to inhale the fresh morning air. It was certainly a lovely day; the atmosphere seemed impregnated with the delicious stillness. Not a sound was audible, not a foot seemed to have pressed the dim grey dew upon the lawns. I still lingered, feeling almost reluctant to break the spell, when all of a sudden it was shattered to pieces by a frightful crash—a crash from somewhere within the house itself.

I positively jumped at this outrage, as it were, on the quiet morning. Then I became rigid, listening. The noise had evidently proceeded from the west wing; I thought it was followed by a confused sound of feet and voices, but I could not be sure. A few seconds only, I suppose, can have passed in this way; then, quite unmistakably, I heard a female scream.

Hesitating no longer, I threw on my dressing-gown and, without even pausing to find my slippers, hastened in the direction of the tumult. A somewhat intricate length of corridor separated me from the west wing, which was usually reached by another stair, but I was, of course, thoroughly acquainted with the building, and I lost no time. Just at the corner of the west wing I encountered the flying figure of Frampton, who positively threw me against the wall in his hurry and confusion, and would not stop to make any reply to my inquiries. A moment later, however, I found myself in the very centre of commotion. One of the doors in the corridor was open—had been broken in; before it stood my old friend and two women, whom in my agitated state—and partly, no doubt, because they were, like myself, attired in dressing-gowns—I did not immediately recognize as Mrs. Fairfax and Phyllis Winter. The house was suddenly full of the noise of running feet, and just as I drew near I observed another woman—one of the housemaids—hastening up from the opposite direction.

Matthew, on catching sight of me, came hurriedly forward and said:

"Don't *you* make a scene, Joseph. Malvern's been gassed."

"You don't mean——?"

"Stone dead," said Matthew. "Stiff. For God's sake don't *you* make a scene."

He looked very ill; his face was blue. As for me, I could say nothing, but leaned against the wall, momentarily unable to support myself.

Just then the housemaid uttered a loud shriek. The sound seemed to restore Matthew to activity.

"Shut up!" he barked, turning upon her almost ferociously. "Go straight down to your own quarters without another sound, or you may walk out and not come back again. And when you get there, stay there, do you hear? and go about your work. Tell the others the same. And look here," he added as she was about to depart, "you'd better wake Miss Barry. Don't scare her into fits. Tell her there's been an accident. And by the way"—as she was again going—"you can tell the other girl—Violet—I want to speak to her presently." In a hurried undertone, as if talking to himself, he went on: "I know she does these rooms—I've seen her at it."

While this was passing, I had advanced to the doorway and looked in. Lord Malvern's body was lying almost flat on the floor, near the fireplace, with the carpet rucked up under it; he seemed to have been leaning against an armchair just behind, and to have slid gradually down. He was in evening dress, and a glance showed that the bed had not been disturbed since the day before. The window was wide open, but a distinct smell of gas still hung about the room.

I stood gazing in a kind of fascinated horror, barely conscious of the two white-faced and silent girls just at my elbow, when Phyllis unexpectedly glided past me into the room, and, bending down, touched Lord Malvern on the arm. I supposed it was the rigidity of the body that frightened her; she gave a scream, turned her eyes for one moment with a dreadful vacant look on Mrs. Fairfax, and then burst out sobbing and shrieking in the same breath.

"Hysterics next—good God!" said Matthew in the same impatient undertone, unaware, I imagine, of being heard. He seized hold of the shrieking girl and led her, not very gently, out of the room. "Which is her door? Anne, can you do anything to shut her up?"

He and Mrs. Fairfax got her into her bedroom, but

the hysterics seemed to continue. After a moment or two Matthew reappeared in the doorway, exclaiming:

"Where the devil is Susan? Susan could stop her. . . . Thank God!"

"What is the matter, Matthew?" his sister was calling out rather indignantly from the top of the stairs. "Will someone kindly tell me in a sane manner what the matter is?"

"Come in here, will you, Susan? Phyllis is taken ill."

Miss Barry hastened into the bedroom, and after a few hurried words of explanation Matthew and Mrs. Fairfax came out again, leaving her, as I supposed, to tranquillize her young protégée. Just then I heard a footstep behind me, and Colonel Lawrence's voice exclaimed:

"What the devil is the matter, Barry?"

I turned round, and was astonished at beholding the Colonel in full evening dress. He was extremely dishevelled, and had an almost ludicrously self-conscious air.

"Malvern's dead," replied Matthew very shortly. "Gassed."

"Good God!" said the Colonel.

His tone would, on a less tragic occasion, have been really laughable; for, though he was evidently shocked, it betrayed the over-emphasis of one labouring under a social anxiety to display the right feeling. He stepped forward and looked into Lord Malvern's room.

"Good God!" he repeated. "That's an unlucky thing!"

24

"Isn't it?" said Matthew rather drily.

"Who found him?"

"Frampton and I."

The Colonel had taken a step or two into the room.

"Must have happened last night," he remarked after a short silence. "Before he went to bed. And by the way," he added with more excitement, "it's a funny thing—I woke up like this." He indicated his evening clothes. "Sitting in my armchair; must have fallen asleep like that. Now that's a thing I've never done before." He paused, as though becoming aware that he had not paid sufficient attention to the matter in hand. "Not the time to mention it," he concluded hastily.

"Anne," said Matthew, "don't hang about that room—it's still gassy. You'd better go and get dressed. Why the devil haven't the police come?"

"Did you send for them?" I asked.

"I told Frampton to phone for them—and for the doctor. Williams has to get over from Oxon, of course, but the bobby should have been here half an hour ago. Hullo!"

We all started. The door of the room next Lord Malvern's had suddenly opened, and Edward, still in his pyjamas, appeared on the threshold.

I think the others, in the confusion, must have totally forgotten Edward. He had been in my own mind more than once, but I supposed him to have gone for an early morning stroll, as he occasionally though not often did; for it seemed impossible that anyone should be so near what I may describe as the uproar of the morning, and not be awakened by it.

There he stood, however, looking bewildered and still more than half asleep. There was a peculiar silence.

"What's the matter?" he asked at last.

Matthew told him.

"Gassed!" repeated Edward with a vague air. Then he added, in the same bewildered manner: "I thought I smelt gas last night."

"*What!*" exclaimed Matthew furiously. "You *smelt the gas*, and you—— Oh God! and to think that this drivelling idiot——"

He broke off, absolutely choked with rage. Miss Winter's door opened.

"Matthew," said Miss Barry icily, "please do not shout. Do you want to make Phyllis hysterical again?" The door closed.

Edward, like everyone else, had stepped forward to stare at the dead man. The next thing he said was:

"Where's Judith?"

"What the devil does that matter?" retorted Matthew. "Where were you, is more to the purpose —with this din going on outside your door? You slept through it, I suppose?"

"No," said Edward after a slight pause, still vaguely. "I thought I heard something."

Matthew was speechless. Suddenly Mrs. Fairfax spoke.

"You smelt the gas?" she asked Edward in a curious faint voice.

"I don't know. . . . Has nobody told Judith?"

"*Damn* Judith!" exclaimed Matthew, himself, as it seemed to me, on the verge of hysteria. "I want to know——"

Miss Winter's door opened again.

"I am taking Phyllis to my own room. You may shout when we are gone, Matthew, if you *must* shout —for which I do not myself see the necessity."

There was a dead silence under this reiterated rebuke; and Miss Barry presently issued from the room, with Phyllis, still white and trembling, hanging on her arm. They walked away with slow steps down the corridor.

"Well, that's a good move," said Matthew. "It's time we all did the same." He gave something like his usual ironical glance at the half-clad figures round him. "And when we have our naked frailties hid——"

I thought there was a strain of rather ill-timed levity in the quotation, and Mrs. Fairfax's expression seemed to indicate that she felt the same.

"Yes," I agreed, with some reproach in my tone, "we had better go and dress."

"Got to undress first," said the Colonel. "Ha, ha!" He let out an abrupt guffaw, which broke off in the middle, and then, as if to cover his own impropriety, walked hastily away. Matthew and I followed him; Edward had already re-entered his bedroom and shut the door. We had barely turned the corner of the wing, however, when we heard a thud, as of a falling body. One catastrophe seems to pave the way for others; I think we all three felt a dreadful sinking of the heart as we rushed back to see what was amiss. We had not far to seek. Mrs. Fairfax was lying on the floor of Lord Malvern's room, in a dead faint.

Matthew did not, on this occasion, betray the impatience he had shown when Phyllis Winter became hysterical.

"Poor girl," he said, "no wonder. Lawrence, help me to carry her into her room."

"Let me do it," I remonstrated. "Your heart——"

"Confound my heart!"

He and the Colonel lifted her up and laid her on her own bed.

"I suppose we ought to throw water over her," said Matthew rather helplessly. "Why isn't Susan here? Two women in a fit is too many."

Just then, however, Mrs. Fairfax, unaided, began to show signs of returning consciousness. I offered her a glass of water; she drank a little, and then said faintly:

"I shall be all right . . . go away, please."

"Can't we do anything for you?" said Matthew.

"No, thanks. I shall be all right."

"But we ought not to leave you like this," said I.

"Yes, really . . . please go away."

We yielded reluctantly to her insistence. Outside the door, Matthew said:

"I'll send Susan to look after her." And with that we separated.

I was by this time in a state of agitation which made dressing very difficult; my hand actually shook as I picked up the garments. Moreover, my anxiety to be quicker than usual had, as always, the contrary effect. I had not made much progress, and had, indeed, just sat down upon the bed to compose my nerves a little, if possible, before proceeding, when a deafening report, like a pistol shot, shook the entire house.

The House Awakened

I am not, I trust, a man habitually lacking in self-command, but on this occasion I am afraid I screamed. I was not conscious of it at the time, but that is the impression which I find remains with me. My first coherent thought was Edward: could anything have happened to Edward? Half-dressed as I was, I rushed from the room, and the first person I met was Edward himself, also half-dressed, who flew past me, exclaiming in a frightful tone of agony and suspense:

"Judith!"

In my previous horror I had not paused to reflect from what quarter the noise came: I now turned, equally without question, and hurried after my young friend. Almost immediately another sound met our ears. We exchanged glances of dismay.

"Phyllis!" I said. "She's in Miss Barry's room—she must be hysterical again."

"It's next to Judith's," said Edward hoarsely.

He had stopped dead, and was trembling visibly. Extremity of terror seemed to have taken all strength from his limbs; he leaned shakily against the wall, and I really began to fear that he might faint.

"You mustn't come any farther," I said. "Go and lie down, and I'll find out what has happened. Do go, my dear boy."

"No, no," he replied, just able to articulate: and with an obvious effort he hurried on again.

Before we had reached Judith's room, however, we were arrested by a gesticulating group in the geyser bathroom—so called because it contained the only bath worked in this way. The Colonel, still in his evening clothes, and with a purple face, was saying vehemently:

"Never done such a thing in my life, I tell you—can't understand it. Nerves, I suppose. A man's nerves——"

"*Nerves!*" repeated old Miss Barry with bitter sarcasm. "You are aware, Colonel, that there are three other bathrooms in this house?"

"Certainly, but——"

"And you feel obliged to select the geyser bathroom when you are suffering from *nerves*. Really, Colonel, if it were not that I must return at once to that poor child, I should have more to say to you!" And she swept past us with an air of unapproachable resentment.

"Well, Colonel," said Matthew, "you seem to have roused the house again effectually. What's the matter, Edward?"

Edward had sunk down on the bathroom stool, looking as ill as though his worst fears had been realized.

"Do you mean to say", he began faintly, "that it was only the *geyser*?"

"Yes," said the Colonel with a mixture of confusion and alacrity. "I thought I must have a dip—wash off all *this*, you know." Again, this time somewhat inappositely, he pointed to his incongruous evening clothes. "And all of a sudden the damned thing went off. Very sorry, of course—bringing you all here again, and all that. But, you know, really——"

"Where's Judith?" asked Edward, interrupting him.

30

"My dear Edward," said his father, "you had better go and dress. You'll see Judith at breakfast, no doubt. As for you, Lawrence, I think you ought to try another bathroom. As Susan pointed out just now, there are three of them."

He seemed, I thought, to have wonderfully recovered his self-possession. At that moment Mrs. Fairfax came up, fully dressed, but still very pale.

"What's happened?" she asked in a strained voice.

"Only the geyser. The Colonel tried to light it, and he happens to be suffering from nerves; so it exploded and nearly blew his head off. But what about you, Anne? Are you feeling better?"

"Much better, thanks. If that's all, I'll go and have some breakfast."

Matthew took my arm and walked with me back to my own room.

"The doctor should be here any moment," he remarked. "Frampton's a fool, though. I told him to ring up the police at the same time, and he rang up the *Oxon* police—because Williams is in Oxon, I suppose. However, it can't be helped now—the whole gang ought to be here directly."

"I suppose it was necessary to send for the police?"

"Of course it was necessary. It's a confounded nuisance, I agree."

"It was a very odd accident. Poor young man! Was it Frampton who first noticed something wrong?"

"No—I thought I smelt gas in the hall, and Frampton was drifting about looking like a pickpocket, as he always does—thank God he's going!—so I told him to come and help me to locate it. There wasn't much mistaking where it came from. The door was locked on the inside, so we bashed it in—Frampton rushed to open the window while I turned off the gas. It was no use moving him; I thought we'd better not touch him at all for the present." He gave a heavy sigh, and added in a different tone: "Poor Charles!"

We were in my bedroom by this time, and I was engaged in completing my toilet. Matthew sat down, and remained for a few moments plunged in thought.

"I suppose it was time someone said that," he remarked presently. "There seems to have been no time to think it so far. Well, I must be off and have a word with that girl—she seems to be keeping out of my way. It's a queer business—poor Charles! If it had to happen, I wish to God it had happened somewhere else."

With these words he got up and left me.

CHAPTER THREE

How did it happen?

Breakfast at Friars Cross was usually a cheerful and informal meal. Miss Barry did not come down to it; and the other inmates dropped in irregularly, at what hour they pleased. Matthew was always the first; indeed he had almost invariably finished eating before anyone came down to join him, but he was seldom in haste to quit the morning table, and would sit smoking and chatting with his guests till a late hour. The breakfast-room was one of the pleasantest in the house; its windows looked out on the front lawn and the gravel sweep, so that any external comings and goings were easily visible from within, and a feeling of liveliness and animation was added to that of leisured idleness. As a lonely, and—if I may say so without boasting—a hard-working man, I found a peculiar relish in these care-free, social hours, reckoning them, indeed, among the happiest of my life.

But on the morning I am now to describe, what a change was there in the atmosphere of the once cheerful meal! Miss Barry, contrary to her custom, presided. Phyllis Winter was sitting by her, and looked, though no longer much agitated, very weary and depressed; the Colonel had by no means regained his usual poise—a stranger would certainly have suspected him of an uneasy conscience; while neither Edward nor Mrs. Fairfax seemed to me enough recovered to be up at all. I was surprised to observe Miss Grant's continued absence: to be sure, she habitually rose late, but on a morning like this curiosity, if nothing else, ought to have brought her down betimes—it was impossible that she should have heard nothing. My old friend's chair was empty, and the conversation, which he usually led, seemed unable to sustain itself, and was dying away in occasional dejected undertones.

I helped myself to coffee, and sat down next to Edward, almost with the sensation of appearing at a public function: for my entrance had been followed by a general hush, and all eyes were bent on me.

"Where is Matthew?" I inquired, in as natural a manner as I could command. "Has he breakfasted already?"

"No," replied the Colonel, attempting a robust air, "he's talking to Williams—didn't you hear the car?"

I replied in the negative, at the same time glancing involuntarily out of the window. The back of Dr. Williams's Buick was just visible.

"Drove up not five minutes ago. The police are here, too; man from the village—what's his name?—and another man from Oxon. Don't know what they want two for—always the way with those fellows. If a thing's done at all, it's overdone." The Colonel's loud tones sounded rather hollow in the general silence; he seemed to become uncomfortably aware of them himself, and, hastily changing his communicative countenance for one of greater solemnity, added with a shake of the head: "It's a sad business. Poor Malvern! Who would have thought of it yesterday at this time? Such a lively young fellow, too; last man one would have expected such a thing to happen to. Well, well."

I did not, I must admit, perceive the cogency of this reflection; the young man's liveliness could hardly be supposed to render him less susceptible to noxious vapours. I contented myself, however, with agreeing that it was very sad.

"How do you suppose it happened, Mr. Colchester?" asked Mrs. Fairfax. "Has Matthew any idea?"

"I imagine he suspects some carelessness on the part of the maid who does the room. I know he intended to question her."

"Ah, yes," said the Colonel. "Fooling about with the gas fire—turned the gas on by accident."

"But surely", I said, "that cannot be possible in the circumstances. When would she be in the room last?"

"Some time before dinner," said Mrs. Fairfax.

"But Lord Malvern did not retire till after ten. If the gas had been on for several hours——"

"He'd have smelt it!" broke in the Colonel, with the triumphant expression of a rapid thinker. "Bound to have smelt it, if he had a nose at all. So that won't do."

"What do you say?" inquired Miss Barry unexpectedly.

"I was saying", replied the Colonel, raising his voice, "that if the gas had been left on before dinner, poor Malvern would have smelt it."

"The gas was not on before dinner; therefore it could not have been left on."

"No," shouted the Colonel, "that's what I say. He would have smelt it."

"I was not aware", returned Miss Barry, "that there had been any question whether the unfortunate young man had all his faculties."

The Colonel grew very red, and remarked in an undertone to Mrs. Fairfax, who sat next him:

"Bit deaf, you know—doesn't quite follow. Makes conversation a bit awkward sometimes."

"If you wish to say anything about me, Colonel," said Miss Barry pitilessly, "it would be more gentlemanly to raise your voice, or wait till I have left the room."

Colonel Lawrence was now purple.

"No, really," he protested, correcting his former error by a voice of thunder, "I assure you, Miss Barry —upon my word, you know, I didn't mean——"

Miss Barry raised a hand, and said icily:

"Please do not bellow."

This remark was followed by a silence of acute discomfort. Then Mrs. Fairfax began:

"You're quite right, Colonel Lawrence; it couldn't very well have been the maid who turned the gas on. But what about the window? it must have been shut, I suppose?"

"Yes," said I, "it was certainly shut."

"That's a funny thing," said the Colonel, but with a considerably chastened air. "Very funny on a night like last night."

"You mean," said Edward, speaking for the first

36

time, "Violet might have shut the window for some reason while she was doing the room, and forgotten to open it again?"

"Yes, that's what I was thinking of."

"But," objected the Colonel, "Malvern would have opened it. First thing he'd have done. On a hot night like last night, what's more."

"If the curtains were drawn," said Edward, "he might not have noticed that it was shut."

"Well, I suppose that's possible. Though on a night as hot as last night—besides," added the Colonel, interrupting himself eagerly, "you don't see the point, Edward. If the window was shut, and the gas hadn't been turned on, Charles might have had a headache—couldn't have been gassed, you know."

"I imagine", said I, "Edward's theory is that, the window being shut through some carelessness of Violet's, Lord Malvern himself somehow turned the gas on by mistake."

"Well," admitted the Colonel, rather crestfallen, "if you put it that way I dare say it's possible. Sounds a rum business. The window happened to be shut, and Charles happened not to notice it, and then he happened to go and turn the gas on——What about Violet? Does she say it was open?"

"What is all this about Violet?" asked Miss Barry.

It was repeated to her.

"Nonsense! Of course Violet left the window as it should have been. The maids in this house do not go about shutting bedroom windows."

"Not habitually, of course," I ventured to say. "No

one thinks of such a thing. But a mistake of this
kind——"

"Stuff and nonsense!" said Miss Barry. "The girl
gads. If I send her on an errand, I have learnt by
experience that she is sure to gad. Well, I put up
with it. But do you think I should have her in the
house if she left bedroom windows shut?—let alone
shutting them, which is arrant nonsense."

We were all silent.

"May I ask who is responsible for this idea? It was
you, Colonel, I suppose?"

Colonel Lawrence made haste to disclaim the suggestion.

"No, no, I assure you—Matthew's idea, not mine.
I said from the first it was a rum notion."

"I am glad to hear it; and in future, when such
insinuations are made, I shall be obliged if you will
not leave me to find it out by accident. Now I have
no doubt Matthew has been bullying the girl, and
allowing policemen to bully her, and she will be unfit
for her work for the next month or so. Upon my
word, Colonel!" Miss Barry rose and pushed back
her chair. "I suppose I must go and see what can be
done about it. Will you come, Phyllis?"

"No, thank you, aunt," replied Phyllis in a low
voice. "I feel all right now. I think I'll stay and have
some more coffee."

"Just as you please, child." And she swept out of
the room.

"Great character there!" declared Colonel Lawrence in awed tones. "A little hasty sometimes, but
what character!"

How did it happen?

"I didn't know you were actually related to Miss Barry," said Mrs. Fairfax, addressing Phyllis.

"Oh, I'm not. But mother is a great friend of hers, and I call her aunt sometimes—she likes it."

"Very strong attachments," said the Colonel. "An amazing woman."

"Do you really think", said Mrs. Fairfax, "that there's nothing in that window business?"

"My aunt seems sure enough about it," replied Edward. "Of course she may be mistaken all the same."

"But look here," began the Colonel, "if the maid didn't do it, it's a rum thing. I suppose Malvern *might* have turned the gas on by mistake somehow—but hang it all, he couldn't have shut the window by mistake."

For a moment no one made any reply to this.

"You mean", said Mrs. Fairfax, "that he did it on purpose?"

"Suicide!" I exclaimed.

"But surely", said Mrs. Fairfax, "that's too unlikely. Why should he have done it? And even if there was any reason, would you have expected *Charles* to commit suicide?"

"No," said Colonel Lawrence, "it's a rum thing. Still, you never know, you know. But, as you say, who'd have imagined it! Poor young fellow! Money, I suppose. He was hard up, you know—told me so himself."

"But he was engaged to Jane Elliston," said Mrs. Fairfax. "She must have money."

"Quarrelled, perhaps," said the Colonel. "Suppose she jilted him," he continued eagerly. "Lost his girl—no cash—turned the gas on."

"But she didn't jilt him," objected Mrs. Fairfax. "He was meeting her to-day." There were tears in her eyes as she added: "Poor Charles!"

"He may have said so," said Edward. "Perhaps they quarrelled and he didn't want it known."

"Why not?" said the Colonel.

"If he meant to kill himself, he wouldn't want her to be blamed. He may have meant it to look like an accident."

"Don't let us forget", I put in, "that it may have been an accident in reality. We are making a serious charge against the poor young man. I am afraid we are talking unjustifiably."

There was a brief silence.

"Of course," said the Colonel, "it *may* have been an accident. It's an odd thing, though. Window shut, gas turned on—both by accident on the same night."

Another pause.

"But the *door*," said Phyllis in a low and distressed voice. "The door was locked—surely he wouldn't have locked it unless——"

"I see," said Edward. "You think he was making sure no one would interrupt him?"

"Yes, but look here," interposed the Colonel, "if anyone had come along and smelt anything, they wouldn't simply have walked away because the door was locked."

"They might have come before it was bad enough to smell."

40

"They might, of course. By Jove!" exclaimed the Colonel, "I believe there's nothing in it! Don't you remember the other day—I know some of you were there—we were talking about something or other, and Malvern said he'd spent so much of his life in shady places that now he locked his door as often as not from force of habit?"

"Yes," said Edward, "I hadn't thought of that—but I remember he did say so."

"Well, there you are," said the Colonel, "it *must* have been an accident."

This inconsequence was too much for Mrs. Fairfax.

"Nonsense!" she rejoined. "That only proves that it may have been—which was admitted all along. At the same time——"

Just then, however, the door opened, and Miss Grant walked in.

I think her appearance and manner startled us all. She looked fresh, cheerful and composed; her colour was as good—or perhaps I should rather say her toilet was as elaborate—as usual.

"Good morning, everyone," she said airily, though with, I noticed, a somewhat uneasy glance at her betrothed. "Am I fearfully late?" She looked into the coffee-pot. "Empty again! I wish I could contrive not to be *always* the last down—I'm sure Rhoda detests me."

Was it possible, I thought, that she had heard nothing?

She rang the bell, and then sat down in her usual place.

"You all look rather solemn! It really wasn't my

fault this time—nobody woke me up. At least they did really—I think someone must have knocked a table over. Oh, Rhoda, *is* there any more coffee, please? Thanks awfully."

To us who knew, there was something shocking, almost unnatural in her serenity. We looked at each other aghast, all equally reluctant to enlighten her.

"*Why* do you all look so shaken? It was that frightful din, I suppose. I heard it in my bath—it gave me such a fright I nearly drowned myself. What was it? Did the boiler burst?"

"No," I replied, feeling it really necessary to say something, "it was the geyser that exploded."

"Oh! I didn't know anybody used the geyser bathroom." She gave another glance round the table, and added, for the first time with alarm: "What *is* the matter? Was anybody hurt?"

Edward fixed a strange gaze on her.

"Do you mean to say, Judith, you've heard nothing?"

"Edward! What *is* the matter? Do, somebody, tell me what the matter is!"

"It's poor Malvern," said the Colonel at last. "He's had an accident."

"Charles!" she exclaimed. "Was he hurt in the explosion?"

"No," replied the Colonel, after waiting a moment for someone else to speak, "he's been gassed, unfortunately."

Just then the maid came in with the fresh coffee. Miss Grant took no notice, but continued to gaze at

How did it happen?

Colonel Lawrence with a bewildered, almost a stupid expression.

"Gassed!" she repeated in a blank voice.

"Yes—his gas-fire, you know, in his bedroom. It's a sad thing—a very sad thing. Let me pour you out some coffee, Miss Grant. Afraid this has been a shock to you. Shock to us all, naturally. It's a sad business."

Still Miss Grant eyed him stupidly. Then she looked round us all, as though vainly seeking for enlightenment, and said:

"Charles has been gassed!"

"My dear Miss Grant," said I, "as the Colonel says, this must be a great shock to you. Indeed, none of us are quite ourselves yet. Nothing was noticed until about an hour ago; but the gas-fire had been on all night. It is a heavy calamity—we must all feel it so; but——"

"Calamity!" she repeated. "Is he—is he very ill?"

"He's dead," said Colonel Lawrence.

"*Dead!*"

There was a silence.

"But—but how did it happen?"

Another silence.

"Why," said the Colonel, with what I sincerely think he meant as tact, "we don't quite know yet—but of course, as I said, it may have been an accident."

"*May* have been! Then . . . but. . . ." Her voice faltered; she said no more.

"Yes, yes," said the Colonel reassuringly, "we hope it was nothing but an accident."

Miss Grant rose unsteadily to her feet.

"*Oh!*" she said, in a breath like a deep sigh. She

43

gave Edward one look, and burst into a flood of tears.

We were all horror-struck. Edward started up with an exclamation, and at the same moment Miss Grant rushed from the room.

"Dear me!" said Matthew's voice in the doorway. "What does that mean?"

He came in, accompanied by Dr. Williams.

"Stay where you are, Edward; the Inspector wants you in a minute. Williams, you know everyone, I think. What's gone wrong here?"

"Miss Grant had not heard of the accident," said I. "It has upset her a good deal."

"Very natural," said Matthew drily, with a glance at Edward. "I suppose this coffee's cold?"

"No, it came in a few minutes ago."

"Good," said Matthew. "Williams, you like it pretty black? The bacon and eggs will be here presently."

"I feel like breakfast," said Dr. Williams, "I must say. It won't do for me to be long, though."

"Sad business this, Doctor," said the Colonel.

"Very sad—very sad. I hardly knew him, of course; but I should never have thought of his doing such a thing. He seemed a particularly cheerful young fellow. But these things do happen very oddly sometimes; I've known as queer cases before now."

"You think it was suicide?" asked Mrs. Fairfax.

The doctor put down his cup and gave her a look of surprise.

"Why, I'm afraid I was assuming that. I hope my imagination has not run away with me. But really I scarcely see how it could have been an accident; and then the position of the body——"

"You think *that* means suicide?" said Mrs. Fairfax.

"Well, it's an odd position, whatever one may think of it; but he might have sat down like that, just in front of the fire, with an idea of facilitating the process of asphyxiation—and then he would naturally slide forward a bit afterwards. And then, of course, the door was locked. I don't want to pronounce, you understand; it's not my business. But if it wasn't suicide, it certainly looks rather like it."

At that moment the maid brought in the eggs and bacon. When she was gone, Dr. Williams resumed:

"Well, it's a sad business—must have been a nasty shock. But I understand none of you knew him very well?"

"We hadn't known him long," replied Matthew. "But I've known many people longer that I'd rather it had happened to."

This was an uncomfortable speech for his old friends. I imagined Colonel Lawrence was trying not to look as if he felt it so.

"Ah, yes," said the doctor condolingly, between two mouthfuls. "An engaging young man. Yes, yes, it's a sad thing."

"Engaging!" repeated Matthew with unexpected vehemence. "Good God!"

The doctor looked at him in astonishment.

"He was engaged," said Matthew. "He was to have met the girl some time to-day. I suppose I've got to let her know somehow."

"Dear me, how tragic! Yes, I suppose you ought."

"I'd better wire her. It seems a brutal thing to do."

"Why not wire to her father?" I suggested. "Or her mother—her mother is alive, is she not?"

"Yes, I think so. Well, thank God, that's not so bad. I don't know who his relations are exactly, but they'll know. What, are you off already, Doctor?"

"Can't wait, I'm afraid. Don't come out, Barry; I know my way. Well, good-bye, everyone."

He hurried out, and a moment later we heard his engine starting.

"I wish to God the Inspector would go with him. You must all prepare for a cross-examination, I'm afraid; just at present he's hectoring the servants, but it seems we're all to have our turn. And by the way, no one is to leave here without permission; no one was going anyhow, so that's all right."

We all looked a little blank at this announcement.

"Well," said the Colonel, "must obey orders, I suppose—but what the devil is the fuss about?"

"I should ask the Inspector," returned Matthew.

CHAPTER FOUR

Light from the Servants' Hall

"Well, well," said the Colonel, rising, "no use hanging about here all morning. If I'm wanted, Matthew, I'll be in the billiard-room."

The influence of Sunday was, unhappily, little felt at Friars Cross.

Just then a message came from the Inspector: he wished to see Mr. Edward Barry in the library. Edward rose, and followed the Colonel from the room.

"Come for a stroll, Phyllis," said Mrs. Fairfax, getting up in her turn.. "You look a bit seedy still—I think fresh air would be a relief."

Phyllis gave her a doubtful, almost a frightened glance, and seemed to hesitate. Then she replied faintly: "All right."

As the door closed on them, Matthew looked up from his breakfast, and said: "What a house!" Then he returned to his toast and marmalade.

We were both silent. Presently he finished eating, and sat motionless for some time, evidently deep in thought.

I was just about to speak when he exclaimed

abruptly: "Oh God, that wire!" He got up, and, calling over his shoulder: "Wait for me a minute, Joseph!" strode out of the room.

Left alone, I walked to the window and gazed on the intensely quiet scene. Within doors, the day seemed to have grown old in stir and agitation, but the dreaming stillness without at once reminded me that it was still early—I should think scarcely nine o'clock. It was certainly a lovely morning. Not a soul was in sight. Under that deep sky the lawns, the rivulet, the heavy encircling trees had an intent, self-engrossed air, almost bewilderingly alien from the petty turmoil, as it now seemed, within the house. I brooded long and painfully on the strangeness of man's position in the universe; the differences between his own mind and his habitation seemed to me at that moment irreconcilable, a hopeless problem, and the whole of human life trivial and pointless in the comparison. Religion, indeed, teaches us how we should understand it all; but there are moments in every man's experience when religious teaching becomes shadowy and inconclusive, sickening, as it were, before the unanswerable yet inhuman beauty of earth and skies. Such moments are, I have no doubt, wisely sent as a trial of our faith: but they are a severe temptation. I began to think of the poor young man who had died. The creed I receive told me that he had just entered on a fuller existence; yet I could think of him only as one who had that morning ceased to be. And the other members of the household seemed like ants scurrying hither and thither, bewildered and ridiculous, on the scene of some minute catastrophe.

Light from the Servants' Hall

These are no thoughts for a Christian priest upon a Sunday morning. I was relieved when my old friend rejoined me; his entrance—such is the feebleness of mental effort in comparison with the most trivial external force—dispelled my brooding in an instant, and I became once more fully sensible of the importance of human events.

"Well," said Matthew, "I've done that. Let's have a turn in the garden."

I silently accompanied him, and we strolled down a gravel walk in the direction of the orchard. For some time neither spoke. I think he felt it a relief to be alone with me, and to enjoy a short respite from his anxieties.

"It's going to be hot again," he said presently. "What a day! I wish to God I could enjoy it."

We strolled on in silence. When we had reached the orchard, Matthew said: "Let's sit down here."

We seated ourselves accordingly on a rustic bench at the foot of a tree. The day had not yet lost its early freshness, but there was hardly a breath of air, and the ruddy apples hung unstirred among the boughs.

"I don't suppose", said Matthew, "that the Inspector's veto means you can't go home; but you'll stay here a day or two?"

"Certainly, if you would like to have me."

"I'd like to have someone in the house who isn't a hysterical female or a dithering idiot. It seems there's going to be more trouble about this."

"Indeed!" said I with concern. "But what has happened? Has anything more been found out?"

"It's that fool Violet's doing. I chivvied her a bit

about the window; of course she swore she left it open, but how can anyone tell whether she did or not? Then she had hysterics, as you may suppose. She seemed to think something was intended to be done to her, and the sight of the Inspector was the last straw. She positively howled with terror, and said it was cruel, and she ain't done nothing, and she don't know nothing, and her belief is it was that there Frampton that went mad and done it."

I listened to this recital with horror and astonishment.

"But . . . you don't mean . . . you mean she insinuates that the young man was *murdered*?"

"Not insinuates. It appears to be the received opinion in the servants' hall."

"But surely the Inspector does not take it seriously? Why, the door was locked on the inside."

"I suppose someone *might* have slipped in and turned the gas on just before Charles went to bed."

"But gas poisoning is not instantaneous. Surely he would have been bound to smell it almost at once."

"That's true; and it does for the accident theory, I'm afraid."

"Then the unhappy young man must have killed himself. No one could have turned the gas on through a locked door."

"Very true," said Matthew gloomily, "but there may be ways of locking doors from the wrong side. I rather imagine the Inspector thinks so."

I remained silent for a minute, pondering this idea.

"But, my dear Matthew," I exclaimed presently, "the position of the body! If that had happened,

Lord Malvern would have been in bed. Why should he have gone up to his room and sat down fully dressed upon the floor? It appears to me that the doctor's explanation is the only one."

"I put that to the Inspector," returned Matthew, "but he was unimpressed. He said he would like to have a word with Frampton."

"Murder! but it cannot be possible! How does *he* explain the position of the body, in that case?"

"He doesn't. I think he flatters himself that he looks inscrutable, but what he does look is infernally self-satisfied. Some idea he must have, of course, if he'd come out with it. I suppose this is a piece of luck for him."

After a pause he added: "I wish to God there were fewer women in the house. Not that Lawrence is much better; but at least he doesn't swoon and shed tears."

"Murder!" I repeated. "Surely it must be impossible! Why does Violet accuse Frampton?"

"Well, in the first place, he's a socialist, you know."

"My dear Matthew!" I remonstrated. My friend was once more, as it appeared to me, betraying a levity somewhat ill-timed; and moreover, I have myself considerable sympathy with the socialist movement.

"He seems to be in the habit of declaiming against the idle rich, and Charles was worse, of course, on account of his title. And on top of that—I told you about Milly Baker?"

I assented. Milly Baker was the gardener's daughter; they lived in a small thatched cottage just outside the grounds, and Milly came up three or four days a week to do sewing, mending, and some of the lighter household tasks. She was a very pretty girl, good-tempered and obliging, and a general favourite. Some months before—in fact, not long after he was first engaged at Friars Cross—she had begun "walking out" with Frampton, rather to the displeasure of her parents, who doubted his steadiness, and perhaps also his intentions; and less than a week before the period of which I am writing, she was found to be with child. It had been a great blow to her parents, respectable, serious-minded people, in every way superior to their rank in life. Owing to my indisposition I had not seen them since, but I could easily believe what I had heard of their distress. They could have little satisfaction in the prospect of Frampton for a son-in-law, for, though an intelligent servant, he was intemperate in his habits, and actually under notice to leave at the time; I believe Edward had detected him stealing whisky.

"Well," Matthew went on, "we now come to the old-fashioned melodrama. It appears Frampton's latest is that the baby's none of his."

"Matthew!"

"Do you remember when Charles was here a couple of months ago?"

"Certainly I remember it."

"It seems to be a fact that he paid some attention to Milly at that time. They were seen kissing—now, Joseph, don't let your professional feelings get the better of you."

"My dear friend," said I gently, "do you really think this tone is quite appropriate?"

"Well, perhaps I ought to say that Malvern was seen kissing *her*. It got round to Frampton, of course, and it appears they had a row about it—he and the girl, I mean. For some time afterwards he let off socialist maxims with a peculiar zest, and used to hint about what Charles's fate would be in a proper state of things. I heard something about it at the time from Susan, who hears everything."

"But surely you don't mean to suggest——"

"Not at all, it's not *my* theory. Well, Frampton's not popular in the servants' hall; he's considered supercilious. And the other day when he was expounding his philosophy of life someone brought Milly's condition up against him. Frampton apparently grew very hot and denied flatly that it was his doing. I haven't heard the details—I'm not even sure that he mentioned Charles by name; but there was something anyhow about high-born and parasitical seducers——" Here Matthew broke off with a groan. "Lord, what a farce!" he said. "Poor Charles!"

I respected his emotion—was, indeed, rejoiced to see it; for his previous flippancy had pained me.

"Then they gibed at him for allowing a gentleman to steal his girl, and apparently someone hinted that he wasn't really man enough to resent it. Frampton stormed a good deal, but afterwards he subsided into dark suggestions—he was only waiting for an opportunity, and time would show. Really, when things had got to that point I don't blame him. What else could the man say?"

"And the other servants imagine that Lord Malvern's death——"

"Was the vengeance of an honest man. Precisely."

"But surely, Matthew, you yourself don't suppose it possible?"

"Of an honest man, certainly not. But I suppose even dishonest men have their susceptibilities."

"But even supposing him to have had designs upon the young man's life, how is it possible? The position of the body——"

"I told you the Inspector has some notion of his own on that point."

"Then you are seriously inclined to believe Frampton is guilty?"

Matthew rose and began walking up and down.

"I don't know. Frampton's a fishy character—it's a long time since I met a fishier; and by the way, he certainly returns to the scene of the crime. When I took Williams up just now to look at the body, we had a good view of him slinking off in the opposite direction. On the other hand——"

For a moment I waited vainly for him to continue. Then I asked:

"Do you believe what he has been saying about Milly?"

"On its own merits I should call it humbug. It may be an excuse for not marrying the girl now he has got her into trouble, as the saying is. In fact, that appears to me extremely likely. Or he may simply have been goaded into it by zeal for his own character. It's a sound principle not to believe a word Frampton says at any time. But the unfortunate thing is——"

"Yes?" said I.

"The Inspector seems to have made up his mind that *somebody* killed Charles."

We were both silent.

"He may be mistaken," said I at last, "may he not?"

"I hope so," returned Matthew.

"It still appears to me that he *must* be mistaken."

"Quite so; but don't you think it at all possible that he knows best?" He paused for a moment, and stopped dead in front of me. "My dear Joseph, this is a damned, infernal, hellish business. If it was really Frampton who turned that gas on, I should rejoice to wring his neck; but even then I must admit I'd prefer not to see him hung. So would Charles, you may remember."

I could find nothing to reply.

"On the other hand, if it wasn't Frampton—it must have been someone else."

The gloomy significance of his tone appalled me.

"My dear Matthew, don't forget it is still possible that the Inspector is mistaken."

I got up and took his arm. He gave me an intent look and said:

"Do you really think Charles committed suicide?"

I was at something of a loss under the direct question.

"Surely", I replied, "it is at least possible. Dr. Williams himself said——"

"I heard him. But what do *you* think? Do you sincerely believe that he committed suicide?"

"You press me very hard, Matthew. But you must allow that Lord Malvern was a young man of expensive habits. He had never been used to work, and he had never, I suppose, wanted for money. If he found himself at the end of his resources——"

"Stick to the facts. He was engaged to an heiress, and if she *had* quarrelled with him—which she hadn't —there are plenty more."

"But if he was attached to Miss Elliston?"

"Nonsense, Joseph. However, I see you won't pronounce, and I don't blame you. I'm sorry for that girl, by the way."

"Miss Elliston?"

"No, Milly Baker. It'll be her turn next, and we shall have another hysterical woman on our hands."

By this time we had turned and begun to stroll back towards the house. Matthew looked ill and weary; I felt anxious to say something which might comfort him, but scarcely knew how.

"Try not to take it too hardly," I said at length. "These things are all in the hands of Providence."

"Amen," he replied with a fervour that considerably astonished me; for, as I have said, he was not precisely a religious man.

We walked on in silence a little way, and then he began unexpectedly:

"Do you remember Charles last night?"

I looked inquiry, wondering what could be in his mind.

> *How oft when men are at the point of death*
> *Have they been merry! . . .*

Do you know, Joseph, I think I must have been a little in love with that young man."

I could say nothing. We emerged on to the gravel sweep before the house.

"I feel religious this morning," he said, "but there's no time for it. I must go and talk to Susan now. The Inspector may want you, so don't stray too far."

I promised to be within call, and Matthew went upstairs to look for his sister. I glanced into the breakfast-room; it was empty. So was the drawing-room. No one seemed to be about at all. The Colonel, I thought, might still be occupied with billiard practice, and I went to see: the billiard-room also was deserted. Friars Cross had suddenly the appearance of a stricken house, an abode of eeriness and desolation. I found myself strangely wondering if, after this, it would be haunted. It was vain to recall how often, on a fine morning, everyone was out of doors; the knowledge of what had happened filled the atmosphere, and changed the very look of the deserted rooms.

I returned to the breakfast-room, and was attempting to distract my mind by a perusal of the Sunday papers when Rhoda, the parlour-maid, interrupted me.

"If you please, sir, the Inspector would like to see you in the library."

The information was by no means unwelcome; indeed, I felt it a relief. I had a natural curiosity to see the official in charge of the case, and to form my own judgment of his abilities.

Inspector Lockitt was not prepossessing. His features were harsh, his manner that of a man accustomed to command and not disinclined, I thought, to tyrannize. To me, however, he seemed to wish to behave pleasantly. After begging me to sit down, he proceeded:

"Now, Mr. Colchester, I want you, if you please, to give me your own account of what happened this morning. Let me have all the details—everything you can remember."

Accordingly I related to him, in substance, what I have already written here. The Inspector seldom interrupted, and showed no surprise, or indeed interest, at any moment of the narrative. When I had finished he said:

"Thank you, Mr. Colchester. Now what about last night? Will you kindly describe exactly what happened between dinner-time and the time you went to bed?"

Once again I complied. When I came to mention Edward's return from the mothing expedition, the Inspector interrupted me.

"What time would that be, do you know?"

"Really, I cannot be certain; but I should think somewhere about twelve."

"Thank you—go on, if you please."

He made a similar inquiry as to the time Matthew and I had gone up to bed, and once again had to be satisfied with an approximation.

"I heard two o'clock strike, and I think also the half-hour—but I cannot be certain."

"Very natural," said the Inspector heavily. "So it was past two o'clock, and most likely nearer three."

"Exactly."

"You were not intimately acquainted with Lord Malvern?"

"No, very slightly. I saw him once or twice when he was here in the summer, and once before during this visit."

"But as far as you could judge, would you say he was in his usual spirits yesterday?"

"He seemed in excellent spirits. I understand that he was habitually so."

"Ah. . . . Would you say that he drank much?"

"Do you mean last night," I asked, "or as a rule?"

"As a general thing, I mean."

"Why . . . I should not think he could properly be described as abstemious; but I have never heard that he drank to excess."

"I see. Well, Mr. Colchester, I'm much obliged to you. For the present that's all I want to know"

I could not help reflecting, as I left the library, that Inspector Lockitt certainly kept his own counsel. He had not so much as mentioned Frampton throughout the interview, or let fall a word which could have led me to suppose that a possibility worse than suicide was in his mind. For my part I had, of course, said nothing of the disagreement between Edward and Judith, or of the supposed connection between Judith and Lord Malvern in the past.

CHAPTER FIVE

The Colonel's Thunderbolt

It was a long morning. As I sat alone, after my interview with the Inspector, trying to fix my attention on the *Sunday Times*, I could hear through the open window the familiar, yet now strangely alien and indifferent sound of the church bells. They ceased; and the hush that followed was, to my imagination, a counterpart of the hush within the sacred building, where my curate was just then beginning morning worship. Not merely was external nature unmoved by "this great gap of time"; even in the world of human life, the eddies of tragedy died away into smoothness within a few yards from the centre of commotion. As I sat there unoccupied, and thought of the service going on as usual in the little church, I felt an eerie conviction of essential solitude; I felt stranded, as it were, by a spring tide, where no return of ocean would ever reach me. A morbid fancy; for how could I be affected, except momentarily, by what had passed? I glanced at the clock; the minute hand seemed to be moving very slowly, and there were still more than two hours before luncheon. A difficult crossword puzzle might, perhaps, do something to beguile my thoughts. I had just doubled the paper down at the right place, when I was arrested by the sudden pealing of the telephone bell almost at my elbow.

There is always, as it appears to me, something heartless and almost brutal in the sound. I made haste to lift off the receiver.

"Is that Wampish 7?"

"Yes."

"Will you hold on, please?"

I waited a moment. Then a female voice, but quite unlike the first said: "Hullo—is that Friars Cross?"

"Yes."

"I want to speak to Mr. Barry."

It was, I thought, a young voice, but deep and a little husky in tone. I hesitated, feeling it not right that poor Matthew should be harassed, at a time like this, by social calls.

"Ah, yes . . . do you particularly wish to *speak* to him? If you could leave a message——"

"Isn't he in?"

I could not bring myself to reply falsely.

"I believe so—but he is rather preoccupied. If it is not urgent——"

"It *is* urgent!" said the unknown woman, with great emphasis.

"In that case——"

"Wait a minute." There was a pause. "Who are you, please?"

I was surprised, but gave her the required information. Another pause followed; then she said:

"This is Jane Elliston speaking."

"Miss Elliston!" The name startled me; I felt

greatly moved, but, I am afraid, extremely awkward. "I am so sorry, Miss Elliston; of course, if you——"

"I was engaged to Lord Malvern. I want to know what happened, please."

This was an uncomfortable question indeed: and there was no time to consider how much the poor girl ought to be told.

"I am so sorry! But you have heard the sad—the terribly sad news? I understood that Mr. Barry——"

"Yes, he wired. I want to know *how* it happened."

"Why . . . we are not quite sure as yet. The police——"

"The *police*! . . . Wasn't it an accident?"

"Why . . . I trust so, Miss Elliston. I trust and believe that we shall find it was an accident."

"You *trust*. . . . What do they think it was, then?"

I could see no possibility of evasion; and, after all, the truth could not now be long delayed.

"Remember it is mere conjecture. I cannot believe——"

"*What* do they think it was?"

"It is difficult at first to see quite how the accident ——"

"I can't *hear*!" said Miss Elliston in a voice of anguish.

This interruption confused my mind.

"I say they cannot see quite how the accident—if, as I trust——"

"Oh, God!" said Miss Elliston, "I can't *hear*!"

Thus thrown out a second time, I entirely lost my head.

"They are afraid it was his own doing."

In my anxiety to be heard, I communicated this news, I fear, with brutal sharpness. A dead silence followed.

"Miss Elliston!"

There was no answer.

"Are you there, Miss Elliston? My dear Miss Elliston, I entreat you——"

Her voice came again, not, as I had expected, grief-stricken, but tremulous with anger.

"They think it was *suicide*?"

"Miss Elliston, I entreat you to remember it is only a theory. For all I know——"

"I can't hear," she returned, not now in suspense, but as though impatient to silence me. "Do the police think so?"

"Really, I am not sure. If you would like to speak to the Inspector——"

"I—— No," she returned suddenly, "I'm coming down. Will you tell Mr. Barry?"

"But, my dear Miss Elliston——"

"Good-bye."

I addressed her again, but there was no answer. Clearly she had rung off.

I feared my anxiety to spare Matthew had turned out unfortunately: his views on the proposed advent of yet another distressed woman were easily to be imagined. Had I managed the conversation with more skill, I might perhaps have succeeded in averting it, but such thoughts were now too late. I did my best, therefore, not to give way to them, and returned to my task.

Crossword puzzles have in my experience no slight

power of absorbing, even if they do not satisfy, the mind. Mine served to shorten the rest of the forenoon though it left me rather more dejected than before. At last the luncheon bell rang, and I obeyed its summons with relief, tempered, however, by discomfort, at the thought of the news I should have to break to my old friend.

The morning meal had been, as I said, far from cheerful, but a deeper gloom was now visible on every countenance. I could not doubt that the suspicion of murder had become generally known. Miss Barry sat at the head of the table without opening her lips, and indeed for some time very little was said by anyone. Frampton did not appear, though it was customary for him to wait at luncheon. In a pause between two courses, and, I almost believe, with an idea of making conversation, the Colonel rather tactlessly remarked on this.

"As a suspect," said Matthew, "he feels above such menial tasks."

The observation was not calculated to increase our gaiety.

"Oh—an—ought to have thought," said Colonel Lawrence.

"No, no," returned Matthew, "no one expects it of you."

The Colonel, I think, did not understand, but everyone else looked uncomfortable. There was a profound silence.

"I heard the telephone bell," said Matthew at last. "Who was it?"

"Miss Elliston," I was obliged to reply.

Matthew laid down his knife and fork, and looked at me.

"What did you say to her?"

I evaded this question.

"She is in great distress, naturally. I am afraid she seems to have an idea of coming down to Friars Cross."

"Oh God!" said Matthew in a voice of uncontrollable despair.

"Matthew," rapped out his sister, speaking for the first time, " it is bad enough to have an inspector in the house; you might at least spare us profane language."

Matthew said nothing, and, to my surprise, asked no more about Miss Elliston. Under the disaster of the morning he seemed to have lost all resilience, and to seek refuge, as far as possible, in a passive waiting on events. The others, however, actually revived a little, and the Colonel said with an air of improved spirits:

"Ah, poor girl—nasty shock to her, no doubt. I dare say she was very fond of him."

"I wonder what she's like," said Miss Grant curiously.

"I've met her, I think," said Mrs. Fairfax.

Every eye was turned to her with interest.

"Have you?" asked Miss Grant. "What *is* she like?"

"Very handsome," said Mrs. Fairfax. "Rather muscular."

"She hunts a lot, doesn't she?"

"Four times a week, I should imagine."

"May I ask if the young lady is dark?" I asked involuntarily.

Mrs. Fairfax looked surprised.

"Yes, she is dark—but why?"

"Really, I don't know," I replied, somewhat confused. "I am afraid it was an idle question. But from her voice on the telephone—rather a deep voice for a young lady—I had somehow formed the impression that she was dark."

"Oh, but you can't tell by that," said Miss Grant. "Think of Greta Garbo."

"Fair women", said Matthew, "are not called handsome as a rule."

"Very fond of poor Malvern, was she?" asked the Colonel, who seemed to derive satisfaction from this idea.

"I dare say she was—I don't know her at all."

"Must have been, poor girl, no doubt. And you say she's coming down here, Colchester?"

"I understood so."

"Wants to see him again, I dare say. Well, it's quite natural, poor girl. Seemed badly cut up, did she?"

"She seemed in a good deal of distress."

"Poor thing!" said Miss Grant, conscientiously rather than with feeling. Then with a sincerer accent she added: "Why, she was meeting him to-day!"

"She will," said Matthew.

There was an abashed, almost a remorseful silence. Miss Barry rose.

Coffee was always served in the drawing-room, and the change of place proved, on this occasion, a relief. Miss Barry, on leaving the table, had gone immediately upstairs, and when the coffee came in Matthew said:

"Will you pour out, Anne?"

Mrs. Fairfax complied. The Colonel, walking about the room cup in hand, presently began:

"Well, no need to hang about now, I suppose? Lockitt's seen everyone?"

Matthew assented.

"Born fool," said the Colonel "—that is, if you ask me."

"Is he?" said Mrs. Fairfax.

"Told him what an odd thing happened to me this morning—well, it cropped up, you know——"

"Quite so," said Matthew.

"Well, and what do you suppose he asked me?"

No one professed to have the least idea.

"Asked me how much I drank last night! Confound his impudence! Seemed to think I was too drunk to go to bed."

"Perhaps", said Matthew, "he thought you were still drunk this morning, when you blew the geyser up."

The Colonel, to my surprise, did not appear to resent this.

"Ha ha!" he ejaculated. "I've been thinking about that, you know. My belief is there's something the matter with the thing. You ought to get a man to look at it."

"You think that would do it good?"

"Colonel," said Mrs. Fairfax, "some more coffee?"

"Ah—well, yes, thanks, I will. Yes, two lumps. Thank you."

67

"Mr. Barry," said Phyllis Winter timidly, "why doesn't aunt come down? Isn't she well?"

"Yes, yes, it's only the domestic problem. The Inspector's been turning Malvern's bedroom upside-down, and she can't keep her mind off it."

"Has he?" said Miss Grant in a faint voice. "What . . . what for?"

"Hunting for clues, doubtless. Don't you know it's always done?"

"Oh, yes, of course," returned Miss Grant, with an effort at vivacity, "how stupid of me!" Then with increased agitation, which she seemed unable to repress: "What sort of clues?"

"Oh, letters from the criminal, I imagine, outlining his plot—or any little thing of that sort. What's the matter?"

This was addressed, not to Miss Grant, but to Colonel Lawrence, who had just struck his forehead with a dramatic air.

"By Jove!" he ejaculated. "Never gave it a thought till this moment."

"Gave what a thought?"

"It's an odd thing, now I come to think of it— damned odd! Upon my soul," said the Colonel with growing excitement, "I shouldn't wonder if it's the very thing that fellow's after!"

"Do, Colonel," entreated Mrs. Fairfax, "be less enigmatic."

"Well, you know, two or three days ago—can't be sure just when offhand—poor Malvern gave me some papers to hang on to for him. Don't know what they were, of course—good-sized envelope—might have been letters, or something of that kind. Said he was always losing things—asked me to hang on to them till he went up to town. Poor Malvern!" said the Colonel parenthetically. "Can't have had the least idea!"

"And . . . and you've still got them?"

Miss Grant's voice shook. She was clutching the arm of her chair as though in a death-grip.

"Yes—locked them up in my trunk. Malvern's notion. Said he'd lost the key of his suit-case, or he wouldn't bother me."

There was a short silence. Colonel Lawrence was entirely wrapped up in his discovery, but everyone else, I think, looked at Miss Grant.

"Lawrence," said Matthew in a curious voice, "don't you realize that you ought to be telling all this to the Inspector? Don't you realize that before us you ought to shut up like a clam?"

"Nonsense," said the Colonel, rather disconcerted, however. "No harm in mentioning it. I'll go straight up now and dig them out. Well, what do you think?" he added, unable to tear himself away without some assurance that his disclosure was appreciated. "May throw some light, eh? I shouldn't wonder if it's the very thing the police are hunting for."

"In that case", said Mrs. Fairfax, "the Inspector may be annoyed that you didn't mention it earlier."

"Tut, tut—a man can't think of everything at once. Better see him now, though, and be done with it. Where is he, Matthew?"

"I don't know—try the library. If he's not there, you'd better ask the housekeeper."

"Colonel!" said Miss Grant, almost inaudibly.

The Colonel paused with his hand on the door-handle.

"Don't go just yet. I want to speak to you."

The Colonel took a step back into the room. With a visible effort Miss Grant rose; but her knees seemed to fail beneath her, and almost immediately she sank back into her chair.

"You're not well," said Edward, in a low, strained voice. After a moment's apparent hesitation he crossed the room and sat down close by her.

"Yes, quite well . . . I only——" She made a second attempt to rise, and then, covering her face with one hand, burst into tears.

For a moment no one spoke. Then Colonel Lawrence said uneasily:

"Great shock—very natural. All of us a bit knocked up. Well, Miss Grant, any time you feel up to it, I shall be honoured—honoured and delighted. Must see the Inspector now, though, I'm afraid."

He backed once again towards the door.

"Colonel!" said Miss Grant in a choked voice.

He stopped again, looking more and more uncomfortable.

"You mustn't go—I——" Sobs interrupted her for a moment. "Those are my letters. I assure you they are. Oh, *won't* you give them back to me?"

She broke down altogether, and wept bitterly.

No one moved a muscle; there was no sound in the room except her sobs. I glanced at Edward; he had become very pale, but his face was rigid, empty of expression. The Colonel, on the other hand, stood transfixed in ludicrous uncertainty. It was evident that he had not the least idea what course this extremely awkward situation demanded of him. For almost a minute, I should think, the scene prolonged itself; no one spoke, and Judith Grant wept audibly. At last Matthew said in a bitter undertone:

"Well, well."

Miss Grant looked up at this. The Colonel's immobility, and perhaps also his manner, seemed to give her hope.

"You *will* give me them? They're only a few letters —letters of mine; I promise you they are. You won't let the Inspector see them?"

Colonel Lawrence was now red with embarrassment; he glanced round the room furtively, as though for a hint of what he ought to say. Miss Grant sobbed again. It seemed to impel him into speech.

"Well, really," he began, stammering a little, "in that case—as I have your word, Miss Grant—'pon my soul, I can't see that it's his business."

"Oh, Colonel——"

"*No!*" said Mrs. Fairfax.

The interruption startled us all.

"Eh?" stammered the Colonel in bewilderment.

Mrs. Fairfax got up and leaned on the table-edge facing him.

"You're not really going to suppress those letters, Colonel Lawrence?"

"Suppress! . . . No, no, nonsense—nothing of the kind. But as Miss Grant says they belong to her——"

"That doesn't matter, Colonel. Don't you see we're *all* mixed up in this? What are our private

71

affairs to the Inspector? If the letters have nothing to do with this, he won't blazon them abroad; but unless he sees them——" She paused, and then added in a low voice, but with unmistakable finality: "Colonel Lawrence, if you *do* suppress them I shall tell him so."

There was a silence of consternation. Then Miss Grant uttered an inarticulate little cry, and collapsed with her head upon her arms.

"Lawrence," said Matthew rather wearily, "hadn't you better go?"

"On my soul, Miss Grant—Oh God!" said the Colonel, and bolted—I can use no other expression—from the room.

"Well, Anne," said Matthew, in the same curious tone of bitterness, "is that all right?"

"I'm sorry," said Mrs. Fairfax. "I'm sorry, Judith. It's not that I want to—Oh God!" And she, in her turn, burst suddenly into tears.

Matthew groaned—with rage, as I judged from the intonation. Edward, white-lipped, rose and began pacing up and down. I looked from one to the other, feeling that I ought to say something, yet completely at a loss.

CHAPTER SIX

Confession

Mrs. Fairfax got up and left the room. No one made any comment on her departure; but almost immediately Matthew turned to Miss Grant and asked with suppressed vehemence:

"Why the devil did you let him keep them?"

She gave him a dumb look of terror and misery, but could not answer. For a moment Edward seemed about to intervene; then with, apparently, an abrupt change of feeling, he turned from her, and went out with hasty steps. As he did so, Miss Grant made a wretched gesture of appeal, and her lips moved; but no sound came from them, and as her lover was not looking at her he saw nothing.

Matthew suddenly took hold of my arm.

"Come out of this!" he ejaculated.

Almost with reluctance, for it seemed a cruel desertion, I complied. We went out, leaving Miss Grant still huddled in her chair, and Phyllis Winter, pale, motionless and silent, in her remote corner.

Matthew continued to hold my arm, and led me, without speaking, out on to the lawn before the house. Then his grip relaxed, and he said meaningly:

73

"A Pleasant Sunday Afternoon!"

His tone made me uncomfortable.

"It's very hot," I replied, conscious instantaneously of my own feebleness.

Matthew did not seem to hear.

"If that girl had had the sense to get hold of Lawrence quietly, we'd have heard no more about the letters." He paused for a moment, and then added: "I begin to think she'll suit Edward after all."

"Matthew! I entreat you, if only for my sake——"

"Nonsense, Joseph." He walked on a few paces, his eyes bent on the smooth-shaven turf. "I wish to Heaven I could clear the house of them!"

"Of Edward and Miss Grant?" I inquired, startled.

"Of the whole gang. I thought at least Anne had some sense."

"My dear Matthew, after all we have no right to blame her. We must acknowledge ourselves rebuked by her attitude. Doubtless it is our first duty to conceal nothing which may tend to throw light on this most unfortunate affair."

"Nonsense: what have Judith's amours got to do with it?"

I winced at the unkind levity of the expression; but my old friend was evidently not himself, and I forbore to remonstrate.

"But", I suggested, "do not forget that Mrs. Fairfax is an unprotected young woman. Until these suspicions are cleared up, it is only natural she should feel uneasy."

"Why? *She's* not involved in them."

"No, no, of course not—I had no idea of implying such a thing. But at a moment like this——"

"Anne's not the kind of girl to get into a panic about nothing. She may be a fool, but she's not utterly invertebrate."

"Then, as I said, surely it can only have been public spirit——"

"Public spirit! When did you know a woman who had any? It's the usual thing, I've no doubt—jealousy and curiosity. I dare say she was in love with him herself. No doubt she detests Judith for that reason."

It seemed to me that he was jumping wildly to most improbable conclusions. I had not observed in Mrs. Fairfax any symptoms of attachment to Lord Malvern, and I could not help thinking that my friend's own affection for the poor young man led him to view the conduct and probable feelings of both young women in a false light.

"My dear Matthew," I said earnestly, "it is unfair to suggest such things. You are not well—this morning's dreadful business has been too much for you."

He made no answer.

"After all, are we not both giving way to unreasonable apprehensions? Try to look at it more calmly. What foundation is there for the shocking report that has been spread abroad? You imagine Inspector Lockitt has some idea of his own; but after all, the locked door, and the position of the body—— Really, Matthew, I do not see how they can possibly be explained away."

Matthew heard me out, but did not appear to derive much comfort from my reasoning. He was by nature, as I knew, of a somewhat desponding turn of mind, prone to fear the worst, and to anticipate evils. We took another turn or two on the lawn without speaking; then he remarked:

"Well, there's nothing to be done. It's strange to think Charles was alive yesterday." He stood still, and, grasping my arm again, added with increased excitement: "Joseph, when I think back into yesterday this whole morning seems incredible. I wish to God I could wake up from it."

"My dear friend," I replied with great compassion, "in the true glimpses given us from time to time, does not our entire life reveal itself as a kind of dream? These terrible changes in it have nothing permanent. At the worst, by God's mercy, we can say to ourselves: 'This also shall pass away.'"

Matthew listened to me, as he had done in the morning, with unusual patience, but he made no answer. I did not venture to say more. Presently Matthew broke the silence, exclaiming:

"Well, well—at any rate loafing is no use. If anyone wants me, I'll be in the study."

"Surely you are not going to work this afternoon?"

"Why not? I shall get through the day."

I could not approve it, but it would, perhaps, have been heartless to object; for, after all, nothing was so likely to take my friend's mind from other things. He was engaged on a work to be entitled "Theology and Morals in the Greek Drama", and to this employment he gave, with almost unbroken regularity, three or four hours every day. He could not endure the slightest disturbance when thus occupied, and did not choose to monopolize the library; therefore, some two years before, he had caused the small dressing-room which opened from his bedroom to be new-furnished with a desk, an armchair, and such books as he required. The tiny chamber was hardly more spacious than a monastic cell, but from its use it was now invariably called the study.

Left alone, I did not, it may be supposed, lack food for thought. Yet the afternoon, as it dragged its leisurely course, made somehow a different impression from the morning. It seemed, in my solitude, profoundly ordinary. Wrapped in their still, warm, rather hazy atmosphere, the lawns and gardens, which earlier in the day had expressed a cruel indifference to human woe, now seemed a calm embodied refutation of anything abnormal within their sphere of influence. All around me was, in fact, so irresistible an assertion of the commonplace that the dreamlike feeling I had spoken of returned more potently; I was half charmed into toying with the fancy that nothing had happened after all. The mere idea, however, was accompanied by such a sense of relief, such a wonderful lightening of the spirits, as instantly shattered its own force, and gave way, not only to a full consciousness of the real state of things, but to a torrent of vague fears and apprehensions, more acute than any I had before experienced. Matthew, I thought, had been wise to seek refuge in employment; for in a pause like this it became unhealthy to think or be alone, and external nature, no matter what its aspect, seemed to nourish the disease.

I had been straying aimlessly about the grounds,

meanwhile, to indulge my reverie, but at this point I turned back, intending to re-enter the house by a side door. Just as I reached the door, however, to my astonishment it was thrown violently open, and Miss Grant, rushing out to meet me, clutched me with both hands, and gasped out:

"Oh, Mr. Colchester!"

I was dumb with amazement. In the same frantic manner she continued:

"What shall I do? Oh, Mr. Colchester, tell me what I ought to do!"

I was more shocked and startled than ever by this adjuration. Had the light-minded, unhappy girl resolved to confide in *me*? Did she, perhaps, hope to induce me to mediate between her and Edward?

"Miss Grant," I said, "I must really beg you to compose yourself. If there is anything you wish to say to me——"

"Oh," she returned with a sob. "I know you hate me—everyone in this house hates me now. Even Edward——" A burst of tears finished the sentence.

"Miss Grant," I replied somewhat sternly, "you have no right to make these accusations against any of us. As for Edward, if he is displeased with you, I fear I must ask your own conscience whether it is without reason."

"Oh, Mr. Colchester, don't—don't talk like that to me! Oh, *what* shall I do? I've nobody to go to now."

"Well, well," I said, "if you have anything to say, you must at least realize that this is not the place for it. Come indoors, and then, if you wish it, I shall be prepared to listen to you."

I drew her into the house, and opened the nearest door, which chanced to be that of the billiard-room. The room was empty. I led her to a chair, and then, having first closed the door, myself sat down.

"Oh, Mr. Colchester, tell me what I ought to do! Oh, I'm so miserable!—I *am* so miserable! I know it's all my fault. And I've no one to go to now that poor Charles is dead. Oh, poor Charles! how could anyone have *m—mur*—dered him!"

I could not contain my indignation at this outburst, so unbecoming in itself, and before me, a clergyman and Edward's friend, so peculiarly unbecoming.

"Really, Miss Grant," I said, rising, "I am afraid you have mistaken your audience. You have evidently nothing to say which it can be necessary that I should listen to. I beg you to excuse me."

I was about to quit the room when, to my horror, Miss Grant flung herself at my feet, and, seizing my hand, ejaculated:

"Oh, don't go! It isn't that—it isn't about Charles. At least—Oh, you don't understand! Oh, Mr. Colchester, you *can't* leave me!"

I raised her, not without difficulty, and made her sit down again.

"Very well," I said, "I will hear what you have to say; but on condition, Miss Grant, that you make some effort to control yourself. Try to check your tears; they will only exhaust you, and can do no good."

"Yes, I know I look awful," she replied with strange inconsequence and levity, dabbing her eyes, "but oh, what does that matter now?" And at the idea, apparently, that her own beauty was now un-important, she began to weep again.

Something childish and, if I may venture to use such a word, innocent in her folly, began to soften me a little, almost against my judgment.

"Come, come," I said with less harshness, "you must not give way in this manner. Be composed, and explain what it is you want with me."

"Yes, yes, I will—but oh, Mr. Colchester, don't be too hard on me! I—before I met Edward—really before I'd ever seen Edward at all—— Oh!" she ex-claimed suddenly, with an air of collapse, "oh, what shall I do? I don't believe I dare tell you."

"Is it about Lord Malvern?" I asked with a return of displeasure.

"Yes—no—it wasn't *Charles*! I know people used to say that Lord Malvern and I—and I suppose—but oh, Mr. Colchester, it wasn't Charles!"

"I fear I do not understand you, Miss Grant. You mean to say——"

"It was the *other* Lord Malvern—Charles's uncle. You know he died last year."

I got up hastily.

"Do you mean", I said, "that between you and the late Lord Malvern——?"

"Y-yes," replied Miss Grant, nodding, with a con-fused, anxious glance at me.

I began pacing up and down the room.

"And Edward knew nothing of this? You did not tell him?"

"Oh, Mr. Colchester, how could I? He knew no-thing about it, but afterwards he thought that

Charles—I met Charles several times when—— And Edward knew I used to know him. I know a lot of people said that Charles and I—but it wasn't true, Mr. Colchester. There was never any truth in it at all—never!"

She made this assertion with great eagerness, and seemed to think that it was almost a complete vindication of her character. I could see she was relieved at having got through the first part of her story; but as I said nothing, she asked with a return of anxiety:

"Oh, Mr. Colchester, are you very angry with me?"

"It is not for me to judge you," I said at last, "but —you would have let Edward marry you in ignorance of this?"

"Y-yes—but oh, how could I have told him? He mightn't have wanted to marry me at all."

Her moral feelings seemed entirely undeveloped— so entirely that it was difficult to know what to say to her. I was in this uncertainty when she gave way all at once to a fresh burst of grief.

"And how could I ever have expected this? It's all my fault—and poor Charles—and it was nothing but an awful, terrible mistake!"

"*What* was a mistake, Miss Grant? What do you mean?"

"Oh, if I had only told Edward after all! If he had only known! It's all my fault, and he won't even speak to me, and I've *no one* to go to now poor Charles is dead——!" She sobbed convulsively, more in fright, it seemed, than grief.

"Miss Grant," I said with the firmness she so clearly needed, "will you tell me at once whatever

you mean to tell? If you mean that all this is in some
way connected with Lord Malvern's death, will you
please explain the connection? Unless you can come
to the point, I shall begin to think that your distress
is nothing but hysteria."

"I will—I will come to the point," she exclaimed.
"But I wish you would be kinder to me!"

The piteous tone of this appeal, and the utterly
woebegone look accompanying it, again softened me.

"My poor girl," I said, "God knows I have no in-
clination to be otherwise. But these outbursts only
harm yourself, and I cannot give advice or comfort
until you have told me what the matter is."

"No," she agreed in a subdued voice, "no—of
course. But oh, it's so awful—it's *so* awful. It was
those letters Colonel Lawrence had."

"Yes," I said a little impatiently, "of course, I supposed that. But", I added with a sudden recollection,
"you have just declared that there was nothing between you and Lord Malvern."

"There wasn't—the letters weren't *that*. They
weren't letters from me—it was that awful Frampton!"

"Frampton!"

"Yes—I got the first one about a week ago. It was
full of awful hints about me and Lord Malvern, and
threatening to tell Edward all about it. And it wasn't
signed or anything, but it said I should hear again
before long, and I'd better get my answer ready. I
didn't know what to do—I was *so* frightened! Of
course I knew it must be blackmail, and I know all
about that—you have to go on paying and paying,

and it's no use, however much you pay you can't get rid of them. And yet I was so terrified of Edward getting to know. I didn't know *what* to do—and so I decided to ask Charles."

"What!" I exclaimed. "You applied to *Lord Malvern*?"

"Yes, why not? Charles knew already—about me and his uncle, I mean—so of course he was the first person I thought of. And—oh, dear, you didn't know Charles! he was *such* a darling! So I showed him the letter, and he looked fearfully surprised, and then he began to laugh."

"He *laughed*?" I repeated in astonishment.

"Yes, and I thought it was awful of him—I couldn't think why he was being so horrid. And then he said: 'What a blockhead the poor fellow is!' And then *I* was surprised, because it sounded as if he knew who wrote it; and I asked him if he did. And he said: 'Yes, he's tried his hand on me already.' I couldn't think what he meant, and then he told me it was Frampton. He'd had a letter just like mine a day or two before, trying to blackmail him about that girl Milly—saying he'd been making love to her, and threatening to write to Jane Elliston. Charles seemed to think it was a joke. And he said: 'Don't worry—if he bothers you again I'll deal with him.' I asked what he was going to do, and he said he'd kept Frampton's letter to him, and if Frampton showed any sign of telling Edward he'd have him prosecuted for blackmail. I didn't see what good that would do if it all came out, but Charles said the threat would be enough, and there was no need for me to worry. And he seemed so cheerful that

I felt almost all right again. I felt it was sure to be all right while he was there. And now he's *dead*," she concluded in a burst of tears, "and it's all my fault. Oh, Mr. Colchester!"

For a moment I was silent, trying to arrange this narrative in my own mind.

"But this letter you received," I said at last, "did it seem as though it might be referring to the supposed connection between you and *young* Lord Malvern? Or——"

"Oh no—I wouldn't have minded that, because of course it wasn't true. Or at any rate, it wouldn't have worried me so very much."

"You mean to say that Frampton was really in possession of the facts?"

"Yes—I don't know how he knew, but he knew somehow. He said——" She checked herself and blushed deeply—"he said things that showed he knew."

"And he wrote to you again?"

"Yes—the next day but one. He said I was to meet him after dinner in the orchard, and bring my reply with me. And I was rather frightened again, but I showed that letter to Charles too. And he said: 'All right, I'll settle him.' And oh, I forgot to say that I'd given him the other letter; I thought I ought to tear it up, but Charles said it might be useful. He said: 'See how lucky it is I kept mine.' He didn't seem in a rage with Frampton at all; he just laughed about it."

"Did he speak to Frampton?"

"Oh, yes—he went that night instead of me. I saw him when he came in—I could see at once it was all right. He told me afterwards he'd given Frampton the most awful fright. And he said he'd keep both my letters just in case he wanted them, though the one Frampton had written to him was the most useful one. Because he didn't seem to mind who knew about him and Milly, and he'd told Frampton that—so he wouldn't have minded prosecuting him, even if it meant everybody finding out. All the same, I was rather frightened at my letters being kept, because I thought how awful it would be if Edward somehow saw them—and I told Charles to be sure and keep them safe. You know he was always losing things. But he said he'd take good care of that, because if Frampton could manage to get back the one to *him*, he might think it safe to begin on me again."

"But", said I, "why did Frampton *write* at all? He was in the same house with you. Why should he have written letters that might be used against him?"

"I couldn't think—but Charles said he thought it was more diplomatic—I mean that Frampton did, you know. They weren't written; they were all in printed capitals, and Charles said he must have thought that if anything went wrong no one would be able to prove he did it. Charles seemed almost to *like* Frampton for blackmailing us. It seemed to give him a kind of friendly feeling somehow. But he used to laugh awfully at the way he'd done it. He said Frampton was a neat hand at his job, but that every other part of his brain seemed to have gone solid."

"Well," said I, "and is that the whole story?"

"Oh, no, no! oh dear, that's just where the awful, *awful* part begins! I thought it was all over, and I was feeling quite all right again—or only feeling a bit frightened now and then, before I went to sleep, or when I thought of Edward perhaps seeing the letters somehow—and then yesterday morning—— Oh, Mr. Colchester!"

"You really must not allow yourself to break down again. Tell me quietly what happened."

"Oh, Mr. Colchester, he wrote to Edward after all!"

"Frampton wrote to Edward! You mean he actually told him——"

"I don't know what he said—but oh, I'm afraid he must have told him everything! At least, not everything—oh, if he only had! But he can't have told him it wasn't Charles, because——" She uttered a wail of such intense, hopeless misery that the hardest heart must have been moved by it.

"My poor girl! But you must go on—you must not keep me in suspense. I entreat you to tell me at once what happened next."

"I saw the letter as soon as I came down in the morning. You know Edward's always late, and I was earlier than usual, and there it was on the sideboard —it was the first thing I saw. I knew what it was at once, because it was just like the others: oh, I felt so awful! I thought for a minute I was going to faint. And I would have taken it, but I didn't dare because Mr. Barry and Anne must both have seen it, and then afterwards I wished I had. I felt so *awful*, Mr. Colchester! I had to sit there and pretend nothing had happened, and all the time I was looking at it and waiting for Edward to come down. And when he did come down, and opened it, I almost expected him to say something right out; but he didn't even look at me, and I was *terrified*. I couldn't think what he might do, he looked so queer. And after breakfast I waited about to be alone with him, because I felt I couldn't bear the suspense a minute longer; I felt I *must* know what he knew, and what he was going to do about it."

"It was then you quarrelled?" said I, remembering what Matthew had told me.

"Edward asked me——" She broke off and blushed as she had done once before. "He asked me something that showed Frampton must have told him, and I didn't know *what* I had better say—I cried."

"Did he seem aware that it was not *this* Lord Malvern who——"

"Oh, no—he still thought it was Charles. And I told him over and over again that Charles had never been anything to me—I swore he never had, because that was true, you know. But he didn't believe me, and I was longing to see what was in the letter, to know exactly what Frampton had said; and perhaps Edward might have shown it to me, but somebody came in—and Edward would hardly speak to me again the whole day. I was afraid he would never speak to me again. All day I kept hoping and hoping for him to say something, and all the time I had to pretend to be enjoying myself, as if nothing was the matter. And I wanted to speak to Charles, and ask him what I could possibly do now—Charles was *so* comforting!—but I didn't get a chance the entire day. Oh, Mr. Colchester, it was so awful! I thought I should never manage to live through it. But *now*—if things could *only* go back and be no worse than that, I should almost think it was heaven!"

She wailed out the last sentence with an utter abandonment to despair, a naive, childish self-pity which forbade reproaches.

"When I came down this morning," she continued with some return of the eagerness which had accompanied all her pouring-out of trouble, "when I heard the awful news, I could think of nothing but Edward's face over that letter. And then I felt so *awful* about having behaved like that—cried, I mean, before everyone. But I couldn't help it at the time, I *couldn't* help it! And afterwards no one seemed to be suspecting anything, and after that they thought Frampton did it; and I began to think perhaps he *might* have done it, for revenge or something——"

"*What*!" I exclaimed. "You don't mean—you cannot possibly mean that you thought *Edward*——?"

She sobbed bitterly.

"What *could* I think? I knew it was all my fault—it wasn't poor Edward—it was my doing really. I almost wished he had done it to me instead—I did wish it. Oh, *how* I wish I was dead, and not poor Charles!"

"Do you mean to say, girl, that you *still* imagine ——"

"Oh, *don't* talk to me like that! I prayed and prayed that it mightn't have been him, and I *prayed* that those letters might never turn up, in case they might suspect him. And then the Colonel—I knew at once it must be those. And Inspector Lockitt sent for me—and I could *see* he thought Edward had done it."

I said nothing, but my face, I think, must have alarmed her.

"Oh, *don't* look at me like that—I can't bear it! He asked me thousands of questions, and I told him Edward knew it wasn't Charles. I thought that was the best thing to say. And then he asked me how *I* knew that, and I remembered I hadn't told him about *Edward's* letter, and I got all muddled, and could only say I didn't know. And then afterwards I tried to invent a reason, and he didn't believe me—I could see he didn't. But he only said I could go. Oh, Mr. Colchester, I'm *so* miserable! I know I said all the wrong things, and Charles is dead, and Edward won't even speak to me, and there's *nobody* for me to go to!"

I laid my hand upon hers—it was impossible to do less for such wretchedness—but I still made no answer. She lifted her head, and fixed an appealing, abject gaze on me.

"I know you don't like me—but there seemed to be no one now but you. I didn't dare go to Mr. Barry. And I knew you were fond of poor Edward—and so I thought—— Oh, say something to comfort me! Tell me what I ought to do!"

It was like the appeal of a child to an infallible grown-up.

"How can I do that, my poor girl? I pity you; I try not to think hardly of you. But what has happened cannot be comforted away. We must all prepare to face the consequences of it, everyone else as well as you. Remember you are not the only, not even the chief sufferer, and try to bear this with more fortitude. My poor child!"

The words, or some of them, may appear rather unfeeling, but I think my tone was not so. She clung to my hand, and seemed quieter, and even grateful.

"But", I said after a pause, "is the case really as you imagine? Are you quite *certain* they suspect Edward?"

Miss Grant nodded; she perhaps would not trust herself to speak.

"And do you, of all the world——"

"What's that?" ejaculated Miss Grant suddenly, with the breathlessness of shaken nerves. Not waiting for a reply, she rushed to the farther window, which looked out on to the drive.

The noise that had startled her was the hum of an approaching car. Remembering Miss Elliston, I followed her to the window, though more slowly, and was in time to see a fashionable-looking two-seater draw up before the house. A glance convinced me that it was indeed Miss Elliston who drove it, but she was not alone. Beside her was sitting a dark young man with no hat on.

CHAPTER SEVEN

An Uninvited Guest

Miss Grant appeared fascinated by the new ar-
rivals, and had fixed Miss Elliston with a look
of intense—I fear I can only call it curiosity. But as
they approached the front door she seemed to experience a change of feeling, and shrank back into the
room as though to avoid their observation.

"Oh, Mr. Colchester, I can't face her!" Then with
sudden horror in her voice: "Oh, do you think he's a
man from Scotland Yard?"

My own glimpse of him had suggested quite a
different idea.

"He is Miss Elliston's brother, more probably."

"But she hasn't one—that's why she'll be so rich.
I'm *sure* he's a man from Scotland Yard! Oh, Mr.
Colchester, *do* find out who he is! I know the Inspector will try and persuade him Edward did it. Oh, do
get him to say that it was really suicide!"

"Miss Grant, you must not upset yourself about
nothing. If he is not Miss Elliston's brother, he is
probably a friend of hers—a cousin, perhaps. He does
not look in the least like an official."

"But you will go and find out who he is? Oh, do
go, Mr. Colchester! I *can't* face them!"

"But what will you do? In this state you are not fit to be alone."

"Oh, yes—I'll go upstairs and tidy myself; I know I look *too* awful. I'll be all right, really I will. Only promise you'll go and find out who he is."

Partly to soothe her, I gave her the required assurance. Miss Grant ran hurriedly upstairs, and I entered the drawing-room, into which I supposed the visitors must have been shown. This proved to be the case; they were in conversation with Miss Barry, who had evidently just come downstairs to receive them.

A second look would have strengthened my idea that they were brother and sister, had I not been told it was impossible. They were both tall and dark, with an air of breeding and of somewhat paralysing reserve. Miss Elliston was, as rumour had asserted, very handsome; but her face now wore a look at once stony and impatient, as though, in the concentration of her feelings, she had scarcely a thought to spare for what was immediately about her. Despite all my anxiety, I found time to wonder at Lord Malvern's having engaged himself to a young woman whose temperament appeared so entirely unlike his own.

On my entrance, Miss Barry performed the necessary introductions, presenting the young man as Mr. Nicholas Hatton, but without any account of him beyond his name. Almost immediately she said, glancing at Miss Elliston:

"Perhaps you will have the goodness to excuse us for a short time."

Accordingly the two women quitted the room, and I found myself alone with Mr. Nicholas Hatton. I am

apt to be somewhat intimidated by the young intel-
lectuals of the present day; Mr. Hatton struck me as
being almost certainly a member of that class, and
the situation was, besides, ill adapted for small talk.
I felt, therefore, considerably at a loss. But after an
obligatory remark or two about the weather, an idea
struck me.

"Excuse me," I said, "but is it possible that you are
related to an old Oxford friend of mine? I was
intimately acquainted with a young man of your
name."

"I should think it was my father," said Mr. Hatton.

Further inquiry put this beyond a doubt, and I
then ventured to ask the young man if he were also
related to Miss Elliston.

"No. She wanted me to come down and look into
this business."

I gave a start of surprise.

"You don't mean that you are connected with
Scotland Yard?"

"No," said the young man calmly, "I'm not a
policeman. I privately detect."

"Of course, of course—I ought to have guessed that.
You must allow me to apologize for the mistake."

"Not at all," said Mr. Hatton.

"It is natural that Miss Elliston should be particularly anxious to have this sad business cleared up.
You may suppose it has been a great shock to all of us."

Mr. Hatton appeared to acquiesce. Then he said
interrogatively:

"Miss Barry's a connection of the Malverns?"

This again took me by surprise, for though I was

aware of the fact it had not hitherto occurred to me. The relationship, through Miss Barry's mother, was a distant one, and had led to no intercourse for many years.

"You didn't know?" Mr. Hatton asked politely.

"I did know, but I had entirely forgotten the circumstance. Of course Lord Malvern was not staying here on that footing."

"No? Jane seems to think he was."

This fact, which Mr. Hatton communicated without apparent interest, seemed to me distinctly odd, but his serene air discouraged me from saying so. I replied: "Indeed!"

The conversation, though languid, appeared likely to attain great length, when Mr. Hatton suddenly observed:

"I ought to look in on the Inspector. Where is he, do you know?"

I told him he would probably find Inspector Lockitt in the library, and described its situation.

"Thank you," said Mr. Hatton. "Do excuse me." And he was gone in a moment.

I am unwilling to form judgments hastily, but I could not help doubting whether the young man was likely to be as useful as Miss Elliston supposed. He seemed to be a personal friend, which would no doubt prejudice her in his favour. It struck me as most likely that he had private means, and had taken up this pursuit as an animating pastime, though little animation appeared, so far, to have resulted from it. I could not understand why Miss Elliston should have trusted the inquiry to an amateur, even though he were a friend, rather than to an official detective from Scotland Yard; possibly, however, she had been misled by detective fiction, in which, as far as I can learn, the police force is often underestimated.

It was not long before Miss Barry and Miss Elliston returned, and almost immediately afterwards tea was brought in. This reassembled most of the house-party, though Matthew, Edward and Miss Grant did not appear; but the presence of Miss Elliston, who had been weeping, checked all freedom of talk, and seemed to create a kind of solitude. I think most of us escaped from the tea-table with relief. Yet on this interminable day each meal wore at least the aspect of an occupation, an exit from long, unappropriated hours in which there seemed nothing to be done: I found myself almost instantly wishing it were nearer dinner-time. Meanwhile, it was only too likely that Miss Grant was waiting for me, yet I could not bring myself to see her again quite so soon. My news of Mr. Hatton was almost certain to strike her as disastrous, and a scene of agitation would follow which my nerves quailed at in advance. Besides, her image revived thoughts of Edward, now intolerably painful to me. I resolved to take the first opportunity of ascertaining Mr. Hatton's theory, supposing, that is, he had begun to form one, and through him to learn, if possible, what the Inspector really thought. Until then, I would not dismiss the hope that Miss Grant had been exaggerating, and with this in view I found it safest to avert my thoughts as far as possible from the whole subject.

But there was another distressed girl who, it

occurred to me, might well be in need of comfort and support. Matthew had said that the police intended to question Milly Baker. To a self-respecting lower-class family like hers, such an inquisition, I thought, must be dreadful; Inspector Lockitt's manner was not reassuring, and Milly herself was young, ignorant and with child. Several times throughout the day I had thought anxiously of her. I now made up my mind to stroll as far as the Bakers' cottage, look in, and say a tranquillizing word or two if I saw occasion.

I was not many yards from the house when there were steps behind me, and turning round I was surprised to see Mr. Hatton once more.

"You're going for a stroll?" he asked.

"I thought of going to see the Bakers. Perhaps you have heard of them by now?"

"Yes, I'm going there myself," said Mr. Hatton easily.

I was considerably taken aback by this announcement.

"To be quite frank with you," I said, "my idea was that Inspector Lockitt had probably frightened the poor girl earlier in the day, and I thought a visit from me——"

"I see," he replied, "very sound. It's lucky I met you."

"You intend to cross-examine her?"

"I might as well get it over, though I don't suppose I shall find much out there. It'll be an excellent thing to have you as a shock-absorber."

"You do not object to my presence, then?"

"Not at all—as I say, it's a good thing."

"I suppose", was my next question, "you have heard the greater part of the story by this time?"

"I know all the Inspector knows, and thinks he knows. In fact my business down here is really over."

"What!" I exclaimed in irrepressible amazement.

"Yes, I'm engaged, you know, to prove that Lord Malvern didn't kill himself, and that seems to me quite a clear thing. But as I *am* here, and Miss Barry has asked me to stay, I'd rather like to make a job of it."

I was astonished to find him so communicative. It confirmed me in the idea that his present occupation was not serious, but it offered an opening too welcome to be overlooked.

"You think", I inquired, "that it was an accident after all? I hope you think so."

"Out of the question," said Mr. Hatton. "He was murdered."

"What!" I said, "have *you* also reached that conclusion—and so very rapidly? Mr. Hatton, I cannot understand it. The door of the room was locked; the gas cannot have been turned on beforehand, or Lord Malvern would have smelt it. The position of the body seems to me absolute proof that it could not have been turned on later, when he was asleep."

"Apart from the locked door," Mr. Hatton murmured.

"Exactly—even if, as I have heard suggested, the door might have been locked afterwards from the other side. Yet, in spite of all this, the Inspector believes that he was murdered—and before you have been in the house two hours, you say the same. Certainly, either of you should be a far better judge of such things than I am; yet I confess I am utterly bewildered. How is it possible—how is it physically possible that he can have died as you suggest?"

Mr. Hatton seemed to think a minute. Then he said:

"Would you rather know at once?"

I looked at him in surprise.

"I mean, you are prepared to give up the idea of an accident? I'm afraid you must sooner or later."

"Mr. Hatton," I returned, "your manner—forgive me for saying so, I am an old man—your manner is so considerate that I am sure you have very bad news. I entreat you not to keep me waiting for it."

"Very well. In the first place, there are no finger-prints—except of course Mr. Barry's—on the gas-tap."

I could only stare at him.

"On the other hand, the gas-pipe comes through the wall from Edward Barry's room. As you know, they both used to have open fireplaces. Where it comes through, there's a gap in the bricks filled up with plaster. Well, a chunk of that plaster's quite loose, and it was the first thing the Inspector noticed. It had evidently been disturbed not long ago. One would only have to take out some of that, and turn the gas on quite comfortably through the wall—not by hand, but with a poker or anything of that sort. In fact, it seems clear enough that that's what happened—— only. . . ."

I struggled for breath a moment, and then said:

"You mean—it was done from *Edward's room?*"

"I'm pretty sure of it."

"But Edward was out all the evening—he was out till after twelve! Someone must have entered his

room while he was away. It must have been meant
to throw suspicion on him."

The young man shook his head.

"Lord Malvern went to bed at ten o'clock, didn't
he? and Edward Barry was in the house till half-past
ten at least. It's admitted that he was away for nearly
two hours after that—the Inspector's gone into the
mothing business very thoroughly; but then the doctor
will have it that the gas was turned on early in the
night. He can't be certain; but he says *almost* certainly
not *after* twelve, and the earlier the likelier. And remember, Edward Barry admitted he smelt gas at
twelve."

"And surely that proves that he can have had
nothing to do with it?"

"The Inspector thinks it was his artfulness. Nothing in the whole business has damaged him as
much as that."

"But the body!" I cried. "The position of the body!"

"Yes," he answered unexpectedly, "I wish I knew
why the carpet was rucked up like *that*. . . . Look here,
shall we put Milly Baker off for half an hour? I was
intending to speak to you."

Though more and more astonished by a frankness his
exterior had done so little to suggest, I agreed eagerly.

"Then let's sit down somewhere."

I led him to the orchard, and we sat down where
Matthew and I had sat earlier in the day. Then, instead of enlightening me further, Mr. Hatton said:

"Will you give me your account of last night and
this morning?"

I could not refuse, but in my impatience I made the

narrative as concise as possible. Mr. Hatton was not, apparently, dissatisfied; he forbore to interrupt, and, when I had finished, said:

"Yes, nothing new. So that only three people had any whisky, and of those, Edward had none to speak of. That leaves Lord Malvern and the Colonel."

"Yes, but how can that possibly affect the case? They were not intoxicated, Mr. Hatton. The Inspector appears to have suggested it, but I can assure you it was not so."

"No," said Mr. Hatton, almost absently. Then after a pause: "Edward Barry takes pills to make him sleep?"

I gave a violent start at these words.

"Pills which contain morphine. He never exceeds, I suppose?"

"No, no—but I *entreat* you to be more explicit. Do you mean to imply——"

"Well, there are a number missing," said Mr. Hatton. There was a brief silence. I felt dizzy.

"He got a new bottle from the chemist on Thursday, and he has somehow managed to get rid of five pills which ought to be still there. Of course they were accessible; I mean he didn't lock them up. Still, taken with everything else it's unfortunate."

"You mean that they—you mean the whisky was *drugged* last night?"

"Of course it was. To suggest that they were both too drunk to go to bed is sheer nonsense, when they weren't drunk at all downstairs. They may have been tired, and no doubt the whisky was a soporific, but in the drowsiest condition one can take one's clothes off.

And if they were drugged, it was the whisky: it was
the only thing nobody else had. The only question is
what was put into it. Unfortunately, Edward Barry's
pills are highly soluble."

"But if it *was* so—you admit anyone might have
taken them!"

"There we come to the motive, I'm afraid."

"Mr. Hatton," I said earnestly, "you do not know
Edward. He is incapable of this horrid crime. Surely,
even his attachment to Miss Grant makes it impossible. He would not, in a cooler moment—I mean at
any time after the first shock—repose complete faith
in such charges against her, on the sole evidence of
anonymous letters—blackmailing letters?"

"Ah," said Mr. Hatton, "you know what was in
them?"

I was a little taken aback.

"Why, yes—after her last interview with the Inspector—just before you arrived—Miss Grant confided the whole story to me. She was greatly
agitated; and I should judge her to be a young woman who must confide in someone. As a friend of
Edward's, perhaps also on account of my calling, I
was selected."

"Yes." Mr. Hatton gave his usual calm assent.
"What did she tell you exactly?"

I hesitated.

"We know the worst," said Mr. Hatton. "It can
do no harm."

Thus urged, I repeated the substance of Miss
Grant's story.

"You heard more than the police did," he said

afterwards. "She didn't tell *them* that Edward had been written to."

I must have looked very blank at this reminder, for he went on hastily:

"It came out, of course. Several people noticed all those letters; they were bound to. Wampish postmark, block capitals—nothing could be more ostentatious in a quiet way. And as we have the first three, the inference about the last was obvious. It seems to have vanished, though, which is exceedingly unlucky. She did tell the Inspector that Edward knew about the *other* Lord Malvern; but as she justly says, he didn't believe her. I think it may have been evident from the letter, all the same."

"You think so? It appeared to me a strange story; in fact, I could not help wondering if there had actually been another Lord Malvern in the case. May she not have invented that with a confused idea of weakening the suspicion against Edward?"

Mr. Hatton shook his head.

"No; if she'd merely had an affair with Charles, I dare say she could have faced Edward's hearing of it. But the letters make it quite clear that she was *kept*; kept pretty handsomely. That was what she was so afraid Edward would find out."

I gazed at the young man with horror.

"Charles had no money till last year; it was as much as he could do to keep himself in any comfort. And besides that, the dates are wrong. The letters don't mention Lord Malvern more specifically, but they make it clear enough that it wasn't Charles."

"Wretched girl!" I exclaimed with undisguised bitterness and indignation.

"Oh, she didn't mean much harm. She's been unfortunate, you know. But as it is, Edward Barry is in difficulties."

There was a silence.

"Excuse me," I said at last, "under all these dreadful revelations my head is not clear. But I cannot yet see that murder must necessarily have been committed. Even if a drug was used, as you believe, may not that consist with the theory of suicide? Lord Malvern may have been anxious to obviate all possible suffering."

"He might have taken a drug himself for that reason, but he would hardly have drugged Colonel Lawrence. Doping the whisky was a furtive, troublesome business. He could have dissolved the pills afterwards in a glass of water with no trouble at all."

I was again silent.

"It was murder: I'm afraid you must assume that."

"And do *you* think—have *you* made up your mind that it was Edward's doing?"

I spoke bitterly; but the young man said without resentment:

"Not at all. He *could* have done it; and almost anyone else in the house could have done it too. His room was entirely accessible from half-past ten to twelve. He isn't even the only person who had a motive for doing it. But I won't deny that he's Inspector Lockitt's favourite."

I groaned.

"You, Mr. Colchester, are more or less out of it

from the beginning; you didn't know Charles. And as you confirm each other's alibis, you and Mr. Barry are in it or out of it together. But anyone else in the house may have done it, and Edward Barry was the obvious person to incriminate, even if he *was* innocent; he was known to be jealous of Charles. That's the situation from my point of view. And I think you might be useful to Edward, if he *is* innocent."

"How is that?" I asked eagerly.

"You get confided in. There's no temptation for anyone to confide much to Inspector Lockitt, either officially or personally, and I think you may hear other things that don't reach him. You can see that the more is heard the better for Edward, if he didn't do it; and it seems to me there are one or two clams in this house. The Inspector, as I say, has unfortunately put his money on Edward already, but I haven't, and I'm willing to consider any other suspect that can be produced. Will you do what you can for me?"

"You mean that if I should happen to hear anything——"

"Let me know it if you can."

I reflected a moment.

"Very well—anything I may hear, and can honourably repeat to you, I will. With me, Edward's innocence is beyond question, so that I cannot see any possibility of his being injured by such openness. Mr. Hatton, all this has been a great shock to me; but at the same time I am very grateful to you for having told me so much. It is terrible to go about in ignorance."

"Well," said Mr. Hatton rising, "what about Milly Baker?"

"Certainly, if you wish it." I also rose, and we set off again in the direction of the Bakers' cottage.

"I hope", I remarked on the way, "you do not think Milly is likely to get into trouble over this?"

"No—she knew nothing about the blackmailing, it seems. Frampton is a master mind, and scorns accomplices. I'm told the girl's character, as they say, is excellent?"

"Excellent; and her parents are very industrious, self-respecting people. This must all be dreadful to them."

"Do you suppose Frampton had any ground for his insinuations against Charles?"

"I should think it unlikely—but of course I cannot say. Matthew is inclined to think he was not even sincere in making them. He imagines Frampton may have seized on that as an excuse for evading his obligations to Milly."

"And decided on blackmail as an afterthought. Well, it's quite plausible; and in that case he wouldn't be likely to confide in her. Anyhow an accomplice—and a young female accomplice—would increase the danger. Milly, of course, says it's Frampton's baby, which may not be true, but at any rate seems to show that she's concerned for her reputation, and not mercenary."

"Unless", I suggested, "she was afraid of injuring Frampton if she told the truth."

"But she's apparently insisted it was Frampton's all along, which would be absurd policy for a blackmailer. Well, we'll see."

We had reached the Bakers' cottage by this time, and I knocked at the door.

CHAPTER EIGHT

A Talk with Milly

By a piece of unexpected good fortune, Milly was alone in the house. Her mother, she explained to us, had just gone off to church, and her father was doing a bit of gardening: did either of us wish to speak to him? She could fetch him in a moment.

"No, no," I replied, "we came to see *you*, Milly. This gentleman is Mr. Hatton. He is a friend of Miss Elliston's—the young lady poor Lord Malvern was engaged to be married to."

Milly looked rather frightened, I thought, on hearing this; but Mr. Hatton's detached manner, disconcerting to one of his own class, seemed, curiously enough, to reassure her. She made a shy acknowledgment of the introduction, and then said:

"Won't you sit down, please?"

We did so, when I had induced Milly to do the same. She looked from one to the other of us, not without some apprehension.

"I have been feeling anxious about you, Milly—I called, in the first place, to inquire after you. This terrible business, I fear, must have been a shock to you all."

"Oh, yes, Mr. Colchester—terrible! Father and mother——"

She broke off in some distress; I was afraid she would shed tears.

"Of course," I hastened to say, "of course—they cannot but feel it. I know you must all have felt it very much; but I am glad to find Mr. and Mrs. Baker can exert themselves, and to see you, Milly, looking better than I had expected."

"Thank you, Mr. Colchester—it's very kind of you. I'm quite well, thank you."

"Inspector Lockitt was here this morning, I believe?"

"Yes, Mr. Colchester," she replied, with another frightened look. Mr. Hatton, who had been observing her in silence, now asked:

"He's not been here again?"

"No, sir, only this morning."

She looked perplexed and anxious, but I had at once caught his meaning: in that case, she did not yet know about the letters. The distressing communication rested, evidently, with me. In a way, of course, I was glad to spare her the Inspector's blunter methods, yet I felt the task to be an awkward one.

"Then I am afraid, Milly," said I, "we have bad news for you. Do not be alarmed—it is nothing which concerns you directly, or can get you into any trouble; but you will be sorry and shocked to hear it, I am afraid."

"Oh, Mr. Colchester," she exclaimed, "what is it? Has anything more happened?"

"Something more has been found out, unfortunately, since the Inspector was here. As I said, it does not concern you directly—not in any way which need frighten you at all. It is about Frampton."

"Oh, Mr. Colchester, not—— They haven't found out that he did it? Oh, Mr. Colchester, it can't really have been him?"

"No, no, Milly—I trust not. But you know what Frampton believed, or pretended to believe, about your own relations with poor Lord Malvern?"

Milly blushed crimson.

"Yes, Mr. Colchester—but it wasn't true. The Inspector doesn't think it was true, does he, Mr. Colchester?"

"I really cannot say; I hope not, Milly. But I am sorry to have to tell you that Frampton——"

I paused, in some doubt how to express what must come next.

"Yes, Mr. Colchester?" Milly was gazing at me wide-eyed, and half breathless with suspense.

"I am sorry to say that Frampton actually wrote a letter to Lord Malvern repeating his accusation, and threatening to tell Miss Elliston unless he were given money to be silent."

"Oh, Mr. Colchester!"

"You know that that is a serious offence, Milly? You have heard of blackmail?"

"Oh, Mr. Colchester!" exclaimed Milly, with a catch in her breath. "Will he—will he be sent to prison?"

"I am afraid it is possible. You see, Milly, it has not been his only offence of the kind."

Milly looked thoroughly frightened, and began to cry.

"Do not let yourself give way, my child; you must be brave, and listen to what I have to say. Frampton thought he had found out something about Miss Grant which would displease Mr. Edward if he knew it. And we have just learnt that he wrote to Miss Grant also, threatening her in the same way as he had threatened poor Lord Malvern."

The terrified girl broke out into sobs.

"You must not distress yourself so, Milly. Remember, you are quite safe; nothing can possibly be done to *you*. But we wish to know if Frampton said anything to you about these letters—if he hinted at them at any time."

"Oh, no, sir, not a word! He durstn't have done it, Mr. Colchester—I wouldn't have let him do it if I'd have known. Oh, Mr. Colchester, whatever will father and mother say! Do you think he'll really be sent to prison?"

I could give her no reassurance on this point.

"Oh, whatever shall I do!" At the remembrance, I suppose, of her condition, poor Milly began to cry again. I soothed her as well as I could, and when she was a little calmer she asked suddenly:

"He doesn't say *I* knew about it, Mr. Colchester? I don't know what father and mother would do if they was to think *I* knew about it."

"No," replied Mr. Hatton, in his unemphatic way, "he says you didn't. But you knew his idea about Lord Malvern?"

Milly blushed again.

"You mean—you mean about me and him, sir?"

Mr. Hatton assented.

"Oh yes, sir—he accused me to my face. More times than one he did, sir."

"And what did you say?" asked the young man.

"I told him", replied Milly with a flash of spirit, "that he'd no need to say it, and no right to, and no gentleman would have asked me such a thing."

"That annoyed him, I expect," said Mr. Hatton.

"Yes, sir, he was wild. He didn't like me comparing him to a gentleman, you see, sir, and he said he supposed I thought Lord Malvern was a gentleman, and that was why——" She broke off in confusion, and blushed deeper. "But it wasn't true, sir—it was only his jealousy. And we made it up in the end, and he said he was sorry—but he was always coming back and hinting about it, and making my life a perfect misery, till I said I'd have nothing more to do with him—and then he said he was sorry, and we made it up."

"Ah, yes," said Mr. Hatton. "And he was never jealous of anybody but Lord Malvern?"

"No, sir—you see he'd run away with that notion at first, and it seemed to keep him going, if you see what I mean, sir. I think it was partly his lordship being a lord, you see. He didn't like gentlemen, sir, not even ordinary gentlemen—he was always thinking people were thinking they were better than him. And so his lordship being a lord he seemed to think I was bound to like him best. It was no use anything I could say, sir—it was just words wasted, if you see what I mean."

"And you never heard him threaten Lord Malvern in any way?" I inquired.

A Talk with Milly

"Oh, yes, Mr. Colchester—he used to say what he'd do to him if he found out there was anything wrong between him and me. He used to say he'd be even with him if he was the Prince of Wales. But I never thought nothing of that—I thought it was only his talk, Mr. Colchester. He never said nothing to me about letters—I wouldn't have allowed it, and Lord Malvern such a nice young gentleman, and always so much the gentleman to me. And Mr. Edward, too—and father and mother been in the family so long, and me born in it, as you might say. I wouldn't have had him making trouble between Mr. Edward and his young lady, Mr. Colchester, if I'd have known about it. But it was different with Frampton, you see, sir." (She turned eagerly to Mr. Hatton again.) "He was new to the place—and anyhow, he never seemed to think it matters how you treat a person that's well off. I shouldn't wonder if that's why he did it, sir. He might have thought it was all right to do it as they was well off—he might have thought they could spare a little money. You don't think they'll be very hard upon him? Couldn't you say a word to the Inspector not to be too hard upon him?"

"I will if I can," replied Mr. Hatton, "but I'm afraid you must count on more trouble."

His serious tone seemed to remind Milly of the worse suspicion resting on her lover. She turned very pale.

"Oh, sir—does the Inspector truly think he did it? That it was him killed Lord Malvern, I mean, sir? They *can't* think it was him did that! Oh, I *know* he'd never have done that, sir! Surely the Inspector can't think it was him?"

"No, no, he doesn't," said Mr. Hatton, distant as ever, yet to her, I could not think why, obviously reassuring. After a pause he added: "But I hope you don't still think of marrying him?"

Milly looked painfully confused; she lowered her eyes and murmured, reddening:

"I—I can't help myself now, sir." Then with a burst of grief and humiliation: "If he'll marry *me*."

I felt somewhat indignant with the young man for his thoughtless question, and was about to turn the subject as hastily as possible when he said:

"You don't mean you're in any doubt of that?"

"He—he used to say he wouldn't, sometimes, when he'd had a jealous fit. He used to say——" She broke off in tears and confusion, but presently resumed: "I don't believe he really meant it, sir. Frampton isn't a bad sort—not really, when he can get ideas out of his head. He's not really the sort to go off and leave a girl."

She seemed to be convincing herself rather than her questioner, but now she glanced eagerly at Mr. Hatton, as though to be assured that she was right.

"Well," he replied, "all the same, I should advise you to think twice about it. It's not my business, of course, but I'm sure you would regret it. Frampton's bound to get into trouble some time, if not now."

"Thank you, sir—it's very kind of you, but—but what can a girl do?" She hung down her head, and sniffed pathetically.

"You can do much better than Frampton," he said, rising. "Don't let one mistake rush you into a worse one. And in the meantime, don't let the police worry you; you may have another call from the Inspector, but I should think that'll be the last."

Milly thanked him again, and after another word or two of encouragement from me we left the cottage. I was in some doubt what view to take of Mr. Hatton's parting advice to the poor girl. It seemed only too likely that Frampton would turn out a bad husband; but that might be her just punishment for the unsanctified love she had bestowed on him. Her sin might be extenuated if, at the time, she had honestly looked on herself as his wife, but if that were so, her duty now was beyond question: she ought to cleave to him, for better, for worse. Yet it seemed hard to condemn her, for a single error, to a life of probable misery. Sceptics, I remembered, have much to say about the inhumanity of religion. If Milly could accept her lot as a chastisement, a probation, a brief trial of faith, she might certainly be blest in it; but I knew too well, alas, that adversity does not always purify. As we walked away, I was so full of these thoughts that I could not resist some audible allusion to them.

"Ah, well," said Mr. Hatton, "if Frampton is hanged, the difficulty won't arise."

I was somewhat pained by this speech, which reminded me of Matthew, and at the same time greatly startled by it.

"You really think that is possible?" I inquired.

"He may have done it. He had opportunity enough—access to the room, the whisky, and everything else. He had motives—almost a plethora of motives."

"What can you mean by that?" I asked, again conscious of disapproval.

"I'm not sure of their strength, but numerically they're quite impressive. In the first place, revenge, of course. He certainly thought Charles had been making love to his girl, and whether he wanted to marry her or not, there's no doubt he was jealous. Then, of course, Charles had made him look a fool. Charles's coolness under blackmail may have been the last straw."

"Yes," I replied doubtfully, "I see that that is a possible motive."

"It's the same motive as Edward Barry's, after all. But he had others—I can think of two others at the moment. Very few people are as high-handed with a blackmailer as Charles. If it hadn't been for Charles, he could probably have made a very good thing out of the other two."

"Out of Miss Grant, perhaps," I conceded, "but why Edward? I cannot imagine why he wrote to Edward at all; it was surely madness from his point of view. How could he have hoped to profit by a secret Edward was already acquainted with?"

"Well," said Mr. Hatton, "unluckily Frampton's a stupid man. It means one can't work his mental processes out by pure reason. But when his designs on Miss Grant were put a stop to, he may have thought Edward was the next best; he may have thought Edward was enough in love to stick to her after all, or at any rate not to want her exposed publicly. In fact, that appears to me reasonably sound. That unfortunate letter to Charles was still a pitfall; it was the only effective hold they had on him, and I think there's no doubt he spent a good deal of his spare time hunting for it. Still, he may have reflected that Edward at any rate wouldn't confide in Charles, and that Miss Grant wouldn't dare to admit she'd confided in him. So he risked it, and wrote the letter."

"But", I objected, "Miss Grant would certainly have told Lord Malvern, and he would have threatened Frampton as he had done before. Edward need have known nothing of it."

"Yes—and what I'm suggesting is that Frampton thought of that a little too late. And by that time I'm inclined to suspect that he didn't believe Charles had kept the first letter after all. It wouldn't take long to conduct a pretty thorough search for it. In that case, there was only Charles's personal testimony to be afraid of, and he murdered him."

"But the danger!" I exclaimed. "If the letter had been discovered afterwards, as it actually has been ——"

"Oh, he must have intended it to look like suicide. And then if Charles had been carrying the letter about with him, which probably seemed the one chance left, he would have nipped in and abstracted it. He was hanging about there this morning, you remember. After that he could have gone on blackmailing Edward to his heart's content."

"It is ingenious," I admitted, "but does it not seem to you—forgive me—a little thin?"

"Pretty thin," replied Mr. Hatton with great coolness, "but we're considering possibilities."

"You said there was a third motive—what is that?"

"It's a variant of the last, really. He may simply have been in a panic. When he'd written to Edward it occurred to him that Charles was bound to hear of it, and might prosecute him as he'd threatened. So he killed him, meaning it to pass for suicide—or accident —and of course to get hold of the letter if it still existed."

I reflected for a minute or two.

"The first motive appears to me the strongest," I said at last.

"Yes. By the way, Frampton admits that letter to Charles—indeed the internal evidence leaves him nothing else to do—but he denies all the others flatly. Says he didn't write either to Miss Grant or Edward, and it's the first he's heard of it."

"Indeed!" said I. "Is that possible?"

"Not as far as Miss Grant's concerned; nobody's seen Edward's letter. I wish you would try to bring Edward to reason; he insists that he got no letter of the kind, which is mere obstinacy—several people noticed it, they even noticed that it put him out. And as no one else knows what was in it, it's exasperating. It's doing Edward harm, too. If you could get him to produce it——"

He filled up the sentence with an inquiring glance. I began to see what was expected of me in return for his surprising openness, but on reflection it did not appear to me that in this case he was asking too much.

"If you assure me that I cannot injure Edward by doing so——"

"Not at all; as I say, his obstinacy is against him."

I promised to see him, and to persuade him if I

could. We had almost reached the house by this time, and Mr. Hatton replied promptly:

"Will you do it at once?"

A little taken aback, I again assented, and we parted in the doorway. Before going about my mission, however, I thought it my duty to write a brief note to Miss Grant. I told her who Mr. Hatton was, and why he had come to Friars Cross, adding, however, that he seemed well disposed towards poor Edward, and that his presence ought rather to relieve than to augment her anxiety. This note I entrusted to Rhoda, begging her to take it up immediately to Miss Grant's room. When she had gone, I felt at liberty to turn all my thoughts to Edward.

I had hardly expected to find him downstairs at all, but to my surprise he was sitting alone in a corner of the drawing-room. Nothing could have been more disconsolate than his whole attitude; and his face expressed, in addition, a deep sullenness which offered little hope of his being induced to confide in me or anyone. I approached, however, and sat down by him.

"My dear Edward," said I, "why are you alone like this? You must not avoid us because you are unhappy. My dear boy, I cannot express half the sorrow I feel on your account; surely you will not refuse to let me share this grief with you?"

"I'm not avoiding anyone," he replied, without looking at me, and in a tone at once of dejection and bitterness. "This isn't the world's end. Anyone could find me here if they wanted to see me."

It seemed plain enough that Miss Grant was in his

thoughts, and I wondered if it could be possible that he still loved her.

"My dear boy," I returned, "you know that very often there is no one here between tea and dinner. Why should you be hurt now by their absence?"

I used the plural from a feeling of delicacy, but I could see he understood me. He made no answer, however, and his countenance wore the same look of determined sullenness.

"You did not come down to tea," I pursued gently. "That is what I meant when I said you were avoiding us."

"I didn't want any tea," he replied, "so I preferred to spare everyone my company."

"Edward, Edward! why are you resolved on increasing your own burden? We are all concerned for you—we are all unhappy about you. Why have you made up your mind to treat us as enemies? Though your trust and affection have been so cruelly deceived in one instance——"

"In *what* instance?" he interrupted. "What do you mean?"

I looked at him in astonishment and some confusion.

"I thought", said I, "that my meaning was unhappily too clear."

"If you are talking of Miss Grant," he replied with assumed composure, "I know perfectly well that she doesn't care about me, and no doubt everyone but myself has realized it for a long time. But as for any other stories about her, I know nothing of them and don't care to hear anything. Those who choose to gossip about Miss Grant can surely, at least, do it in my absence—I'll take care that they have plenty of opportunity."

There was what, in spite of my affection for Edward, I can only call a weak mulishness about his tone and manner which it gave me pain to observe. I felt that, for the moment at least, nothing could be done with him; still I could not make up my mind to leave him in that despondent mood.

"My dear boy," I said again, "I respect your attitude, believe me; but are you quite certain it is wise? In your anxiety to shield Miss Grant you forget that the police are already acquainted with the facts, and that your silence can only prejudice them against you. Mr. Hatton assures me——"

"Mr. Hatton?" he repeated quickly, with a glance of suspicion—the first direct glance he had bestowed on me.

"Yes, Edward—Mr. Hatton is sincerely anxious for you. He assures me that by producing the letter you received yesterday morning——"

"Did he tell you to speak to me?" asked Edward.

I was rather disconcerted.

"Why—yes," said I, "I cannot deny that he suggested it."

"Ah, I was wondering why anyone had come near me. I'm sorry I can't give you any news for him; but I've already told the Inspector that the letter was a receipted bill and as I didn't keep it I'm afraid there's nothing to be done. I expect he's waiting to hear what you've got out of me—I'd better go."

"Edward!" I called after him.

He took no notice, but walked out, shutting the door behind him with great precision. Almost immediately, however, it opened again, and Mr. Hatton walked in.

"I wasn't eavesdropping," he said, "but I gather it's no use just yet?"

"No," I replied, "I am afraid not. I fear he is utterly unreasonable."

"Ah, well," said Mr. Hatton, "very likely——"

He was interrupted by the sound of feet and—more surprisingly—of laughter. The Colonel and Mrs. Fairfax entered the room.

CHAPTER NINE

All Suspects

They stopped short on observing my companion, and Colonel Lawrence hastily effected a change in his somewhat too jovial expression.

"Perhaps you have not met Mr. Nicholas Hatton?" said I.

"The new detective?" said Mrs. Fairfax, looking surprised. Then, addressing Mr. Hatton, she added with a peculiar smile: "Eton and Oxford?"

"Cambridge," he replied, not at all discomposed, but eyeing her, also, with an expression I did not understand. "And you are Mrs. Fairfax?"

"Quite right," she answered approvingly, "a good beginning. No doubt you've identified the Colonel too?"

"Oh, yes. I've been expecting to see you both, you must remember."

"Haven't kept you waiting, I hope?" said Colonel Lawrence. "Just been having a game of tennis." He seemed afraid that this occupation might not strike Mr. Hatton as funereal enough, and added hastily: "Just knocking a ball about, you know. Exercise. Trying to keep our minds off the thing."

"I see," said Mr. Hatton.

"Played a rotten game, I'm afraid, though—both of us. Nerves, you know. Can't get it out of one's head. My nerves have been in a rotten state all day—dare say you heard how I blew that wretched geyser up."

Mr. Hatton appeared to assent.

"And then those letters—bad business, Mr. Hatton; very awkward business!"

"Yes—you noticed them at the time, didn't you, Colonel? I mean when they arrived."

"Yes, yes—thought they looked odd, you know. Addressed in capitals. I'm an observant man, I believe—a fairly observant man. Been told so many a time, Mr. Hatton. Well, an observant man couldn't miss a thing like that; addressed in capitals, local postmark—very odd indeed. Felt like mentioning it at the time, I assure you; but I'm not a busybody. Shady side to all families—questions not wanted—no business of mine."

"You saw them too, Mrs. Fairfax?" Mr. Hatton inquired.

"I'm not particularly observant," returned Mrs. Fairfax, with an expression which was not quite a smile, "but I did see them."

"You saw the one Edward Barry got yesterday morning?"

"Yes."

"Ah, yes," repeated the Colonel, summing up, "an awkward business. Really a tragedy, of course—poor Malvern! Such a pleasant young fellow, never out of spirits, and engaged, too. By the way, we passed Miss

Elliston's car in the drive just now—not gone for good, is she?"

"Yes, Lady Elliston insisted that she shouldn't stay."

"Very natural—bad for her nerves, poor girl. Very fond of poor Malvern, I've no doubt?"

Mr. Hatton offered no opinion. The Colonel, a little disconcerted, hastily said:

"Well, have you begun to see through all this? Got any suspects?"

"Colonel," said Mrs. Fairfax, "don't you realize that we're all suspects from Mr. Hatton's point of view?"

The Colonel looked still more disconcerted, and turned rather red.

"Nonsense!" he replied bluffly. "Beg your pardon, Mrs. Fairfax, but really, you know—all stuff! Detective novels—I'm afraid you've been reading detective novels. Not the way things happen in real life."

"I'm sorry," interposed Mr. Hatton calmly, "but in this case Mrs. Fairfax is quite right."

He and Mrs. Fairfax again exchanged one of those odd looks whose significance, just then, escaped me.

"What!" exclaimed the Colonel. "You don't mean to say you're going about suspecting all of us?"

"More or less. Almost any of you could have done it, Colonel."

"*Could* have done it! Why, you don't mean to say, sir, that you think yourself at liberty to pester anyone who *could* have done it? You're not going to make it your business to harass Mrs. Fairfax, or Matthew, or —or Miss Barry, for instance, because they *could* have done it?"

"As to pestering or harassing," replied Mr. Hatton without anger, "I hope not. But I have certainly an open mind about Mrs. Fairfax—and Miss Barry—at the moment. Mr. Barry, I think, couldn't have done it; he wasn't there."

"Why, good heavens, sir, you don't pretend that—that Miss Barry, for instance, is a *suspect*? I protest against it! In the name of reason and decency, sir, I protest against it! Why, good heavens, because Miss Barry has had a murder in the house, is she to be followed about by a detective for the rest of her days? Nonsense, sir!"

We were astonished at this outburst. No one spoke, and the Colonel himself, apparently, began to feel uneasy.

"Sorry," he said after a moment, "no wish to appear warm. But really, Mr. Hatton, common sense—mustn't lose sight of common sense, you know, even in these matters."

"I suppose you realize", said Mr. Hatton amiably, "that you've turned the limelight of suspicion full on Miss Barry now?"

The Colonel choked.

"Nonsense!" he reiterated feebly. "Took her as an example, that's all—only an example." He seemed to intend further protestations, but thought better of it, and jerked out instead: "Better go and change." With these words he hastened from the room.

When the door had shut behind him, Mrs. Fairfax laughed. It was not unkindly mirth, nor of long duration, but it seemed almost strange in the cloud of horrors involving us.

"You don't really suspect poor Miss Barry?" she inquired.

"Why not? She's a relation of the family."

Mrs. Fairfax looked puzzled.

"Of Charles's family, I mean."

"Is she? And you look on that as a dark circumstance?"

"Any sort of connection", he replied, "is a possible clue. I suppose you have no idea where Miss Winter is?"

"In Miss Barry's sitting-room, I dare say. The first door on the right at the top of the stairs. You're not going to make her hysterical again?"

"I want to know why she was hysterical in the first place. A repetition of the outrage——"

"——might supply a hint," she finished promptly. "I see. But isn't she just a hysterical subject, very likely?"

"Very likely," agreed Mr. Hatton. "I'd better go now—it must be nearly dinner-time."

"But don't scare poor Phyllis out of her wits," said Mrs. Fairfax. "She's a nice thing, and easily frightened, I should say. Don't be too sudden with her."

Mr. Hatton smiled, but left us without a reply.

"Is he any good?" Mrs. Fairfax asked me as soon as he had gone. "You've seen a good deal of him, haven't you?"

"Yes," I replied, "I have had some conversation with him. But really, I do not quite know what to say. He is exceedingly communicative—more so, I should have thought, than is quite professional or wise. And then he is scarcely the kind of young man one would expect to see engaged in work of this description. It cannot be much more to him than a hobby, I suspect. I am afraid, Mrs. Fairfax, you will think me hopelessly conservative; but I do feel that investigations like this are perhaps better left to the established police force."

"There's something in that," said Mrs. Fairfax, "but I'm afraid in this case the police force has made up its mind. And really, Mr. Colchester, I *can't* think that Edward is guilty. Surely you don't think so yourself?"

"God forbid!" I replied earnestly. "I believe him to be incapable of such an act. I believe it so firmly that, whatever the Inspector's theories are at present, I feel sure his innocence must be established before long. In the meantime——"

"In the meantime," said Mrs. Fairfax, "things are looking bad. I'm told the latest is that Charles and the Colonel were both drugged last night. Edward takes sleeping-drugs, doesn't he? I hope they made nothing out of that."

I considered a moment, but could see no real reason for evasion.

"Unfortunately," I answered, "the Inspector believes that Edward's pills were used. He purchased a fresh supply on Thursday, and five pills are missing from it—that is, assuming that he took no more than the dose prescribed."

Mrs. Fairfax looked grave.

"And did he ever?" she inquired.

"I cannot say; I must admit that I have never before heard of his doing so."

"Well," she said after a pause, "I should think Edward's the kind of person who might exceed sometimes, and wouldn't like admitting it. How many was he supposed to take?"

"One pill every night, I believe."

"Oh, dear," said Mrs. Fairfax, "then five would be a lot since Thursday—five extra, I mean. Still, of course it *is* possible. And in any case, I suppose someone might have stolen the pills from Edward's room?"

"Very easily," I replied. "Even if his pills were used, I cannot see that the fact is of any value as evidence against him."

"Not in itself—it's the *cumulative* evidence. I wish he hadn't smelt that gas, or had done something about it; it looks funny."

"My dear Mrs. Fairfax," I protested, "is not that wisdom after the event? How easily he may have decided that it was imagination!"

"Yes, I've no doubt that's what actually happened, but it's extremely unlucky." She paused for a moment, and then continued: "I didn't know Miss Barry was related to Charles."

"Very distantly," I answered. "Surely Mr. Hatton does not really attach weight to the circumstance! He mentioned it once before; he said Miss Elliston seemed to think that Lord Malvern had been staying here on that account, which is an odd thing, surely."

Mrs. Fairfax reflected.

"I don't know," she said at last, "I think perhaps I can explain it. I don't know Jane at all well, but she's spoilt, certainly, and exacting. I should think she expects to be danced attendance on most of the time.

There would probably be scenes if Charles absented himself too often, and he wouldn't have liked being always in tow; so very likely he said he couldn't get out of this visit, on Miss Barry's account. People like the Ellistons have an immense respect for that kind of obligation. Even Jane wouldn't try to prevent Charles from doing his duty to his family."

Something in this reminded me of Matthew's wild conjecture about her own feelings for Lord Malvern.

"You don't like Miss Elliston?" I inquired.

I thought she looked slightly confused.

"I don't dislike her, but I'm sure she's very possessive. And Charles evidently lied to her about why he came down here; he must have had some reason."

"Ah, well," I replied, "an only child—she may be a little spoilt, naturally, as you say. And so you are satisfied that there is nothing relevant in Miss Barry's connection with the Malverns?"

"I shouldn't think so," she said doubtfully. "It's a very distant one, you say?"

"I have always understood so."

"She wouldn't be likely to inherit anything?"

"Oh, dear, no!" I replied, shocked at the implication. "I should think it most improbable."

"There's a first cousin, I think," Mrs. Fairfax said after a pause. "That would be nearer?"

"Certainly, I imagine."

"I'm only thinking of possibilities," said Mrs. Fairfax. "Remember Mr. Hatton suspects everyone."

"Surely", I said, "he was not entirely serious in that remark."

"Well, anyhow, Miss Barry seems to have no possible motive. If one rejects Edward, there seems nothing to do but to fall back on Frampton—only after all this blackmailing it doesn't really sound as if vengeance had engrossed his thoughts. What's your own theory, Mr. Colchester?"

"Really, I cannot pretend to have formed one. For Edward's sake, I am anxious that the guilty person should be discovered, but it is terrible to suspect anyone, who may be innocent, of so horrid a crime. No, Mrs. Fairfax, I dare not allow myself to *hope* that Frampton—even Frampton—is guilty of murder."

"Charles said he hoped they would get off," said Mrs. Fairfax suddenly.

I remembered it—indeed, it was not the first time it had recurred to me; and for a moment I said nothing. As I was about to reply, Mrs. Fairfax spoke again.

"Still, he wouldn't have liked the real murderer to get off at Edward's expense. Oh, there's the first dinner-bell—I must go and change."

Having no change to make in my own attire, I washed my hands and returned immediately to the drawing-room. It was still empty, and as I waited for the others I could not help reflecting that though ages seemed to have passed, and the world to be quite different, since the previous night, yet outwardly there would be little to distinguish this dinner assembly from the last one. The presence of Mr. Hatton would make even our numbers the same. One personable young man in evening dress substituted for another: a dead man replaced by one seeking for his murderer; with that exception, there would be no change from the night before. It was an exception appalling to the mind, but very trifling to the eye. Once more I brooded on something unreal in human terrors and agitations, something trivial in the whole course of human life. The same dinner-table, almost the same party round it; only a dark young man, instead of a fair one, on Miss Barry's right. This alone represented the crisis which had driven Matthew to piety, Edward and Judith to despair.

Thus considered, Mr. Hatton's image began to take on a sinister shade, very unlike the reality; and when he came in a minute later I was almost surprised to observe nothing stern or ominous about him. If he had really seen Phyllis he must have changed in a great hurry, but he looked as though his valet had been at work on him for an hour at least. It evidently pleased him to find me alone.

"Ten minutes yet before dinner," he said. "I've rather rushed things in the hope of another word with you, Mr. Colchester."

I looked at him inquiringly.

"In the first place, have you any idea why the Colonel was in such a fuss at the idea of Miss Barry being suspected?"

"Why," I answered with some hesitation, "to be quite frank, Mr. Hatton, I am always unwilling to disseminate gossip of any kind, and more particularly when it concerns such old friends; but if you really consider it important——"

"It may be," replied Mr. Hatton. "I should like to know whether it is or not."

"I may rely on its going no farther?"

"Oh, yes," he replied, "if it's not relevant."

"I do not see how it can be. Well, Mr. Hatton, the fact is that Colonel Lawrence has always had an interest in Miss Barry—a great interest. Of course they are very old acquaintances; but he has a stronger interest in her than mere friendship. In their youth ——" I broke off in some embarrassment. "Really, Mr. Hatton, even at a time like this I scarcely feel justified in confiding such things to a stranger."

"Do go on," said he. "I won't repeat it."

"In their youth, he several times proposed marriage to her. Miss Barry was then decidedly handsome, and though her manner was not conciliating, he was by no means her only suitor; but in his case it was, I may say, the attachment of a lifetime. I am not aware that she ever gave him any reason to hope; still she must always have had an affection for him, and, as you see, they have remained intimate ever since. He visits here, really, upon her account."

"I see—and you think that's why he is so sensitive about her being pestered?"

"I should think it most probable."

"Miss Barry, from what I've heard, isn't so tender about him. She seems to be pretty sharp with him."

"Really, Mr. Hatton, I think it is almost a mark of attachment in her case. I am quite sure she is fond of him. It is natural that she should regard him with somewhat proprietary feelings, if I may say so, after all these years, but her character is not sentimental, and I should think it would not be easy for her to give them any other outlet. I have known many such cases, particularly in her sex."

"Yes," said Mr. Hatton absently. Then with more alertness he continued: "Just by the way—it's not impertinence, I can't tell what may be useful—do you happen to know why she refused him, and the other men?"

"Dear me," said I, "it is a curious coincidence! But you will promise me to let it go no farther, Mr. Hatton?"

"I assure you I won't, if there's no cause."

"Miss Barry, in her youth, had, I believe, a romantic passion for Lord Malvern—the late Lord Malvern's uncle, it must have been, I suppose. It is a very old story—I believe they met only two or three times, and he was probably quite unaware of it; she had not seen him for many years before he died. But though her attachment was of such an ideal character, it must have been extremely strong—all her feelings are so; and as they are also very tenacious, she never outlived it sufficiently to think of marrying anyone else. That is really the whole story. He was, from what I heard at the time, a most unsuitable object for such a passion. Indeed, it seems strange to me that a woman of strong principle like Miss Barry should have loved him at all."

"Thanks awfully," said Mr. Hatton. "The next thing is—— Oh, bother!"

Miss Barry and Mrs. Fairfax had entered the room almost at the same time. Seeing them fall into conversation together, he gave Mrs. Fairfax what struck me as a look of appeal, and drew me unostentatiously a little farther off, towards the window-seat. Turning over the pages of an album which lay there, he went on in a slightly subdued voice:

"It's very useful to have you, Mr. Colchester. Do you mind attempting something more?"

My role of detective's assistant was beginning to weigh on me a little, but when I considered Edward's danger it seemed impossible to refuse.

"I want a little more openness from Phyllis Winter," my companion explained. "There's no doubt she knows something. It's transparent—Lockitt saw it at once, and that was why I wanted to speak to her as soon as possible. I might have got it out of her, perhaps—someone will in the end; but her nerves are in a bad state, and I'd like it done without hysteria."

"If that is all," I replied, "I should be glad to spare her as far as possible; but I really doubt if I can induce her to be open with me. In this case, I think you had better apply to Mrs. Fairfax. Phyllis is greatly attached to her—has a schoolgirl admiration for her, I believe. I think Mrs. Fairfax might persuade her to speak out."

To my surprise, his countenance darkened at the suggestion.

"You forget", he said drily, "that Mrs. Fairfax is also a suspect. I can't apply to her, I'm afraid; but I'm always hearing something from you, Mr. Colchester." He was silent a moment, and then asked: "Phyllis Winter slept in the same wing as Lord Malvern?"

"Almost opposite," I replied.

"And Mrs. Fairfax was next door to him. Well, if you can do anything about it, you will?"

I assented, repeating, however, my doubts of my own influence in this case.

"I was unsuccessful with Edward, you must remember, with whom I might have expected to do more. Therefore I cannot reasonably hope to prevail with Phyllis."

"She's not so obstinate—but for Edward's own sake, will you try him again? I want to see that letter of his —I feel hopelessly in the dark about it. If he *has* got it stowed away somewhere, try and make him bring it out; it may do him an enormous amount of good, I assure you. Anyhow, he's behaving suspiciously— he couldn't behave worse."

I was again assenting when we were interrupted. By this time one or two more people had come in, and Mrs. Fairfax, detaching herself from the group, walked up to us.

"As a suspect, Mr. Hatton," she said, "I begin to feel uneasy. I saw you mention my name just now."

Mr. Hatton had risen, and was looking oddly at her.

"I only remarked that Phyllis Winter must be concealing something, and he told me that you were her likeliest confidante."

Mrs. Fairfax started.

"It sounds flattering," she returned, "but why?"

"On account of her particular affection for you."

Mrs. Fairfax bent her head, and began trifling with the album in her turn.

"*Very* flattering," she remarked with assumed composure, "but not justified by facts, so far. Phyllis has shown no sign of opening her soul to me."

He said nothing. After a moment she asked: "Are you staying here?"

"Yes."

"And the Inspector has to seek refuge in the pub. Doesn't that make bad blood at all?"

"Oh, I have excellent credentials. Jane's father is Home Secretary, don't forget."

My interest in politics is so very slight that I am ashamed to say I had been unaware of this; though, of course, I had known him to be eminent in the political world. Mrs. Fairfax only said: "I see."

The constraint between them was obvious, and, to me, incomprehensible. Myself affected by it, I was trying in vain to think of some topic which might revive a more natural manner, when our conversation was cut short by the dinner bell.

"Ah," said Mrs. Fairfax, "a brief escape for the suspect. What a relief!"

At dinner, however, they were seated next each other. And my calculation proved, after all, inaccurate, for Edward did not appear.

CHAPTER TEN

The Inspector's Favourite

It was not the custom at Friars Cross for the servants to remain in attendance throughout the whole of luncheon or dinner. At the present crisis one or two of us, I think, were sorry for it. Had they been in the room, our conversation at least, and perhaps our thoughts, would have been diverted momentarily from the terrible circumstances of the day. As it was, we had not a sufficient incentive to avoid the subject; other topics were brought forward in vain, and dropped almost immediately. There seemed no medium between total silence and discussion of the crime, and though Miss Grant's presence and Edward's vacant place made the latter alternative appear more delicate, they made the former more uncomfortable. Oddly enough, it was Miss Grant herself who broke the ice. After a struggle, I imagine, between natural embarrassment and fear for Edward, she ventured, necessarily in a raised voice, to inquire of Miss Barry if he were unwell.

Miss Barry flared up in a surprising manner.

"Unwell!" she repeated with bitter irony. "Of course he is unwell. He feels obliged to sit in his room and have his meals brought up to him. By to-morrow I have no doubt Frampton and Violet will be doing the same. I fully expect them to keep their beds to-morrow and have the rest of the household waiting on them with beef tea."

"But is he really *ill*?" persisted Miss Grant timidly.

"As I told you, he has been sitting in his room all day, and keeping the maids out of it. If he is not ill, I am at a loss to conjecture what he means by such unsuitable behaviour."

"Hatching the evidence, perhaps," said Matthew.

An awkward pause followed this remark.

"As for Frampton," Miss Barry presently contin-ued, "we have never had such a capable man-servant, and what is the result? In the first place Edward must needs find him stealing whisky; then there is all this disturbance about Milly Baker, and on top of that we have the police in the house. I wish to say nothing against Lord Malvern, who is dead, as I am only too well aware; but he would have acted more becom-ingly if he had remembered his station, and left that girl alone."

"Quite so," said the Colonel. "Dangerous move— vindictive fellow. Got a dangerous look in his eye."

"Colonel," returned Miss Barry, "I can't hear you. If you are addressing me, will you do me the favour to speak up?"

"I was saying," repeated the Colonel in a loud voice, "he's got a dangerous look in his eye."

"*Who* has a dangerous look in his eye?"

"Frampton—Frampton I was talking about. Al-ways said he looked an ugly customer."

"Indeed, Colonel! And may I ask to whom you have been in the habit of saying so?"

The Colonel, as usual on such occasions, began to quail visibly.

"Not in the habit—too strong an expression—much too strong, I assure you. Just happened to mention it once or twice—purely by chance, you know. Happened to crop up, that was all."

"Colonel," said Miss Barry, "if I thought you had really been going about behind my back making these ridiculous comments upon Frampton's eye, I should know how to express myself on the subject. As it is evident that the idea never occurred to you until this moment, I shall let it pass."

Colonel Lawrence grew purple, and applied himself attentively to the cold meat.

"Frampton's appearance", she resumed, "is quite prepossessing enough for his walk in life. I wish I could say as much for the Inspector."

"Hear, hear," Matthew put in.

"If he considers it part of his duty to hector the maids and domineer over the family, I suppose I must submit; but I should be glad to know how long it is to continue. Mr. Hatton, perhaps you can enlighten me."

"I'm afraid not," said Mr. Hatton. "A day isn't much, you know, in an affair of this kind."

"But hang it all," ventured Colonel Lawrence, "what's the man waiting for? He's got a case— clearest case I ever heard of. Motive—documents— man on the spot, ready to be arrested offhand. Why can't he arrest him and be done with it?"

"For once," said Miss Barry, "I agree with you, Colonel. Frampton is of no use in his present state of mind, and if he is to be arrested, the sooner it is done the better. Inspector Lockitt is not paid for this kind of work by the day, I suppose?"

Mr. Hatton very naturally looked surprised.

"No," he answered smiling, "I imagine not."

"Very well, then; there is no reason why he should not execute it with decent promptitude."

"Perhaps", I could not help observing, "he is not yet satisfied of Frampton's guilt."

"Then it is time he was," said Miss Barry.

"Quite so," the Colonel agreed heartily. "After all, Hatton, what more does he want? The fellow threatened to do it—subversive theories—dangerous man—and now he's done it, that's all. *Crime passionnel* —always hearing of 'em on the Continent. He found Malvern tampering with his girl——"

"Colonel!" exclaimed Miss Barry. "Please be more decent in your language!"

The Colonel blushed.

"Really, I'm extremely sorry—I—unfortunate expression. What I meant to say is——"

"Yes, Colonel?" said Matthew.

"He found Malvern had been too thick with his girl——"

Miss Barry sighed, but did not again interrupt him.

"——tried to screw money out of him in the first place—meant to rook him and murder him afterwards, very likely. Well, rooking falls through. Dare say Charles knew Miss Elliston wouldn't make a fuss about it—modern girls take a different view of these things. Not so particular as they were in my young days—may be a good thing, of course, but there it is."

"Lawrence," said Matthew, "you're digressing."

"Not at all, not at all—where was I? Oh, yes, Frampton saw there was nothing to be got, so he dropped the blackmailing idea and got on with the murder. Meant it to look like suicide, I dare say—or if not, hoped suspicion would fall on——" he glanced at Judith, and concluded tactfully, "on someone else."

"Very well put," said Matthew drily.

"Well, he murdered poor old Charles, as we all know. And—and there you are!" wound up the Colonel, unexpectedly finding himself with nothing more to say.

Miss Grant had followed this exposition with glowing intentness, only now and then taking her eyes from Colonel Lawrence to observe what effect it was producing on his other listeners. Now she smiled: a smile of overflowing relief and comfort which she could not repress. I could not doubt that his theory had convinced her, at least for the moment, and that she believed it must convince us all.

"Yes . . ." said Mrs. Fairfax noncommittally. "*How* do we know he murdered him, Colonel?"

The Colonel looked exceedingly taken aback.

"Why, Mrs. Fairfax—why, I've just explained all that, you know! Motive—opportunity—thoroughly bad character—known to have threatened poor Charles more than once. Don't want more than that, do we? Not that that's all, of course——" with a sudden recollection. "Fellow's been caught already hanging about the scene of the crime. They all do that, you know—curious thing. Seems to be automatic."

"But it wasn't automatic in his case," said Mrs. Fairfax. "He was trying to get his letters back."

The Colonel seemed rather gratified by this reminder.

"Ah, yes," he assented with a complacent, not to say gleeful air, "so he was, of course—poor fellow! Hunted all through poor Malvern's things, I'm told—no idea they were in my suit-case all the time. Ha ha!" He abruptly remembered Miss Grant's interest in the letters, shot a guilty look at her, and subsided.

"You know, Colonel," said Mr. Hatton, "I must set you right about Miss Elliston's broadmindedness. She isn't really indifferent to scandal. Don't forget Charles told Frampton he would prosecute him if she got to know."

"Well, there you are!" replied the Colonel. "The fellow had two motives—enough to hang a man twice over. I'd like to know what all this questioning's about. Lockitt sits there all day asking questions and making general unpleasantness, when the whole thing's as plain as a pikestaff. I suppose a butler's not good enough for him—he wants a duke."

This remark appeared to me, in the circumstances, very tactless; it was little better than a direct reference to Edward's unfortunate position. An electric thrill went round the table, omitting, apparently, Colonel Lawrence himself.

"Well, well," said Matthew, "the best of all this interviewing, my dear Lawrence, is that the Inspector will have repeated contact with your saner ideas of criminal investigation. No doubt you've already begun to form his mind?"

I could not help reflecting that Matthew and his sister were extremely like each other. In both, anxiety and distress of mind took the outward form of increased acidity to those around them. Colonel Lawrence was about to reply when Phyllis Winter, with more than her usual timidity, but with much eagerness, interposed.

"Don't *you* think Frampton did it, Mr. Barry?" she asked in a low voice.

Matthew was ill at ease with the very young, of the other sex at least. When Phyllis addressed him, which was seldom, for she dreaded him extremely, he was apt to discard his normal manner and assume a nonplussed and even foolish air, not unlike that of a man who has just been given a baby to hold. He did so in the present case, and replied hurriedly:

"I can't say—he may have done it. But Mr. Hatton's the authority; you should ask him."

Phyllis gave Mr. Hatton a quick glance, but said nothing. She was clearly afraid of him, and I suspected that he had, in fact, been very near extracting her secret before dinner. But though she had not had the courage to repeat her question, Mr. Hatton seemed to think the look enough, and said at once:

"I'd prefer not to commit myself just yet. Very likely we haven't all the facts yet."

Phyllis turned crimson, and looked down at her plate. Mr. Hatton's eyes, however, were on Mrs. Fairfax, who smiled, and inquired very coolly:

"Do you think you ever will have?"

142

It sounded like a challenge, and Mr. Hatton appeared to regard it as one.

"Well," he replied, "I've heard that there's no such thing as the whole truth; still, I think we may dig out another fact or two."

"Can't see myself what you want with more facts," said the Colonel. "But if there are any, I dare say they'll turn up all right. Not so easy to keep anything dark in these times, Mrs. Fairfax. When you've had my experience of life, you'll realize that."

In the presence of Miss Grant, whose own secrets had been so recently revealed to us, these remarks struck me as ill-judged. I could only suppose that Mrs. Fairfax was not, just then, alive to the connection, for she laughed, and the Colonel looked puzzled.

"Come, Lawrence," said Matthew, with even greater indiscretion, "*your* life may have been full of incidents better kept dark, but why should you expect Anne's to be the same?"

I was made very uneasy by this prolonging of the blunder. Mrs. Fairfax rejoined:

"The Colonel's a cynic. His experience has disillusioned him."

"No, no," Colonel Lawrence protested earnestly. "Mere matter of observation—nothing personal, I assure you, Mrs. Fairfax. I've seen a good deal of the world, you know—knocked about among some queer people in my time—and my experience is that shady facts always crop up sooner or later. Why, just look for example——"

He broke off in extreme confusion, and the direction of his hasty glance made it even plainer what case he had been on the very point of instancing. Matthew, though so much to blame himself, looked furious; Miss Grant had become very pale, and her lips trembled. Nothing, I thought, could avert a painful scene: but just then, at the crucial moment, Miss Barry rose. This timely movement saved the situation, and enabled Miss Grant to escape to her own room. It was impossible even for an intimate friend to be quite sure how deaf Miss Barry really was; but I think it most likely that her intervention in this case was not an accident.

Much as I enjoy a cup of coffee after dinner, I could not bring myself to make one of the party reunited in the drawing-room; I had grown too apprehensive of what might be said next. Moreover, I felt it a positive duty to cut short Edward's solitary brooding without more delay. Though he was so determined on avoiding us, it was obvious that, at the same time, he thought himself neglected, and he might actually be waiting for me at that very moment. Immediately on quitting the table, therefore, I went upstairs, and knocked at the door of his room. There was no answer. I tried the door, and found it was locked.

"Edward!" I exclaimed.

There was a silence; then his voice answered rather sullenly: "What is it?"

"Won't you let me come in, Edward?"

"What for?"

"My dear boy, I want to speak to you. Won't you let me in?"

He appeared to hesitate, but presently I heard him

rise and walk towards the door. He unlocked, but did not open it.

In the midst of my concern for him, I could not be blind to something absurdly childish in this behaviour, but it was not the time to point it out. Moreover, when I entered and saw him actually before me I was greatly touched. He looked not merely unhappy, but haggard and unwell; even his clothes—for of course he had not changed—seemed to emphasize his discouragement and isolation.

"My dear boy," was my first question, "have you had anything to eat?"

"Yes, yes," he replied pettishly. "I'm all right."

I could not be sure that he was speaking the truth, or even whether he wished me to believe him, for he wore, at the same time, an intensely injured air. Yet he must certainly, at least, have been offered dinner.

I induced him to sit down, and took a chair close by him.

"My dear Edward," I said gently, "is this right? Why do you shut yourself up from us in this manner? I have had no idea of avoiding you—none of us have; we have been worried about you all evening. Surely now, more than at any other time, we ought to cleave to one another, and ease one another's burdens. My dear boy, I cannot tell you how distressed I am to see you looking so ill."

He said nothing, but I thought there was already a little change, a little uncertainty in his obstinate look. As I have said, his disposition was very affectionate, even what, in a woman, might have been described as clinging; and this aloofness, however voluntary and irrational, could not, I was sure, be at all easy to him.

"You must not turn away from us, Edward. It is unkind to all of us; it is unkind to yourself. Do not think me selfish or unsympathetic if I speak of my own feelings at such a moment; but you know the interest I have so long had in everything that concerns you. Nothing could add so much to my distress at this time as to find myself repulsed by you in your trouble."

This speech was not without its effect on Edward. He replied, still, however, with a degree of sullenness:

"I'm sorry, Mr. Colchester. But I've no doubt you think I did it—I'm aware that everybody thinks so. And if other people avoid me, there's no reason why you shouldn't."

"*I* think you did it, Edward! My dear boy, I have never suspected you for a moment—I am as confident of your innocence as if I had seen the crime committed. How could you bring yourself to imagine otherwise? Not one of your friends thinks you guilty—I assure you of it most solemnly; but if they all thought so, it would not shake my belief in the least. You cannot really have been tormenting yourself with the idea that we suspect you, Edward?"

"Why not?" he returned, yielding more and more to the irresistible desire for sympathy. "One of you does, at any rate; and if *she* can——"

He hoped, perhaps, that I would contradict him; but after my conversation with Miss Grant that afternoon I could not in honesty give him more than a partial reassurance.

"Even in that case, my dear boy, you may be

wrong; but if it is so, is it not your own fault to some extent? You shun all communication; you deny circumstances—forgive me—which we know to be true. Have you considered what effect this may produce on one whose knowledge of you is, after all, comparatively recent—the work of months, not, like ours, of a whole lifetime?"

I thought I could see in his face a gleam of comfort —of a comfort admitted almost against his will; but he replied:

"No one ought to have known me as well as she ought. She might have realized that if I *have* tried to keep anything dark it was because of her."

"Then you do admit—my dear boy, you must know I have no intention of spying on you; I ask only for your sake—you admit that you did receive a letter yesterday morning?"

I was half afraid that the question, which had given him such offence earlier in the evening, might drive him back into obstinate silence even now. He did not, in fact, answer at once, and seemed for a moment much inclined to be angry; but at length he replied with a groan:

"Oh, well, I suppose *you* may as well know about it. Yes, I did get a letter; but as I happen not to be the murderer, I look on my correspondence as my own affair. So if you expect me to go and tell the police about it, I may as well say once and for all that I don't intend to. It's no business of theirs."

"You are your own master, Edward," I hastened to say, "but at least you cannot object to discuss it reasonably, in confidence. I perfectly understand your motive, my dear boy, and I need not tell you I respect it; but Miss Grant——"

He started, and turned away his head, but did not attempt to interrupt me.

"——Miss Grant cannot now be injured by your admitting the truth. It is known already; the Inspector has read the letters she herself received, and she has, I think very wisely, made a full confession to him. You would be revealing nothing—you would only be placing yourself in a more favourable light."

"Would I?" he said bitterly. "The fact that I had just had a letter telling me the whole story about Lord Malvern would convince them that I hadn't murdered him?"

"But, my dear Edward, that fact is also known. Several people noticed a letter like the others, and even saw that you were discomposed by it. The police cannot doubt what it contained. And in that case, must not your denial have a suspicious appearance?"

"And so you expect me to go to Lockitt and repeat what was in it?" He flared up all at once. "Well, I prefer not to. Strange as it may seem to all of you, I don't intend to recite it to the Inspector, or to anyone else. I'm sorry to disappoint his curiosity—or yours, of course—but there it is."

"My dear boy, I don't ask you to. I can easily believe it would be too painful, and there is no need for it. I do not even ask to see the letter myself, but surely it need not distress you too much to *give* it to the Inspector, or at least to let Mr. Hatton give it to him? Remember he already knows anything it can reveal."

"*Give* it to him!" exclaimed Edward. "Why, I haven't got it!"

"Not got it, Edward! But how—did you actually destroy it, then?"

"No—I meant to, and then I decided to keep it, at least until—well, if you must know, I had an idea of showing it to Judith. I thought she ought at least to have an opportunity——" He broke off with a bitter and unhappy look, and then continued: "When I changed into my riding clothes I meant to take it with me, but you never know what may happen out riding, and I left it behind after all. And when I came back I couldn't find it. At first I thought Judith must have taken it, but I don't see how she could—she was out with us, you remember. It must have been that fellow Frampton, I suppose."

I was silent for a moment.

"Edward," I said at last, "this is exceedingly unfortunate. I am afraid—I am very much afraid the Inspector will believe you destroyed it with a view to lessening the case against you."

"Very likely," he replied. "Perhaps you believe it yourself, Mr. Colchester?"

"Edward, my dear Edward!" I exclaimed. "Do not talk like that; it distresses me more than you can imagine. I have not the least doubt of your word; I am only trying to understand this dreadful situation, and to think what can be done."

Edward was silent.

"My dear boy, you will not misunderstand me again if I venture one more question?"

"What is it?"

"Your morphine pills—have you really taken no more of late than Dr. Williams prescribed for you?"

He appeared to hesitate.

"Yes," he said at length, "I took an extra one last night. I couldn't sleep."

"Oh, my dear boy, why did you not say so at first? I am afraid you have behaved very unwisely. But even then—that still leaves four unaccounted for. Are you quite certain you took only *one* extra?"

"Yes, quite certain. Oh, don't believe me—after all, what does it matter whether you believe me or not? I quite realize I'm done for—I quite realize there's no hope for me."

To my horror, he covered his face with his hands and burst into tears.

"My dear Edward—my dear, dear boy!——"

He looked up again, and said very fast, though with great difficulty:

"After all, it isn't so long to put up with me—even if I *had* done it—if *she* had done it, would I have left her alone to think of it all day, when on top of that—— It isn't that I believe she cares a straw about me, Mr. Colchester, but whoever I was—even if she hated me —when she knew I was sitting here all day with nobody to come near me, and thinking of her all the time—*I* couldn't have done it to anybody, and yet *she* won't say a word to me, although——"

Once more, at this point, he broke down completely. The outburst may have relieved him in a sense, but his immediate grief obviously swelled in his own eyes as he gave words to it, and broke away all his powers of restraint. I was more shocked than I can well describe. I uttered what imperfect phrases of consolation I could think of, and putting my arm round his shoulder entreated him not to indulge this passion of distress.

"My dear, dear boy, very likely you take—very likely we all take too dark a view. Since you are innocent, it *cannot* be impossible to prove your innocence. My dearest Edward, you will let me tell Mr. Hatton what you have told me? At least it can do no harm, and at such a moment every scrap of truth is surely of some value. You do not forbid me to tell him, Edward?"

"No," he replied, in a tone no longer of anguish, but of utter dejection, "tell him what you like. It's no good, though; I'm done for. After all, I wouldn't have lived very long; I almost feel I wouldn't mind it, if only—— Well, she'll know afterwards—when she sees afterwards how I loved her, she may be sorry— she may wish she hadn't left me to face it alone. Perhaps *then*, when she remembers——"

His voice died away. There was a low knock at the door, scarcely audible.

"Come in," he brought out with difficulty, looking very white.

The door burst open.

"*Edward!*" cried Miss Grant. "Oh, *Edward!*"

She positively hurled herself on him, clasped his neck desperately, and burst into a flood of tears. I thought I could not do better than withdraw.

CHAPTER ELEVEN

Work for a Casuist

Monday morning is to me, as a rule, the freshest and most hopeful of the week. I have been used to awake on that morning light in spirit, and to begin the day with a certain undefined alacrity and expectation of good. The preference, if I may call it so, is, I have reason to believe, somewhat uncommon, and may result from the nature of my avocations, since the day preceding is for me, exceptionally, one of toil. But whatever its origin, it has become a habit independent of chance pauses in my round of duty, and so powerful that I felt its influence even on the morning of which I am now to write. As I descended to breakfast, I had no formulated idea of what the day might be expected to bring forth; yet I seemed to breathe wholesome air again, and could no longer think it possible that things should turn out as ill as we had feared.

Matthew and Mr. Hatton were already breakfasting. Matthew, though composed and almost normal in manner, looked as if he had slept little, but there was, as ever, something in Mr. Hatton's appearance which discredited emotion, and seemed to negative the fancy that anything unusual had taken place. We talked, not of the crime, but of the weather, the neighbourhood, provincial society, the modern stage —any topic, in short, generally considered suitable and harmless between new acquaintances. It was not long before others of the party joined us, rather earlier than usual, but with a great improvement in their looks. Edward and Miss Grant, in particular, were so much more cheerful, and so evidently absorbed in one another, that I could not doubt their reconciliation had been complete—in spite of the fact that he must now almost certainly know her true story. Phyllis Winter alone did not seem to have profited by the night's respite; there were dark rines beneath her eyes, and she took scarcely any breakfast. Unmistakably she had a secret, and I was inclined to agree with Mr. Hatton that she would be unable to keep it much longer.

After breakfast my first thought was to communicate what had passed between Edward and me the night before, and Mr. Hatton soon gave me an opportunity. As we left the table he proposed a morning stroll, and together we walked off across the lawn.

As soon as we were alone I plunged into my narrative, and he listened with extreme attention, though without much change of countenance. When I had finished he said:

"You're sure he's telling the truth about that letter?"

"I am convinced of it, Mr. Hatton. It is, indeed, most unfortunate; but I am quite sure it is no longer in his possession."

"No," replied the young man, "but are you sure he didn't destroy it himself?"

"Yes, Mr. Hatton, I am even confident of that. I feared the Inspector might not believe it; nevertheless I allowed myself to hope that *you*——"

"Mr. Colchester, I have still some faith in Edward's innocence of the murder, but it's impossible to have any faith in his veracity. You must see that yourself. He's been lying just as it suited him, or rather as he thought it suited him—for they've all been silly lies. If he's innocent, he's extremely tiresome. I wish I could believe him when he says something, for the case might get on then, but he's put it out of the question himself. What did he mean by that lie about the pills, for instance? When the Inspector first questioned him, he said flatly that he'd had no more than usual, and now he suddenly admits *one* extra. One is no use to anyone whatever; it only gives all his other statements a fishier look."

"Surely, at least," I remonstrated, "it makes the whole of his confession last night more convincing. If he had been lying to me, he would have said that he took *five* extra pills."

"Remember," said Mr. Hatton, "if he's not the murderer, he may not be sure how many pills were used. Still he'd have guessed more than one, at any rate. There's something in that, but the fact remains that as a general thing we can't trust him. Well, the letter's out of reach, and whether he destroyed it himself or someone stole it there's very little chance of its being seen again. I'm afraid this is going to be more or less an off day."

154

I asked him why he thought so.

"Well, the next move is the Inspector's. The police are going through Lord Malvern's rooms in town on the chance of something useful, and I believe Lockitt intends to run up himself and take charge of anything there may be. He has his eye on a will, but not very hopefully, of course. Charles's solicitors haven't got one, and I think it's very unlikely there is such a thing. In any case the estate's entailed, and the rest can't amount to much."

"But surely," I said, "there is no question of such a motive?"

"It has to be reckoned with, and there may be other papers of some kind. By the way, the inquest is to-morrow morning."

I must have looked startled.

"Oh," he said at once, "it won't be formidable. I shouldn't think you, for instance, need appear at all. If it weren't for Frampton, the Inspector might think he had a case, but as it is he wants more evidence, and the proceedings are safe to be adjourned quite promptly. He's thinking now of an autopsy—as it happens there's none of that whisky left to analyse, and of course it's a main point."

"Yes," I replied, "I noticed that Matthew emptied the decanter."

"Very troublesome," said the young man. "You realize that's another bad mark to Edward—his pouring away half his own whisky?"

"But, Mr. Hatton," I replied, shocked, "he never drinks more than a little—a very little. Matthew had inadvertently poured out more than usual for him, that is all."

"I don't say it wasn't natural, but like everything else it looks fishy. By the way, what do you suppose became of the little Edward didn't drink?"

"Really," I replied, "I cannot say. It was thrown away, no doubt."

"He poured it into an empty glass, didn't he?" asked Mr. Hatton.

"Yes, I think so."

"Then Frampton probably drank it if he was innocent, and if not, got rid of it otherwise. If he had shown any signs of being drugged too, we should know what to think; but there probably wasn't enough left to do much harm. So his immunity tells us nothing either way."

"I am, of course, very little qualified to judge," said I, "but I cannot help feeling that we are altogether at a standstill. What is to be done next?—what *can* be done next, Mr. Hatton?"

"Well, suppose we turn back to the house, in the first place. I'll have a word or two with Edward myself; now that he's reconciled he may be more communicative."

I shook my head.

"I fear he has little more to tell."

As we passed before the breakfast-room windows we observed Phyllis on the window-seat, and, as far as I could see, alone in the room. She appeared to have been watching us, but now, catching my eye, she at once turned away her head.

Mr. Hatton gave me an expressive look.

"Don't you think", he said, "that perhaps there *is* something to be done? I'll see you again presently."

Work for a Casuist

It was impossible to ignore so broad a hint; moreover, I reflected, Phyllis's secret, whatever it was, evidently weighed greatly on her spirits, and to induce her to impart it might be a kindness to her as well as a public obligation. With this idea I re-entered the breakfast-room. She started up as I did so, and I feared she was about to make her escape.

"My dear child," said I, "do not let me disturb you—I hope you are not going on my account? Though, indeed, it is a beautiful morning again; perhaps I ought rather to be surprised at finding you indoors at all."

"No," replied Phyllis in great confusion. "I—I wasn't going out. I—I think I want to speak to you, Mr. Colchester."

"Certainly, my dear," said I. "I am quite at your disposal. But you look very serious; I hope nothing unpleasant has occurred?"

"N-no," replied Phyllis, "at least it's not about me really. It's—it's about Saturday night."

"Do you mean", said I, "that it has some connection with this dreadful business?"

"Oh, I don't know—I hope it hasn't! Yes, I suppose it has in a way."

"But if it has," said I, "ought you not rather to speak to the Inspector, or to Mr. Hatton? They have a right to any such information, remember, and they will know best how to deal with it."

"Oh, but that's just it!" she exclaimed. "I don't know whether—I don't think it has *really* anything to do with the murder at all. It's—it's a point of conscience, I think, Mr. Colchester." She blushed as she uttered this rather lofty phrase.

"In that case," said I, repressing a smile with some difficulty, "of course I shall be glad to advise you as well as I can. Won't you sit down again, my dear?"

She complied, and when we were both seated went on:

"I didn't know what to do—I didn't know if it would be right to tell the police. And then I thought if anything should happen to Edward—— But I'm sure it hasn't *really* anything to do with the murder. And then I thought I must ask someone. I thought of aunt, but somehow she's difficult to tell things. And then I thought as it *was* a—a point of conscience, Mr. Colchester, it would be better to ask *you*."

"It was very wise of you to decide on consulting someone," I replied. "And what *is* this point, my dear, which has been troubling you so much?"

"Well, Mr. Colchester, supposing someone knew something about—about that night—something the police didn't know. And supposing she was sure it had nothing really to do with the murder, because— well, because she was sure it couldn't have; only if she told it the police might start suspecting someone who hadn't really anything to do with it——"

She paused. "Well, my dear?" said I.

"Well, in that case, ought she to tell, Mr. Colchester?"

"Really, my dear child," I replied, "I fear I can only answer you if you will tell me what it is you *do* know."

She looked somewhat alarmed.

"But if I did, Mr. Colchester—wouldn't *you* tell the police?"

"My dear Phyllis," said I, "when you decided to consult me on the abstract question—on the point of conscience, let us say—did you mean to abide by my advice?"

"I—yes, I suppose so, Mr. Colchester."

"Then if you were prepared to go to the police yourself on my advice, why should you hesitate to confide in *me*? My dear, you must see that I cannot resolve such a question in ignorance of the circumstances."

"N-no, I suppose not. But I feel it's so awful of me to tell! Even if they weren't suspected, I should feel so awful!"

"Come, my dear, let me know what it is; it will be a relief to your own mind, if nothing more. Remember this is a very serious matter—terribly serious. If your silence were to have the fatal consequences it might have—if you even imagined it had determined the course of events—how could you ever forgive yourself?"

"Oh, but, Mr. Colchester, how could I ever forgive myself if I told, and then things went all wrong? Oh, I don't know what I should do, if——"

"Whatever happened, my dear, you could have no cause to reproach yourself for telling the truth. Be wise, and let me know what is troubling you; I promise I will not urge you to make it public if there seems to me any other course."

Phyllis hesitated a little longer, and then breathed a deep sigh.

"Very well, Mr. Colchester—only if you don't think the police need be told, *you* won't tell anyone?"

"Of course not, my dear. Surely you cannot doubt that I will respect your confidence?"

"Oh, no—I'm so sorry. But I'm so worried, Mr. Colchester—I feel so awful!"

I said nothing, but quietly waited for her to begin.

"Well, you see, it was on Saturday night—you know where my bedroom is, Mr. Colchester?"

I assented.

"I went along to have a bath—you know the bathroom just round the corner, at the top of the stairs?"

"Yes, my dear, of course I do."

"Yes, of course—well, I went along to have a bath, and after I'd turned the water on and everything I found I'd forgotten my pyjamas." She pronounced the word with a slight blush. "So I thought I'd go back and fetch them. I don't suppose anyone could have heard me, because I don't think I'd shut the door properly, and the water was on, and it was making a good deal of noise, of course."

"Yes?" I said, as she again paused.

"And just as I turned the corner I saw that Anne's door was open, and I was just going to call out to her when she came out, and she was *dragging* something.'

"*Dragging* something!" I repeated.

Phyllis nodded, with an expression of intense unhappiness.

"Yes, and it looked so funny that I stopped—I think I stepped back so that she wouldn't see me. I couldn't think what she was doing. And the next time I looked—you know those rugs in the passage, Mr. Colchester?"

Once again I assented. That part of the house was furnished, not with a long strip of carpet, but with a succession of beautifully soft woollen rugs, worked by Miss Barry herself.

"Well, she pushed one of them out of the way, and she dragged this thing—it was bundled up in her own carpet—along to Lord Malvern's door—you know it was just next to hers. And you know how slippery the floor is underneath—the thing just slid along, and you couldn't hear anything with the water running."

"My dear child," I exclaimed, "this is a most extra-ordinary story! Are you sure—forgive me—but are you quite *sure* that it is not, in part, the work of your own imagination? All these terrible events——"

"No, *no*, Mr. Colchester—I really saw it. I *swear* I really saw it! She opened Lord Malvern's door and went in, and then almost immediately afterwards she came out again without—without *it*—just carrying the carpet—and she went back into her own room and shut the door."

I was so much astounded that for a moment I could say nothing at all. Then with an effort I pulled myself together and inquired:

"But this—this *thing*, my dear Phyllis—have you no idea what it was?"

With a very white face she stammered out:

"Oh, yes, Mr. Colchester—I—I'm afraid—oh, Mr. Colchester, I'm afraid it was *him*!"

"*Him*? My dear child, what do you—what can you possibly mean? Are you quite well?"

She began to cry, in a frightened, whimpering manner, with few tears.

"Oh, Mr. Colchester, it was a *man*—I could see it was a man! I couldn't see who it was, but I saw his knees distinctly, and one of his feet, and who else *could* it have been? And I was so *terrified* next morning —I was frightened at the time, but I was so *terrified* next morning—and oh, what ought I to have done? Oh, Mr. Colchester, tell me what to do now?"

I could only, just then, form one opinion—the poor girl's mind must be unhinged. The events of the day before had been too much for her; she had been hysterical at the time, and had since given way to morbid fancies. I looked at her with great compassion, endeavouring to decide how it would be wisest and kindest to treat her at this juncture.

"I can see you don't believe me! Oh, Mr. Colchester, I did see it, I *swear* I saw it, and at first I thought she *must* have had something to do with it—that was why it was so awful. But afterwards when I heard he'd been drugged I could see what must have happened—he'd been in her room and fallen asleep like the Colonel did, and perhaps she was afraid someone would find him there—she might have thought he was drunk or something—and that's why she did it. I'm sure that must have been why. And I'm sure it was all right him being there—there must have been some proper reason, but she can't want it known about, or she'd have told it herself. Perhaps she thinks they'll suspect her, though she had nothing to do with it. And so it seems so awful my telling it, when she's been so nice to me and everything. And after all it might only put them wrong—people who don't know her, I mean—so do you think they *need* know?"

My first impression was staggered by this speech. Lord Malvern *might* conceivably have been in Mrs. Fairfax's bedroom that evening, and if so, the rest was equally possible, though unlikely. It was even possible that he had had an innocent reason for going there, but I confess I felt more than doubtful on that head. Could it be that my old friend, in supposing her in love with him, had actually fallen short of the truth? This was a most unwelcome surmise; yet on the other hand, if Mrs. Fairfax were innocent, and had an avowable motive for receiving the young man in those conditions, why had she been silent all this time? I was inclined to agree with Matthew that she had too much sense to give way to vague fears. Unquestionably it all looked very bad.

"*Must* I tell the police, do you think?" repeated Phyllis.

"My dear," I replied very gravely, "I am amazed that you should have thought it necessary to consult me at all. If your story is true, the police ought to have heard it immediately, and I cannot suffer you to conceal it a moment longer. I still cannot understand why you did not tell them in the first place, when you thought Mrs. Fairfax was implicated in the murder."

"*Oh!*" she exclaimed with a look of horror, "I couldn't tell when I thought that. I don't think I could ever have told them when I thought that. How *could* I, Mr. Colchester?"

"What!" said I. "Not when you knew that *Edward* had come under suspicion?"

She replied only by a burst of tears.

"My dear child," I said, regretting my severity, "do not distress yourself—you have done quite right in speaking to me at last. But it is essential that Inspector Lockitt should know what you have told me; you see that, my dear?"

I could not be certain that she did see it, even then, but she gave way to my insistence.

On inquiry, however, it proved that Inspector Lockitt had already set off on his journey to town. It only remained, therefore, to seek out Mr. Hatton, with whom I felt personally even more bound to communicate at once. Frampton—he was on duty once more, and looking, to my surprise, much as usual—thought Mr. Hatton was with Mr. Edward in the garden.

"Will you tell him, please, that I shall be glad to speak with him at his convenience?"

"Very good, sir."

"Oh, Mr. Colchester," exclaimed Phyllis when we were alone again, "need I be here? Won't *you* tell him? I wouldn't mind it so much if you told him."

"But, my dear, he will certainly wish to question you."

"Yes, I know that, but will you tell him first? I don't think I could bear to. If I hadn't to tell him, I wouldn't mind being questioned so much."

This seemed to me a little unreasonable, and perhaps irregular, but she was so much in earnest that I thought it wiser not to refuse. She was by no means herself yet, and ought clearly to be spared as far as possible.

"Very well, my dear; if you feel so strongly about it, I will tell him."

"Thank you, Mr. Colchester—thank you *so* much! And I needn't be there, need I?"

"But, my dear," I remonstrated, "why not? Do you not feel well?"

"Yes; but I do feel awful, Mr. Colchester; I feel so —so *treacherous* giving her away like this—going to the police behind her back. It does seem such a low thing to do. I'll never be able to face her again—she'll always hate and despise me after this. Oh, are you quite *sure* I need have done it? It does seem so mean."

Once again I assured her that there was no possible doubt of her duty in the matter.

"I suppose you're right," she agreed sorrowfully. "I suppose you must be right. But I do wish I hadn't seen her. I wonder my subconscious didn't make me forget about it."

I could hardly forbear smiling as I asked her what she meant by this odd statement.

"Well, they say that's why you forget things—because subconsciously you don't want to remember them. And I've been hoping all the time that my subconscious would make me forget this, but it doesn't seem to work at all somehow; perhaps I didn't give it time enough."

"I think", said I gently, "most of us forget a great deal that we should like to remember, and remember what we should prefer to forget."

"Yes, I know," she replied with great seriousness,

"it often seems like that. But really that's only our conscious mind deceiving us—our subconscious is quite different."

I did not think it necessary to argue the question, or to point out the inference in her own case; she would, no doubt, have been shocked to think that subconsciously she was bent on remembering Saturday night's incident. There was a brief silence; then she continued:

"But as I couldn't forget it soon enough, I suppose I *ought* to have told—only I needn't be here, need I, Mr. Colchester?"

On this point also I thought it kinder to give way.

"But you must not be far off, my dear, if Mr. Hatton should ask for you."

"All right, Mr. Colchester, I'll be in the garden, I promise." And she made her escape, just in time to avoid encountering Mr. Hatton, who came in before her steps had died away.

"Well," was the first thing he said to me, "*is* it Mrs. Fairfax?"

CHAPTER TWELVE

Quite Unprofessional

His quickness took me a little by surprise.

"Why, the fact is", said I, "that I have just had a conversation with Phyllis—a most extraordinary conversation. She has made a confession to me which I hardly know how to believe. Really, Mr. Hatton, I feel it awkward even to repeat such things."

The young man seated himself on the edge of the table, and asked again, still with not quite his usual detached manner:

"It's about Mrs. Fairfax, isn't it?"

"Yes," I replied. "I cannot think what has led you to that conclusion, but you are quite right."

"You told me Phyllis had a passion for her," Mr. Hatton explained. "Yet she hasn't confided in her; she's been making great efforts not to confide in anyone. Naturally I supposed Mrs. Fairfax was mixed up in it. My only doubt has been whether it was really anything worth keeping dark."

"I do not believe", said I, "that it throws any light upon the murder—I hope not; but certainly it ought not to have been concealed so long. I will repeat the whole story as nearly as I can remember it, and leave you to estimate its significance."

Accordingly, I told him exactly what had passed between Phyllis Winter and myself, not omitting my first impression that her tale was the offspring of hysteria. I could see at a glance that Mr. Hatton did not share that view. He listened with a darkening countenance, and with occasional restless movements which, in him, surprised me greatly; and when I came to state *what* Phyllis imagined she had seen dragged along the passage, he got to his feet with a smothered exclamation which induced me to stop short.

"All right," he said. "Go on, Mr. Colchester"— and he threw himself hastily into a chair.

"Really, there is not much more to tell. When Lord Malvern's body was discovered, Phyllis at first thought Mrs. Fairfax must have had a hand in his death; but she has since formed what appears to me a more plausible theory."

"Yes," said he. "She thinks he happened to be in her room, and fell asleep there?"

"You are very quick, Mr. Hatton. Yes, that is her idea."

"In that case," he said, "I think she might have kept the whole business to herself."

I was startled, and, I must add, somewhat shocked.

"Do you really mean", said I, "that it is unnecessary for the police to hear about it?"

"Oh, they've got to be told *now*. I'm responsible to Lockitt in a way, and I must tell him. But what can it have to do with the murder? It's an additional red herring, that's all, and Mrs. Fairfax's private affairs are no business of ours." He got up once more, and after a hasty turn or two came to a standstill with his back against the wall, looking strangely out of temper, and, I thought, extremely formidable. "Of course," he went on, "it may be true enough—Charles could never have rucked the carpet up like that by sliding *forward*—— Well, it may take Lockitt's mind off Edward for a bit. I've almost committed myself now to Edward; Mr. Barry——"

These words clearly did not represent what was passing in his mind; they seemed intended rather to hide his discomposure, and failed signally, for he now came to a stop in sheer confusion of ideas.

"Matthew", I said, "is relying on you to dispel these unhappy suspicions?"

"Yes—by the way, did Phyllis insist upon *your* breaking the news, or have you told me without her consent?"

I explained what had been said, and how strongly she seemed to feel upon the subject.

"It appeared to me irregular, as you may imagine, but I could not help fearing that a refusal would make her ill again. She is evidently prepared for questioning, however: she promised to wait in the garden in case you should wish to speak to her immediately."

"Then it had better be done," said Mr. Hatton, jerking himself erect. "Will you come with me?"

"Certainly, if you wish it. I thought you might prefer to see her alone."

"No, I don't want to risk another fit—your presence may have a sedative effect on her." As we were leaving the room he added: "How *very* right I was in thinking you would hear more than the police! But I suppose you're used to confidences?"

"Yes, Mr. Hatton, I may say I am used to them. I have, in a sense, no life of my own, and that fact emboldens others to seek counsel of me; a priest who was not also a celibate would, I imagine, hear much less."

"I should have thought——" he was beginning: but just then, as I was about to undo the little gate of the flower garden, we saw Mrs. Fairfax approaching it from the other side.

Her appearance was in strange, almost bewildering contrast to the sinister tale we had just heard. She looked very young and thoughtful; she had an even touching air of nobility and innocence. This might, of course, be the effect only of her personal advantages, and of a pretty summer dress which, though reaching to her ankles, left her arms bare to the shoulder, and displayed the soft outline of her neck. Certainly this attire gave her a fresh and girlish look I had not previously noticed, and it occurred to me for the first time that a connoisseur might perhaps have rated her beauty higher than Miss Grant's. When she caught sight of us, her expression changed, and she called out:

"Oh, there you are, Mr. Hatton! What in the world have you been doing to Phyllis?"

Before he could answer, she pushed the gate open and walked out. He made way for her with more than his accustomed aloofness—almost stiffly—and then said:

"Why do you think I've been doing anything to her?"

"Well, I came across her a moment ago, and she seemed to be moping, so I asked her if she felt like a bathe. She said she couldn't; she said it with so much feeling that I couldn't help asking her why not. She turned very red and gasped out something about Mr. Hatton, and then fled in tears."

Mrs. Fairfax concluded this explanation with an inquiring glance.

"I see," replied Mr. Hatton noncommittally.

"Phyllis is a noodle," resumed Mrs. Fairfax, "but she's a nice thing. I hope you haven't felt it necessary to chivvy her?"

"No," said Mr. Hatton gravely, "I was just about to, but if you'll spare us a few moments instead I'll put it off. Shall we sit down somewhere?"

She glanced rapidly from one to the other of us, and then replied with a smile:

"Oh, certainly—I'm delighted to be the scapegoat. Where shall we sit?"

"I noticed some garden chairs in the porch," said Mr. Hatton. "If I bring them out on to the lawn, we shan't be missing the fine weather."

"You think of everything!" she returned, still smiling. "Just as you like."

There was something very odd, I thought, in their manner to each other; something which was not the result of the present situation, but which I had been aware of from the first. Could it be that they had known each other, or known of each other, before Mr. Hatton's arrival at Friars Cross? And if so, what could there be in either's past to account for this air of self-consciousness, almost of suspicion? I revolved the question as I strolled, at Mrs. Fairfax's side, towards the lawn; I had not dismissed it when we were joined by Mr. Hatton with the garden chairs. But no theory occurred to me which, on a second examination, remained plausible, and the awkwardness of the immediate moment soon claimed all my thoughts. Mr. Hatton must have been fully alive to the suspense he had created; yet the chairs were arranged, and we all seated ourselves, without any remark from him beyond an inquiry whether Mrs. Fairfax would prefer to be in the shade.

"This is a solemn occasion," she observed at last, with every appearance of composure. "Do break it to me quickly, or I may faint again."

"Oh, of course—you fainted yesterday morning, didn't you?" said Mr. Hatton.

"To be sure I did. Well, my comfort is that Mr. Colchester helped to bring me round on that occasion, so he's had experience." And with a resigned air, more impudent than innocent, she closed her eyes.

"Mrs. Fairfax——" he was beginning with the old stiffness of manner.

("Still I'm sure he doesn't like it"), she interrupted parenthetically, ("so you might as *well* be quick, if you don't mind.")

"I was going to," said he, "but I think after all Mr. Colchester had better. He has a more direct knowledge of the facts, and will probably put them more tactfully."

"*Tact*!" exclaimed Mrs. Fairfax. "This looks very bad. Mr. Colchester, do tell me what the matter is."

I glanced at Mr. Hatton with some reproach.

"Is it really necessary that it should come from me? I confess I should prefer——"

"Do tell me, Mr. Colchester," she repeated, now quite seriously. "I'm evidently under suspicion, and Mr. Hatton for some reason chooses to prolong the agony; I know you can't mean to do the same."

"Don't talk like that!" he exclaimed in unexpected confusion, actually reddening a little. "I'm sorry—I had no idea——"

She silenced him with a look and gesture of much dignity. "It's all right," she replied. "As you say, Mr. Colchester will tell me what the matter is." And she turned to me with an air of settled and quiet attention which excluded him, as it were, from anything to be said next.

"Mrs. Fairfax," I began, "you cannot imagine what a painful—what a very painful and unwelcome task this is to me. Pray make it easier for me by considering that I am only about to repeat what I have heard; no belief of my own is involved in it, no idea of condemning or even of accusing you in any way. I hope you will accept my assurance that that is so?"

"Yes, of course," she replied. "Do go on."

Thus urged, I once more, but as briefly as possible, related what I had heard from Phyllis Winter. Any doubts of the story which may have lingered in my mind grew fainter and fainter as I proceeded; it was, indeed, scarcely possible to look at Mrs. Fairfax and imagine that she was surprised. Her face, if it expressed anything, expressed vexation, even perhaps resentment; but she was not shocked, or materially discomposed. In spite of the assurance I had just given her, I began, I must confess, to think of her with great severity: was it possible, I wondered, that Mr. Hatton already knew her by reputation as a woman of light conduct? The delicacy I had at first anxiously maintained seemed quite uncalled for, its object being so much at ease, and I am afraid I even concluded with some bluntness.

"Well," she said when I had finished, "and that's all?"

"That is all," I replied gravely.

"And I am to assume", she went on, glancing for the first time at Mr. Hatton, "that you both believe all this?"

"Not at all," said he. "Mr. Colchester has just said that he has an open mind."

"Oh, yes, of course," she replied with some bitterness. "But you believe it?"

He made no answer.

"If you don't," she exclaimed with a sudden burst of unaffected indignation, "your manner to me is insufferable—and if you do, upon my word I think it's worse. You know that everybody's going to be told this about me, and instead of softening it you take up the attitude—— You'd better go to Inspector Lockitt immediately; I prefer to deal with him. If *his* manners are bad, at any rate it's because he knows no better."

Words cannot express my amazement at this outburst. Mr. Hatton endured it with no more than a slight increase of woodenness, and said calmly:

"Unfortunately the Inspector has gone up to town. I'm sorry you can't see him at once, but he'll be back this afternoon, I dare say. In the meantime, and as a point of curiosity—are we to infer that you deny all this?"

"Just as you please," she returned without emotion.

"But, Mrs. Fairfax," I ventured to remonstrate, "is not your attitude a little unreasonable? If the story is false, you must see that we are not to blame for it. Indeed, for my part——"

"You have still an open mind?" she asked.

"At least," I replied somewhat uneasily, "I am still most anxious to maintain one."

"You know that Phyllis was hysterical yesterday morning?"

"Of course," I said, "and for that very reason I felt some doubt——"

"She was hysterical, and now she's come to you with a hysterical tale which Mr. Hatton apparently finds no difficulty in believing. But I don't really see that I need allow myself to be bullied on that account. I should think in the first place Phyllis ought perhaps to see a doctor."

She was so cool that I felt, in spite of myself, a little shaken.

"Do you really mean", I said, "that this story is an invention of the poor girl's?"

"I didn't say so. If I'd been approached in a less inquisitorial manner—but no, I really think Mr. Hatton had better work it out for himself. If he can establish the least connection between Charles and me, I may think it worth discussing."

"Mrs. Fairfax is quite right," the young man put in, adopting the same indirect method of address.

"After all, this doesn't throw much light on the murder; and it's natural she shouldn't care to admit that Charles was in her room at that hour. It really doesn't concern us in the least."

"Exactly," she retorted with heightened colour. "Though, by the way, it's only because it doesn't concern you that I should dream of denying it—if it were the case. There's no reason why I shouldn't have received Charles or anyone else at any hour I chose."

"Not at all," he assented with an air of polite indifference.

All of a sudden, at the sight of their flushed cheeks and careless manner, a light broke upon my understanding. I was assisting, oddly enough, at a love scene!

The idea once given, I could have no doubt at all; nay, I was inclined to think they had fallen in love, as the saying is, at first sight. The look they had interchanged on first meeting had been one of mutual attraction, and in their peculiarity of manner ever since I had been detecting a slight tinge of flirtation— if I may so call it—nothing more. I was almost astonished at my own obtuseness, for two young people in the early stages of attachment are surely a sight common enough to be recognized without difficulty, even by an ageing celibate; but the truth is, I suppose, that my mind had been too much occupied by the crime and its results. I now understood Mr. Hatton's agitation earlier in the day; I understood why his manner to Mrs. Fairfax had been so stiff, and, to use her own word, inquisitorial; and I realized also why

she had been so hasty in resenting it. Viewed in the
light of this discovery, they both looked a little comic;
but I felt kindly disposed towards them, and instinc-
tively desirous to smooth matters over.

"My dear children——" I began.

The words slipped out unawares; but each turned
on me such a startled look that I broke off in confusion.

"You were saying?" said Mrs. Fairfax, with a
laughable assumption of unconsciousness.

"I was merely going to say that it is a pity this disclosure should have been the occasion of ill-feeling.
Surely we are all united in anxiety to learn the truth
—all those of us, I mean, who are innocent of this
horrid crime; and any coolness among ourselves must
necessarily stand in the way of our main purpose."

"There's no coolness on my side," declared the
young man rather haughtily.

"And there is certainly none on mine," added Mrs.
Fairfax in the same tone. "Besides, not even Mr.
Hatton pretends that this story of Phyllis's is connected
with the murder; therefore nothing I say about it can
affect the real point."

"I did say that," he rejoined quickly, "but after all,
it remains possible—or the Inspector may think so."

"What remains possible?" she demanded.

"That it *is* somehow connected with the murder."

"Well," returned Mrs. Fairfax, "when you have
proved a connection, I may discuss it, as I said. In
the meantime, I'm going to bathe."

And with an air of serenity slightly tinged with
scorn she walked off towards the house.

I turned to Mr. Hatton, who was gazing intently at her retreating figure.

"Surely," I said, "you cannot really imagine——"

Mr. Hatton started.

"Excuse me," he said hastily. "I've just remembered—I'll see you before lunch, I hope?"

And without waiting for a reply he strode off in the opposite direction.

CHAPTER THIRTEEN

Roses and Thorns

I could not but feel this new turn of affairs to be incongruous, and, from Mr. Hatton's point of view, most lamentably unprofessional. He might sincerely wish to view the case with detachment, and to give it his whole energy, but how could that be practicable when he was at the same moment falling in love—in love, moreover, with one of the persons concerned? In the first place he seemed to have entirely forgotten Phyllis Winter, who, I supposed, was still waiting in the garden. This oversight, though doubtless a trifle in itself, might prove only too significant of the conduct we were now to expect from him. He was, I feared, too young to be employed in a case so rich, if I may use the expression, in young women. However, the mischief was now done, and I thought I had better, at least, warn Phyllis not to look for him immediately. With this idea I returned to the garden; but Phyllis was nowhere to be seen.

Her absence confirmed me in the impression that a strangely casual element had somehow introduced itself into this serious and terrible business. It might, perhaps, be due to Inspector Lockitt's absence in

London. Mr. Hatton was an intelligent young man, but he was at best an amateur; his proceedings had not the rigour of authority, and did not command the same respect. He had said, in his colloquial manner, that this would probably be an off day, and the prediction seemed in a fair way to be verified; not even Phyllis's startling disclosure had prevented apathy from setting in. However, there was nothing I could do to remedy this; the Inspector's return would doubtless be the signal for renewed activity, and meanwhile, if a breathing-space was thrust upon us, there could be no harm in enjoying it as best we might.

Edward, I had excellent reason to believe, no longer needed or desired my society, and I made no attempt to seek him out. Indeed, after a little hesitation I thought I could not do better than take a book on to the lawn, where I should be easily visible to anyone who might wish to see me, and in particular to Mr. Hatton if he were really thinking of another interview, as he had appeared to suggest. The morning was bright and warm, though with the refreshment of a slight and fitful breeze, on which now and then a solitary leaf, the first of autumn, would detach itself and flutter, with deliberate and thoughtful pauses, to the ground. At a little distance I could see Baker with his mowing-machine, the steady buzz of which formed an undertone to meditation; otherwise the silence was infringed only, at rare intervals, by the noise of a car on the adjoining road. I was more attentive to the world around than to the substance of my reading, but nothing occurred to ruffle the fair

surface of the scene before me, and no one approached
to disturb me in my solitude. Only, as the luncheon
hour drew near, my notice was caught by one trifling
incident, far from extraordinary in itself, and for that
very reason surprising to me in the circumstances.
Footsteps became audible on the gravel path to the
left of the house, which led out of the grounds by a
side gate: footsteps, voices, and the fresh intermittent
sound of women's laughter. I had hardly had time to
wonder at this when Mrs. Fairfax and Phyllis Winter
came into view, each carrying a towel and a wet
bathing-dress. Mrs. Fairfax, rather unwontedly—for
she was not prone to these intimate gestures—had
linked her disengaged arm with her young companion's, and in this familiar manner they passed on
towards the house. I could but conclude that Mrs.
Fairfax had been at pains to seek the poor girl out,
with the object of reassuring and diverting her; and
the fact was at least an indication of kind-heartedness.
She might, of course, design to play on her affection
and induce her to withdraw her testimony; but it
seemed improbable, and I was most unwilling to
believe it. One of the worst features of this dreadful
business was the suspicion it necessarily fostered on
all sides; surely I, at any rate, might so far withstand
its baneful influence.

Luncheon passed off without any of the unfortunate lapses of the night before, and with nothing more
remarkable than the continued stiffness between Mrs.
Fairfax and Mr. Hatton. In the drawing-room afterwards Matthew pressed me to come out for a stroll. I
felt it was a long time since I had had any conversa-

tion with him, and agreed the more readily on that account.

"Well," he began presently, "have you heard Frampton's latest?"

I suppose I looked surprised.

"You haven't? I thought you and Hatton were all in all to one another. Oh, yes, he's started on a new tack. He now says he did write those letters to Judith."

"Indeed!"

"He found out about her from old Lord Malvern's valet, it appears. But he's prepared to take the most formidable oaths that he didn't write to Edward, and that the whole thing is a conspiracy."

"A conspiracy! But surely the letter to Edward is the main evidence against Edward himself! It can add very little, if anything, to the probability of *Frampton's* guilt."

"Quite so, but you don't realize how the man's mind works—that is, if you can call it working. He's been seeing himself throughout as a victim of the upper classes, and this he sets down as the grand instance."

"But do you really think", said I, "that it is possible he didn't write to Edward?"

"I don't know; I'd rather not pronounce. Of course the letter's vanished, so that it can't be proved against him. We've nothing to go on but its general resemblance to the ones he did write. And he may have realized that, and concluded that his best course was to forswear it altogether."

"But", I again objected, "does he really improve

his position by the denial? He is still admittedly guilty of blackmail, and he may still have killed Lord Malvern out of jealousy and revenge."

"Yes, yes," replied Matthew, "but don't you see, Joseph, that if he didn't write that letter somebody else must have written it?"

I started at the observation.

"To be sure," I said slowly. "But in that case——— My dear Matthew, are you quite certain that the letter *did* so much resemble those Frampton wrote?"

"Quite certain; they must have been meant to look the same. And in that case you can see for yourself it's a queer business. If Frampton didn't write it, someone else must be mixed up in this—someone of an astonishingly fishy character; which makes both Frampton and Edward much more doubtful suspects. But the infernal thing is that after all he *may* have written it."

"But then," said I, "—excuse me, I confess my head is not quite clear—but if there *is* someone else, it must be someone who knew of the relations between Miss Grant and the former Lord Malvern. That is so, Matthew, surely?"

"Yes," he replied, knitting his brows, and unconsciously slackening his pace, "and not only that; they must have known about the *other* letters—in fact, have had a pretty good idea of the whole business."

"And *could* anyone———"

"No one, that I can think of, except of course, Charles and Judith, who are out of it. Someone might have guessed what was in the other letters, I suppose, but it would have been rather a surprising feat of ingenuity."

I reflected for a moment.

"My dear Matthew," I said at last, "is not the whole thing too improbable? Surely it seems more natural to conclude that Frampton is lying again?"

He uttered a groan of vexation.

"It does," he replied, "infinitely more natural; it's the most natural thing to conclude about Frampton in all circumstances. And yet on Edward's account I should like to believe him just this once."

"Of course," I observed, "it is, in a way, strange that he should have had the audacity to write to Edward while Lord Malvern was still in the house. The threat of prosecution seems to have alarmed him greatly, for the time at any rate."

Matthew acknowledged this, but with less eagerness than I had expected.

"If he were only a shade less thick-witted I should call it a strong point; but my dear Joseph, the fellow appears to have no brains whatever. He may really not have seen that it would lead him straight into more trouble. If only Frampton were a rational animal, what an easy case this would have been! or rather I suppose there couldn't have been one at all." His face darkened, and I saw he was thinking of the poor young man who had been killed.

After a pause I asked:

"What does Mr. Hatton think of this new development? He had heard of it, of course?"

"Oh yes," said Matthew, "and he seems inclined to believe there's something in it. Of course, he's bound to look into it for Edward's sake; the misfortune is that there's nowhere in particular to look. As the letter's gone, how *can* it be proved that Frampton did or didn't write it?"

I confessed myself unable to resolve this point.

"But then", I said, "we must not forget that it is in the hands of experts. To a man of special training and ability, modes of inquiry may suggest themselves which would not occur to a mere onlooker. Surely, if it were not so, there would be no object in employing a detective at all."

"Very true, Joseph," replied my old friend rather drily, "but the power of seeing through a stone wall has been denied even to the detectives among us. The paper is evidently no clue. It's a common kind— there was some in the servants' hall, where anyone could have got at it. The letter was posted in the village—that's something; but I'll take my oath it ain't much, as Mr. Boffin said. Frampton, if he *is* lying, must have posted it on Friday afternoon or evening. He had the afternoon off, but no one appears to have seen him in the village, which is rather odd; however, I suppose good luck and a bit of slinking might account for it."

"Has he been asked where he was that afternoon?"

"Yes," replied Matthew. "Part of the time he was certainly mooning about here, but the rest is hypothetical. He says he went for a stroll."

"And on that stroll," I inquired, "did he meet no one?"

"My tale provokes that question," Matthew acknowledged, accompanying the citation with a bitter grin. "I thought he might have had a rendezvous with Milly Baker, but it appears not. He seems doubtful where he went, and thinks he may have seen a farm labourer or two."

We both paused, as though brought to a stop by the hopeless nature of the problem. We had just reached the end of a field-path, and Matthew, instead of opening the gate, seated himself upon it, and began tapping the lower bars aimlessly with his walking-stick.

"I can't say", he observed presently, "that I ever retain a much more vivid impression of my own rambles; but as it's Frampton, and as we particularly want to know about it, it looks fishy."

"Perhaps", I suggested, "we may still find someone who noticed him in the village."

"Very likely," agreed Matthew. "Research can hardly have been exhaustive at this point; but that would only tend to show that he did post the letter— an unfortunate conclusion. And it'll be harder to show he didn't post it. I'm afraid."

"Really," I said after a pause, "my mind is still in a good deal of confusion; but the whole idea, you must remember, is so very recent! I cannot doubt that we shall learn more in time. My dear Matthew, it is your misfortune to despair too readily; you are always too prone to expect the worst."

"Well, well," he returned with some impatience, "I've seen so much of the worst lately that I feel almost entitled to expect it. Shall we be getting back?"

I assented, and we retraced our steps towards the pleasure grounds. Little more was said between us, for Matthew, I feared, was out of temper, and after what he had told me I myself had sufficient food for thought. Yet I was sorry to have annoyed him, although inadvertently, and a longer pause than usual roused me to inquire, by way of introducing a more welcome topic, how his work on the Greek drama had been progressing since our last discussion of it. The effect was instant; he brightened perceptibly, and replied in something more like his usual tone:

"Oh, it's doing well enough; thank God it's out of the sphere of all this hubbub. I shall begin revising it in a day or two."

I had not known it was so far advanced, and expressed my pleasure and congratulations very warmly.

"Thank you, Joseph," he said. "Well, it keeps my afternoons rational, at any rate, and that's something. If it weren't for Susan, even those would no doubt be sucked into the whirlpool; as it is, I may be allowed to work in peace. She's imbued the servants with an excellent notion of routine."

We were just then passing the gate of the flower garden, and I caught sight of Miss Barry herself, armed with a watering-can, and moving to and fro among her favourite rose bushes. It seemed natural to go in and exchange a word with her, but Matthew, when I suggested it, excused himself, saying it was time he got back to his work. I approached her alone, therefore, and made some remark about the beauty of the afternoon. Miss Barry was too much of a gardener to acquiesce.

"It may be very agreeable", she retorted, "to those who have nothing to do but sit down and enjoy it.

For my own part, I should prefer a few days of settled rain."

Somewhat abashed, I agreed that it was very dry.

"In a week or so," replied Miss Barry, "when the well becomes exhausted, as it is bound to do, I shall be prepared to hear complaints of the dry season. In the meantime it must, as you say, be very pleasant to those who have no responsibilities."

"Perhaps", I ventured, "you yourself find the heat a little trying? It has been almost oppressive, certainly; but there is a refreshing breeze to-day."

"The breeze", said Miss Barry "will not fill the well."

I was again discomfited, and would have strolled on but that I felt my departure must seem awkwardly abrupt. Miss Barry's employment put me still further at a disadvantage; for she was constantly moving off a little, and each time I was uncertain whether to move also or to remain in the same place. For some moments I was tongue-tied, feeling extremely foolish, and racking my brain for an unexceptionable topic of conversation; at last, in the hope of propitiating her, I began:

"Matthew has just been speaking of the excellent discipline among the servants here. It must have been severely tried in the last day or two, and he is astonished to find them behaving so well."

"Indeed!" said she, moving a little farther off.

"I think we have all noticed it with admiration. Even Frampton, I see, is going about his work as usual."

"Frampton has the use of his limbs," replied Miss Barry, "and is otherwise in good health, I believe. I have been in charge of a household for many years now, Mr. Colchester; but no one has ever before expressed surprise at my servants going about their work."

"No, no, of course not; but in Frampton's present situation——"

Miss Barry ignored this, and went on:

"Frampton has always been an excellent servant, and I am very sorry to be obliged to part with him. His conduct in other respects may not be faultless, but he is an excellent butler, and a most valuable influence in the servants' hall."

"Indeed!" I replied in some surprise. "I should hardly have thought that—and I certainly understood he was not popular."

"I did not say he was popular, Mr. Colchester; I said he was a valuable influence. The two things are not compatible."

"Is that really so?" I asked. "I should rather have expected them to go together."

"Certainly not," replied Miss Barry, again moving off. "Servants on easy terms encourage one another to neglect their duty. They make a system of it. A little stiffness has the best possible effect."

I could not venture to dispute with her on such a point, and therefore remained silent. After a short pause she said:

"And so my brother has been praising the discipline of the household?"

"Yes," said I, "he mentioned it with the warmest

gratitude to you. A student, Miss Barry, has a peculiar value for domestic order."

"A student", she replied, "ought to have known better, I should think, than to invite Lord Malvern to his house at all. I can say nothing to my brother, who was infatuated with the young man, as we all know; but I should be glad to hear how he reconciled such a step with his value for *domestic order*."

"My dear Miss Barry," I protested, "how could Matthew possibly have foreseen——"

"Nonsense!" said Miss Barry. "When a young man habitually surrounds himself with a harem, anyone with common sense may know what the result is likely to be. Yet my brother not only asks him here, but asks him when we have already a houseful of young women. And what happens next? At every turn I find Mrs. Fairfax whispering to him in corners, and poor Phyllis making sheep's eyes at him across the room; while as for Judith—but unfortunately I need say nothing on that head."

She had grown very warm, and even set down her watering-can in order to give more emphasis to her indignation.

"My dear Miss Barry," I said again, "are you sure you do not exaggerate a little? Miss Grant, at any rate, you must remember, has been cleared from the suspicion of too great an intimacy with poor Lord Malvern."

"So I have been told," she rejoined acidly, "and for my own part, of course, I say nothing. It may be customary nowadays for young women to visit young men's bedrooms at an advanced hour of the night. I express no opinion on the subject, but I hope I may be allowed to entertain my own view of it nevertheless."

"You cannot really mean", said I, greatly shocked, "that you saw Miss Grant entering Lord Malvern's room at such an hour?"

"No, Mr. Colchester, I did not; I saw her leaving it at half-past ten, or very nearly, on the last night of the unfortunate man's life. I naturally conclude that she must have entered it in the first place; but if you think otherwise, it is not for me to contradict you."

I was amazed, not so much by what Miss Barry had just told me as by the fact that she had not mentioned it before.

"But", I exclaimed, "have you said nothing of this to the Inspector, or to Mr. Hatton?"

"Certainly not. I am not in the habit of gossiping, or of spreading scandal about my guests."

"But in a case like this—— You must have been questioned, surely, on the events of Saturday night?"

"I cannot", she replied unmoved, "look upon Judith's behaviour as an event in any sense of the term."

"But surely, Miss Barry, in a case like this the police ought to have been informed of it! I have the greatest respect for your motive—that, of course, I need hardly say; but in these circumstances, and when you were directly asked if you had observed anything——"

"I was asked", said Miss Barry, "whether I had observed anything *unusual* on the night in question. Unfortunately my knowledge of Judith's character made it impossible for me to reply in the affirmative. However, I can place no restraint upon *you*, Mr. Colchester. If you think it necessary to tell this story to the police, do so by all means."

I felt myself in an exceedingly awkward position. There could be no doubt that Mr. Hatton, at any rate, ought to be told; yet, apart from all other considerations, I could not but feel a scruple at disturbing, perhaps, the reunion which had so lately taken place between the two young people, and which was so much to the happiness of both in this dreadful time. Miss Barry had turned decisively away to her rose bushes, and evidently regarded the subject as closed. After a long pause, I said with great, and, I imagine, visible reluctance:

"It is, indeed, very unfortunate; but I really cannot think it consistent with my duty to conceal this."

"Just as you please, Mr. Colchester," replied Miss Barry without looking up.

There was clearly no help to be obtained from her, and I turned, with most unwilling steps, towards the house. At the door I was met by the Colonel and Mrs. Fairfax, who had been playing tennis again.

"Hot day, Colchester," observed the Colonel as we all entered together. "Confoundedly hot. Knocks a man's game all to pieces. Anne's in great form, though —quite got her nerve back—wonderful! Don't know how she does it on a day like this. But I'm getting on, you know—not so young as I was. Wouldn't have turned a hair myself at one time."

I gathered that he had been beaten, and had not quite recovered from it.

"It is certainly very warm indeed," I replied.

"Warm! Hottest day of the year, I believe. Must

have a wash before I do anything else. Phew!"

He left us at the door of the drawing-room; Mrs. Fairfax walked in, and after a moment's hesitation I followed her.

"I must have a wash, too," she said carelessly, "but I must have a cigarette in the first place—I need one."

Accordingly she took one from a box which stood on the table, and lighted it with great composure. Then she flung herself on the sofa with a relaxed air. I was astonished at her coolness, charming enough in itself, but so remarkable in the circumstances as to appear almost brazen.

"The Colonel has just been telling me", she began presently, "that Frampton has revised his story all at once. He now says he wrote Judith's letters, but not Edward's."

"I did not know", I replied, "that the Colonel was aware of it; but certainly I have heard the same."

She looked, for some reason, very pleased: her eyes sparkled.

"Then it's really the case!" she exclaimed. "And —what does Mr. Hatton think of it?"

"I have no idea; I heard of it from Matthew."

Her obvious disappointment made me wonder if she had begun the subject solely with an idea of eliciting Mr. Hatton's views. If so, she recovered herself very quickly.

"Oh, I see," she said. "Does Matthew believe it— I mean, does he think Frampton's telling the truth this time?"

"I really cannot say; he is naturally in doubt what to think. If Frampton did not write the last letter——"

I was interrupted by the sudden entrance of Mr. Hatton himself. He held an open letter in his hand, and looked, for him, almost excited.

"My dear Mr. Hatton," I exclaimed, starting up, "it cannot be that *the* letter—Edward's letter—has turned up at last?"

"Oh, no," he replied, with a fair effort at his usual unemphatic manner, "this is something new; I got it from the Inspector, who's just come back. Do you know it at all, Mrs. Fairfax?"

She took it without moving from the sofa, glanced through it, and handed it back.

"Why?" she asked calmly. "Does the Inspector think I know it?"

"The idea hasn't occurred to him; but then of course he hasn't heard yet about Saturday night. After that he'll probably form his own ideas."

I am afraid curiosity rather overcame me at this point. I made a movement to take the letter from Mr. Hatton, who was still holding it, and then drew back, greatly confused at my own want of discretion.

"That's all right, Mr. Colchester," said Mrs. Fairfax. "It's mine, certainly, and you may read it if you like. It seems to have passed beyond the sphere of private affairs."

Thus encouraged, I glanced at Mr. Hatton, who said nothing, but gave the sheet of notepaper into my hand. It was headed simply "Cambridge", with no date, and the contents were as follows:

My dear Charles—I'm quite ready to do anything you like that's not too inconvenient—in fact I think it's more than time. Ought you to keep Jane in the dark, though? It seems to me a little base. However, you know her, and you ought to know what she can stand. Write to me again when you've made up your mind about it.

Yours with love,
Anne.

I looked from one to the other in extreme amazement. Mr. Hatton had seated himself on the further arm of the sofa, and was studying the hearthrug with a constrained expression of countenance; Mrs. Fairfax, with her eyes on the ceiling, was blowing smoke rings rather badly.

The silence, though very awkward, remained unbroken, I should think, for a full minute; then Mrs. Fairfax recrossed her legs and said:

"I suppose this was among Charles's things in town?"

"Yes—Lockitt thought it looked interesting, and brought it down in case something could be made of it. I'll have to tell him the whole story this evening, I'm afraid—as far as I know it; mightn't you just as well tell me a little more in the first place?"

Mrs. Fairfax appeared to reflect a moment; then she got up and threw her cigarette-end into the grate.

"I suppose I might," she said with an air of resignation. "Very well, after tea."

"Now would be better," said Mr. Hatton.

"It's just on tea-time, and I've been playing tennis. If I have to miss tea, or even wait for it, I shan't be equal to the strain."

She smiled her rather provoking smile, and appeared quite immovable in her decision.

"In that case," he replied, "will you come out to tea somewhere? Mr. Barry has offered me the car when I want it, and we shouldn't be so liable to interruption."

Mrs. Fairfax, to my surprise, looked quite delighted.

"Have tea out!" she exclaimed. "What a good idea! What a *relief!* Of course Mr. Colchester will come too?"

Mr. Hatton had evidently not been prepared for this. He did not answer at once, and I hastened to say that I should not dream of intruding on them—I had no title to learn the secrets of the case.

"It has nothing to do with the case," said Mrs. Fairfax. "You know a good deal of it already, and the rest is bound to come out, I suppose. You must certainly come—it'll look better."

The last words she pronounced with a slight blush. I could easily see that the two young people had already somewhat relented towards each other, but not, on her side, so far as to appear eager for an unchaperoned expedition—if I may use the term in these days. It was all very irregular, very unprofessional; but I felt a degree of human curiosity which made me welcome the idea of going with them, and I was pleased when Mr. Hatton at length said:

"Very well, then—shall we go at once?"

"As soon as I've washed and put a hat on. You can be getting the car out if you like."

And with every appearance of alacrity she left the room.

CHAPTER FOURTEEN

A Revelation

In a very few minutes I heard the car draw up before the house, and presently Mrs. Fairfax, wearing a charming little straw hat and carrying a light coat over her arm, ran downstairs with the air of one bent on a pleasant holiday.

"I've left word that we shan't be in for tea," she said. "And now where are we going?"

"A few miles, I think," said Mr. Hatton. "We don't want to be stared at. Will you get in, Mr. Colchester?"

He evidently expected Mrs. Fairfax to sit in front with him, but she stepped quickly before me into the back of the car, and I took my place beside her. It was impossible to be sure from his expression that he was disconcerted.

"Which way do you think we *ought* to go?" he asked her. "You should know best really."

"Well, not towards Oxon perhaps," said Mrs. Fairfax. "To the right."

At the gate we were stopped by a constable, with whom, however, Mr. Hatton seemed to have no difficulty in arranging matters; after a word or two he stood back, and allowed us to pass through. I was amazed at the relief of driving like this through the open country, away from the now cramped, sinister and, as it were, stale environment of Friars Cross; we seemed to be in another, fresher world, and I was glad that Mr. Hatton had resolved to go some distance. He drove very fast for, I should think, seven or eight miles, and then, slowing down, seemed to be on the watch for a suitable cottage or tea-house. At length, after passing a good many, he found one which satisfied him, and we turned off the road before a small thatched house with a large and pleasant garden, in which a number of little tables were set out.

"Do you like this?" he inquired of Mrs. Fairfax as we drew up.

"Charming—the very place for a dark secret. Much nicer than a village," she added, stepping out and looking round her with approval.

We seated ourselves at a table in the shade, and ordered tea. While we were waiting for it to be brought, Mrs. Fairfax went on:

"What a good thing it isn't raining—or blowing a hurricane! What should we have done if it had been too cold to sit out? I couldn't have told my life history in whispers, with the other customers all silent and straining every ear."

"This is better, of course," said Mr. Hatton shortly. "All the same, you needn't shout."

She had, indeed, spoken in particularly clear and distinct tones, and her attitude altogether was enough to vex him. She received this remonstrance with a laugh which sounded quite sincere, but which extorted no answering smile from the young man; he did not even look at her, but sat with a grave face contemplating the flower-bed a little way off, and said no more until the tea things were arranged and the waitress had again left us. Mrs. Fairfax, looking as calm as ever, began to pour out tea.

"I don't want to rush you," he then observed, "but we ought not to be too long away."

"All right," she said carelessly. "We're allowed to have tea, I suppose; and why should I poison it with my reminiscences?"

Mr. Hatton frowned.

"Have tea by all means," he replied, "and then we can get back at once. I'm sorry I misunderstood you."

To my astonishment, Mrs. Fairfax's composure suddenly gave way.

"*Why* must you take up that tone?" she exclaimed. "Can't you see I'm nervous?"

Mr. Hatton's face changed; he looked bewildered, and almost out of countenance.

"Sorry," he said. "I'd no idea—I'm not in a very placid frame of mind myself."

There could be no mistaking the glance which now passed between them—conscious on both sides, and hastily withdrawn. Had they been alone, the conversation would, I imagine, have become more free, and rather different in subject; as it was, they were quite silent for a moment, each countenance expressing an emotional disturbance not connected with Mr. Hatton's duties as an investigator. I felt so awkwardly superfluous as almost to wish myself away.

"Well," said Mrs. Fairfax at length, "it's got to be

done. I suppose there's no use putting off the evil moment."

"We'll have tea first if you prefer it," he replied hurriedly, in the same conscious manner as before. "Lockitt can wait."

"No, no—better get it over." She sighed, however, and appeared even then reluctant to begin. "You want to know what I have to do with Charles?"

He made no reply; his face darkened with, I suppose, a sudden remembrance of all that we already knew. Mrs. Fairfax evidently observed it. All her levity of manner was gone: she looked for the first time unhappy and, as she had said, nervous. Her fingers had closed on the stem of the sugar-basin, and she was turning it abstractedly round and round.

"Oh, well," she continued presently, with another sharp sigh, "it's easily explained, at any rate. I am his widow."

"Good God!" said Mr. Hatton.

For my own part, I was too astonished for speech. Mrs. Fairfax seemed to think she had completed her confidence, and leaned back, not looking at either of us.

"You—you were *married* to him?" exclaimed Mr. Hatton, after a strange silence. "You were his *wife*?"

She nodded, and I saw that there were actually tears in her eyes—the result more probably of nervous strain than of grief.

"Good Lord!" said Mr. Hatton.

"But—but, my dear Mrs. Fairfax," I exclaimed when I could find my voice, "why have you not said so before?"

A Revelation

"I wouldn't ever have said so if I hadn't seen it must come out. However, there it is. I was married to him in America four years ago."

"But good Lord!" exclaimed Mr. Hatton in consternation, "this brings you right into it. You're the next-of-kin."

"Don't let that worry you," she replied smiling, but with an hysterical break in her voice. "I should think there's nothing to be next-of-kin to."

"But—but in that case——" I said suddenly, more and more overcome. "Why, Lord Malvern was actually engaged to be married!"

She made an effort to reply, but her lips were trembling. Mr. Hatton quickly intervened.

"Have some tea," he said. "There's plenty of time; we can talk about it afterwards. As you say, there's really nothing to worry about. That's cold; have another cup."

With a jerk he emptied her teacup informally into the bushes, and then filled it up again. At first she could hardly swallow; but in a minute or two she had wonderfully regained her self-command, and was eating and drinking very much as though nothing extraordinary had taken place. I remembered Miss Grant's pitiful want of control, and felt grateful for the difference.

We tried to converse a little upon other subjects; it need hardly be said, with poor success. Before long, however, Mrs. Fairfax spontaneously revived the main theme.

"I feel tolerably well-balanced now," she said. "There's nothing like tea. And as we *are* more or less in a hurry, I may as well get on with my revelations."

"Do," said Mr. Hatton, "if you feel up to it."

"I should think you could almost invent the rest. As I said, we were married in America, and no one knew very much about it. I don't think Charles's family even knew where he was at the time. I've none myself except a brother in South Africa, who doesn't count. Charles told me he'd have to keep it dark for a bit, because his mother expected him to marry money—I dare say she also wanted him to marry one of their own set."

"And so", said I, rather shocked, "he was married under a false name?"

"No, of course not. Fairfax *was* his name."

"Good Lord!" exclaimed Mr. Hatton, "I believe I knew that."

Now that it was mentioned, I also seemed to recollect having heard it before. I expressed my amazement that it had struck no one.

"Well, he hadn't a monopoly of it," said Mrs. Fairfax. "It might easily have been an accident. Matthew did speak of it once—asked if my husband were related to Charles. Luckily Charles wasn't there at the moment, and I kept my countenance."

"But why did you go on keeping it dark?" asked Mr. Hatton. "Surely it's years since his mother died."

"Yes, she died within a year after we were married. But the marriage had more or less given out by that time."

I was startled by her light way of saying this; Mr. Hatton, however, looked distinctly pleased.

"It was a great success for a few months," she went

on, "but we oughtn't really to have *married* each
other. Charles was very keen on it at the time—he
thought it was fun; I suppose we both thought it was
fun. A—a mere affair wouldn't have been half so
amusing, and yet as no one knew about it we felt
deliciously free and irresponsible. But when we got
out of the honeymoon stage it really didn't work. I
don't mean we ceased to get on with each *other*—
Charles was very easy to get on with, and we were on
the best of terms. But our tastes were hopelessly in-
compatible—*hopelessly*. I liked his kind of existence
for a month or two, but it depressed me as a steady
thing; and I have a passion for the higher mathema-
tics, and various things of that kind, which he didn't
at all object to, but which were quite out of his line.
So naturally he was bored by a lot of the people I had
most to say to, and I found a good many of his acquaintances rather dull—not all, of course, for he
liked all kinds of people, but still rather a large number. He was restless, too, and I got tired of whizzing
about. We didn't quarrel, but we saw less and less of
each other pretty rapidly, and in the end we agreed
that the marriage had better be looked upon as off."

"How soon was that?" asked Mr. Hatton.

"In about eight or nine months, I should say."

"I see," he said. "But why didn't you get a
divorce?"

"That was Charles's fault mostly. I did suggest it,
but Charles thought it would mean a lot of bother and
he hated bother. He was terribly casual—he didn't
happen to feel the inconvenience of being married at
the time, and so he thought he might as well not

worry. I was back in England, too, and altogether I
didn't feel like tackling it on my own account, or
badgering him into activity. My own friends were
rather at sea about my husband, but I suppose they
thought he'd deserted me, and didn't like to rub it in.
And of course, as Charles hadn't told his family before, there could be no point in telling them when it
was all over."

"But surely", said I, "the situation was very awkward—sadly awkward and irregular?"

"It *would* have been awkward if Charles and I had
been in the way of meeting—in fact it could hardly
have been kept up. But we never did meet; I was
living near Cambridge most of the time, and saw
mostly Cambridge people. In the end I took to saying
my husband was dead—it seemed the easiest thing."

"But what about Jane?" said Mr. Hatton. "That
seems to me almost too casual."

"Yes," said Mrs. Fairfax, "I was coming to her.
Well, Charles and I used to write to each other
occasionally—by the way, I knew nothing about his
going to be Lord Malvern until he actually came into
the title. And about a month ago he wrote and said
he was engaged to Jane Elliston, and he supposed
something would really have to be done about a
divorce."

Mr. Hatton began to laugh.

"It's just like him," he said. "He was extraordin-
arily cool, I must say—it's almost too like him to be
true."

"Poor Charles!" said Mrs. Fairfax with an unexpected change of tone.

A Revelation

Mr. Hatton looked away.

"Remember I knew him very little," he said, as though in self-defence.

"Really," continued Mrs. Fairfax in her normal manner, "I don't think he meant it—he didn't mean to take anybody in. I dare say he hadn't any definite intention of proposing till he'd done it; these things aren't meticulously arranged beforehand, after all. And besides that, I'm sure he'd long ceased to feel that our marriage had any real existence; it hadn't for anyone else, and then having been married in America—I'm sure he had an idea it didn't count. But when he got engaged it must have gradually broken in on him that he *was* married, and that he'd have to do something about it."

"And he asked your advice?" said Mr. Hatton.

"Not exactly. By that time he'd found out he was in a fix; he *had* taken Jane in, however inadvertently, and if she heard at this point that he was already married there was certain to be a grand row. She might even have dropped him—he thought she would, but I'm not so sure of it. Anyhow there would have been the most awful scene, and Charles couldn't bear scenes. His idea was that as we'd been married in America it might be possible to get a divorce there, and no one the wiser. That was really what he wrote to me about; he wanted to ensure my collaboration. Then if I agreed he'd ask a lawyer how to set about it."

"And it was your answer that was found this morning?" said Mr. Hatton with an air of sudden enlightenment.

Death by Request

"Very good work," said Mrs. Fairfax. "Yes, that was it."

"But", I put in, "did you expect to meet your husband at Friars Cross?"

"No, that was pure accident—I didn't know he knew Matthew. He was there when I arrived, and it very nearly gave the whole thing away, but luckily there was no one except the Colonel about when I first came across him—so it passed off all right. I'd have been furious if it had come out then; think of the melodrama. Well, for the moment all was safe, but as Charles was so casual, and I didn't want gossip, I thought the less we seemed to say to each other in confidence the better. On the other hand, I did want to know what was happening to the divorce; I'd had no news at all from him. And altogether, that really was an awkward situation."

"Yes," said Mr. Hatton. "What did you do about it?"

"We found it almost impossible to get each other alone without being noticed; remember we had only a few days. On the first evening we'd snatched an opportunity to agree that we must talk about the divorce before he left—but when it came to the point there was always someone in the offing. By Charles's last day we still hadn't managed it, and then he said the only thing was to come to my room at dead of night. I thought that was rather lunatic after all our caution, but he swore he'd make sure it was quite safe, and after all we were next door to each other. So in the end I gave way—Charles's letters were no good, and it would have been even riskier to arrange

another meeting. He said everyone was sure to go to
bed soon after ten—everyone except Matthew, who
was leagues away—and if so, he'd come along at
half-past; if they *were* later, he'd wait till things were
quiet."

"Perhaps", said I, "it was during this conversation
that Miss Barry received the impression of your
whispering in corners."

"Did she say that?" asked Mrs. Fairfax. "Well,
well; it just shows you can't be too careful, as the
saying is."

"He did come, of course," said Mr. Hatton. "What
happened then?"

"With his usual idiocy he didn't wait till half-past,
and I was in my bath. There's a bathroom attached
to my room, you know. I heard him come in, and I
told him to lock the door and wait a minute. I don't
know how long I was—not very long—but when I
came out he was asleep."

"The drug, of course," said Mr. Hatton.

"Yes, but I didn't know that—I thought it was
exercise and whisky, and I was furious. It did seem
queer that I couldn't wake him, and I suppose it was
very queer he should be in a drunken stupor at this
point, and have shown no sign of it downstairs; but
then I'm not an expert on the combined effects of
whisky and horse exercise. He seemed all right except that he was asleep. I believe it occurred to me
that he might have taken to drugs now and then, but
I couldn't seriously think it. Anyhow he couldn't
have fallen asleep at a worse time, and as I said I was
furious. I'd either have to sit up till he woke and then

pack him off, or go to bed and risk his being found there in the morning. Either was very unpleasant to look forward to, and in the end I made up my mind to something bolder: to the proceeding you heard about from Phyllis."

"But surely," said I, " that was even more dangerous?"

"So it turned out, but I thought not at the time— and besides, I hadn't the patience to sit down and do nothing. When the idea *had* struck me, I felt I must chance it and get it over. It *ought* to have been fairly safe; there were only Phyllis and Edward to worry about. Edward I thought had gone out, and presently I heard Phyllis padding along to the bathroom. I *seemed* to hear her shut the door, which again shows how careful one ought to be. After that I waited a minute, but it struck me that the noise of the bath filling would help to cover other noises—though unfortunately I didn't apply that to any movements but my own."

"You must have found the removal hard work," observed Mr. Hatton.

"It was a strain getting hold of him, but the dragging was nothing; Mr. Colchester, *you* know how those floors are polished. It took almost no time. I had a shock afterwards, though. I'd been sure Edward was out—I'd heard him go into his room, for his tackle I suppose, and then come out and shut the door; but I'd hardly got back when he came upstairs again."

Mr. Hatton's face darkened.

"Very unlucky," said he.

"I know. He may have forgotten something, but it's the worst thing he could have done."

There was silence for a moment; then Mrs. Fairfax added:

"Well, that's the whole story—and I'll have a cigarette."

She took one from the case which Mr. Hatton offered, and he struck a light for her.

"What about a little *fresh* tea", she said, "just before we go? Remember I have an interview with the Inspector before me."

Mr. Hatton looked at his watch.

"Half-past five," he said. "All right; but we mustn't be much longer."

The order was given, and the fresh pot of tea was brought. Mrs. Fairfax poured herself out a cup, and leaned back as easily as the structure of the chair would admit of, looking thoughtful, but far from intimidated. Mr. Hatton, who was also smoking, kept silence for a minute or so, and then said:

"It's almost a pity Lockitt found that letter. It was bound to come out after that."

"Yes," replied Mrs. Fairfax calmly, "so I thought."

"I think," he went on, "I can pretty well guess why you said nothing; but do you mind telling me exactly?"

"Not at all. In the first place, I'm afraid I didn't want to be suspected of the murder. I shall be surprised if Charles has left anything, but he may have; or the Inspector may even think I murdered him to prevent him from marrying anyone else."

"Not very likely," said Mr. Hatton.

"That I should have done it—or that the Inspector should think so?"

"I meant that he should think so," replied Mr. Hatton. "That's the main point."

"Oh, quite," agreed Mrs. Fairfax with a smile. "Yes, it does seem to me improbable, but you can't tell; and I'd have preferred not to run the risk."

"But was that quite right?" said I gently. "Your position was most unfortunate—most unfortunate; still there are others implicated who ought not to be forgotten."

"You mean Edward," she said at once. "But this doesn't affect Edward's case—the chance of his being guilty, I mean. I didn't do it, and I couldn't have said anything to show that he didn't. I should only have confused the Inspector, if anything."

"That may be so," I admitted, "yet I cannot help thinking it would have been wiser and better to let the truth be known."

"Yes, it looks worse coming out now. However, apart from a natural concern for my skin, I hated the idea of suddenly featuring as Lady Malvern—it seemed too silly at this point. And it would have been a horrid blow to Jane—will be, I suppose I ought to say. The whole business is too awful. I suppose there's no chance of the Inspector keeping it to himself, is there?"

Mr. Hatton shook his head.

"I'm afraid not," he answered. "It would be better, if only on Jane's account, but I don't think it's possible."

"Well, I expected as much," said she. "It's a grim

prospect." She sighed, and then continued with more animation: "I had another reason for saying nothing —such as it was. I've begun to have my own ideas about this murder."

We both looked at her in surprise.

"Do you mean", said I, "that you suspect someone?"

"I don't know that I go as far as that yet; but I have ideas I'd rather have followed up unsupervised."

A rather wild theory occurred to me at this point.

"It is not possible", said I, "that you suspect Miss Grant? I happen to know that Miss Barry saw her coming out of Lord Malvern's room that night."

"Oh, did she?" replied Mrs. Fairfax. "And what was Miss Barry doing in that part of the house?"

"I really cannot say."

"Well," said Mrs. Fairfax, "at any rate, I *don't* suspect her; I'm sure it was simply a last attempt to unburden herself to poor Charles. I heard her myself—at least it was probably her—but Charles wasn't there, and she went away again."

"You mean he was still in your room at the time?" asked Mr. Hatton.

Mrs. Fairfax assented.

"But", said I, "she may have returned later. I do not, of course, for a moment think it possible that she is guilty—she had not even a motive for such a crime; but she might, nevertheless, have returned without your knowing it."

"But if the door was locked?" said Mrs. Fairfax.

"It's a queer thing about that door, but it must have been locked some time."

"Never mind the door," said Mr. Hatton. "If we *are* going to consider Miss Grant as a suspect, let's dispose of her. She might in any case have turned the gas on from Edward's room."

"Nonsense," replied Mrs. Fairfax. "She hasn't *savoir faire* enough to gas anyone direct, let alone through a wall. And she didn't know the house; it's the first time she's stayed here."

"Quite so," said Mr. Hatton. "I was only testing your efficiency as an investigator. Now we come to your ideas about that door. You realize that your own story throws a queer light on it?"

"Don't patronize me," she retorted, very amiably however, "it's exasperating. Of course, I see that Charles can't have done it. As he was in a drugged sleep when I left him, he wasn't very likely to wake up and lock the door, and lie down again in the same position. And I don't believe it was locked from the outside, either; there's been a lot of loose talk about that, but it's not such an easy thing to do. However, that's a point of detail; what really interests me is *why* it was locked. It might have been to look like suicide —that's all right if Frampton did it. But *if* Frampton didn't write the letter to Edward, and *if* the person who did write it is the guilty person——"

"That's assuming a good deal," said Mr. Hatton.

"I know; I'm only assuming it as a possibility. Well, in that case suspicion was to have been thrown on Edward—the letter can only have meant that. And so what was the point of making the door look like suicide? Locking it must have involved a lot of trouble, however it was done."

"But", I said, "may not that also have been intended to throw suspicion upon Edward? It actually suggested the possibility of the gas having been turned on from his room."

"Yes, but as anyone could have gone into Edward's room, it's very feeble; it wasn't worth the effort."

"It's possible", said Mr. Hatton, "that the murderer *hoped* it would look like suicide, but had worked up the case against Edward as a second string."

"Well, that would at least show a faint symptom of humanity. I suppose, by the way, you have your own view of *how* the door was locked?"

"Oh, yes," he replied. "I'll develop it some time, if you like, but I'm afraid we *must* go now. Are you feeling all right?" He looked at her, as he spoke, with anxiety and great concern.

"Fit for the cannonade? Oh, yes, I shall come through it. And by the way, do you always discuss your cases with the potential criminals?"

"Yes," he replied, "it gives them a unique opportunity to overreach themselves."

She returned his odd look with a smile of consciousness and evident pleasure, as she said:

"Very well; go on doing it with that view, and I'll take advantage of it—if I can—in pursuit of my own suspect. What could be more rational?"

She rose from her chair; he rose also, but still kept his eyes on her with that unexpressed emotion—wishing, it was obvious to me, that he could say more.

"You're quite sure there's no ill-feeling?" he asked

suddenly, but in his usual unemphatic manner.

Again she met his look with a consciousness which betrayed her understanding of it.

"No, no ill-feeling," she replied composedly.

I thought he was going to take her hand; perhaps I misinterpreted the slight gesture, or my presence may again have acted as a check on him.

"That's all right, then," he said, with the same calmness, and the same legible expression. "I'll go in and pay."

Three minutes later we were on the road back to Friars Cross.

CHAPTER FIFTEEN

Legal Advice

Mrs. Fairfax sat in front this time, but I do not think she and her companion exchanged many words. I had almost said there was no time for them, so short did the return drive appear. Before, as it seemed, I could begin to reflect on what we had just heard, the car was turning in at the familiar gate once more. As we alighted, however, Mr. Hatton said:

"I think Jane had better be your sole reason for having kept this dark—the Inspector may believe it, and it does you credit."

"Very well—anything you say. By the way, if it's coming out who is to break the news to her?"

We looked at each other doubtfully; then I suggested:

"Will not Miss Barry be the best person? As a relative, she is, in a sense, concerned; she might communicate with Miss Elliston, or with Lady Elliston."

"With Jane," said Mrs. Fairfax decidedly. "Yes, perhaps that's the best thing we can do. I ought to see her at once, then, I suppose."

"We'll have Jane down here again," said Mr.

Hatton, not, I imagined, with great eagerness.

Mrs. Fairfax shook her head.

"I don't think so," was her answer. "She'll be too humiliated. But she'll want to speak to *me*, I'm afraid, and I must let her. Well, well."

She was going in when Mr. Hatton said:

"There'll be no difficulty in proving this marriage?"

"Oh, no," said Mrs. Fairfax. "I've got my marriage lines, as the saying is—not down here, of course, but somewhere. I assure you it took place all right."

He was, I imagine, about to protest that he had no doubt of it; but she had already disappeared into the house.

What took place during the rest of the day I could only conjecture. In the interval before dinner the Inspector was informed; I had, of course, assumed that it would be so, and I was confirmed in the idea, not by any signs of discomposure on the part of Mrs. Fairfax, but by Phyllis's air of agitation and misery, and by her continued want of appetite. I could not be sure if she knew the whole story, but that she had come from an interview with Inspector Lockitt seemed beyond a doubt. In Miss Barry, too, I thought there were symptoms of an acquaintance with the facts; her eyes were often on Mrs. Fairfax, and she scarcely spoke. These two might know; it was clear that, so far, no one else did.

The next morning they were still unenlightened. It was the morning of the inquest, and this heightened the tension at breakfast a good deal, though, as it proved, needlessly. I will not enter at length into the proceedings—in fact, I did not attend them; they were without interest, and were soon adjourned for a week, as Mr. Hatton had predicted. Colonel Lawrence, who had been present, seemed to take this rather ill, but almost everyone else clearly welcomed it as a reprieve.

Indeed, Edward confessed to such a feeling. His spirits, so much revived by the reconciliation with Miss Grant, were already beginning to give way again. She appeared in no way responsible for the change; either he had not heard of her visit to Lord Malvern's room, or he was satisfied of its innocence, for he remained on the most tender and confiding terms with her. But the peril of his situation, forgotten or made light of in the first raptures of a mutual understanding, had begun once more, and very naturally, to prey upon his mind. He was even now much happier than he had been during the estrangement; he no longer shunned us, except to be alone with Miss Grant; but he was still convinced that there was no hope for him, and the more he thought of this, the less he could pretend to face it with equanimity.

Though we had had no private talk since the evening of reconciliation, I knew him too well for this return of anxiety to have escaped me; and when, after the inquest, we chanced to be for a short time alone together, his manner of expressing himself was very much what I had expected. Nevertheless, it gave me great pain. Edward's was not a strong character—not a character to shine in any severe trial of patience and fortitude. On this occasion his dispirited air, his obstinate rejection of comfort, even more, perhaps, his bursts of assumed stoicism, were distressing to me beyond measure, and put me almost out of countenance for his sake.

"I've sent for my solicitor," he announced at length, with conscious though gloomy dignity. "I suppose there will be no objection to my seeing him."

"No, no," said I, "how could there possibly be an objection? But, my dear boy, is not this premature? May we not hope, at least, that it will prove unnecessary altogether? Remember, no accusation has yet been made against you—and I still trust and pray that it never will be. If it were time to seek legal advice——"

Edward checked me at this point, with some impatience.

"That's all right," he said, "I'm not under the delusion that *legal advice*" (with bitter emphasis) "can do me any good. I want to talk to him about my private affairs, simply."

It seemed to me there was very little difference: if he were so anxious to arrange his affairs at this juncture, it could only be that he supposed himself in immediate peril. I saw, however, that he attached great importance to the step, and grew irritable at any suggestion of postponing it; indeed, he seemed to resent all efforts to treat his situation as otherwise than desperate. I gave up the point, therefore, and only ventured to hint that it had been unnecessary to summon his legal adviser to Friars Cross. My experience of the day before convinced me that none of us were absolutely prisoners; Edward would not be prevented from driving into Oxon if he chose, and the little expedition might refresh him and improve his spirits.

This proposal, however, did not commend itself to the unfortunate young man.

"What!" he exclaimed. "Go into Oxon to be stared at—and probably trailed by reporters all the way! And have it in all the evening papers that Mr. Edward Barry has thought it most prudent to consult a lawyer! I'd rather be spared that, if you don't mind. No doubt I'll soon have to get accustomed to publicity, but I prefer not to court it just yet, all the same."

I did not remind him that the solicitor was equally likely to be seen visiting the house, and that the same conclusions would probably be drawn from it. Edward, perhaps, did not wish to leave Miss Grant, even for so short a time; or perhaps—the idea, I must confess, occurred to me—morbidly bent as he was on asserting all the horror of his position, he preferred to look on himself as almost under arrest, and prohibited from stirring beyond the gates of Friars Cross. I felt it would be unkind to oppose, or even to reason with him further, and in spite of my private knowledge of the diversion which Mrs. Fairfax had introduced into the case, I was not, myself, entirely uninfluenced by his dark forebodings. The very fact of his calling in a lawyer, for whatever purpose, could not but quicken my sense of the danger in which he really stood. Indeed, when he at last left me to reflection, I almost felt that I had never believed in it till now.

Soon after lunch, when everyone else, except Matthew and Mr. Hatton, had left the drawing-room, an allusion was made to the projected visit. I think it was Matthew who first spoke of it.

"Does that mean", asked Mr. Hatton, "that he's thinking about his defence already?"

I explained Edward's reason for wishing to speak with his solicitor.

"Oh!" said Mr. Hatton, with a look of surprise. "*Has* he private affairs, then?"

"Oh, dear me, yes," returned Matthew in his ironic voice. "He's a millionaire."

Mr. Hatton raised his eyebrows.

"That is, he had no money till the other day," Matthew explained, "but he came into fifty thousand pounds on his last birthday. It was left him by his mother's people."

"And when was his last birthday?" asked Mr. Hatton.

"The other day; I've forgotten when exactly. You'd better ask him."

"In that case", said Mr. Hatton, "I dare say he wants to make a will."

Matthew started.

"Good Lord!" he exclaimed. "Things haven't surely got to that pitch?"

"I hope not," replied Mr. Hatton, looking grave, "but I must tell you Lockitt's getting restless. He's been puzzled and cooled off a little by—recent disclosures; and that leaves us more time. And at the worst I think Edward has a pretty good defence really. But he *is* in danger of arrest; for the moment the Inspector won't venture it, but he's decidedly put his money on Edward, and another suspicious circumstance would probably make up his mind."

There was a short silence.

"Well," said Matthew, "and what are *you* doing—if it's not too personal a question?"

I thought I could hardly be mistaken in the significance of this remark. My old friend, who was exceedingly quick-witted, must have realized the state of things between Mr. Hatton and Mrs. Fairfax, and he evidently shared my view of its distracting influence. Mr. Hatton, however, was not discomposed.

"I'd rather not say," he replied calmly. "There's time enough, and I haven't been talking about Lockitt's attitude merely to prepare you for the worst. The point is that it might be a good thing to keep an eye on Edward."

"What for?" asked Matthew.

Mr. Hatton looked slightly embarrassed.

"You mean," said Matthew with great promptness, interpreting the look, "because he has no sense?"

"No, no," replied the young man, "I'm sure he has a fund of it. But he hasn't given it much play so far, and another indiscretion might just turn the scale against him. It's better not to have been under arrest, for however short a time."

"Infinitely—infinitely better," I agreed with feeling.

"Of course," said Mr. Hatton, "I don't mean that you should warn him to do nothing silly—that would only fluster him. But if you see him in danger, you might pull him up."

"This is a commission for you, Joseph," said Matthew rather drily. "*I've* never been able to dissuade him from making a fool of himself, as you know."

"My dear Matthew!" I remonstrated, pained, as always, by his intolerant attitude to the poor boy.

"Nonsense!" returned Matthew. "Isn't it his own fault that he's mixed up in this affair? I did my best to keep him out of Judith's clutches, but I begin to think he has a passion for being taken in. Even his moral principles give way to it. The late revelations might have been expected to disentangle him, and as far as one can see they've turned out an additional attraction—I've no doubt he means to endow her with his fortune next."

Against the last conjecture I could really say nothing, and on the subject in general he was beyond argument.

Edward's solicitor drove over to Friars Cross early in the afternoon. He was a Mr. Green, the only surviving partner in the firm of Green, Green and Green, long established in the town of Oxon; I had met him before, but had no real acquaintance with him. Groundless suspicion is, I hope, foreign to my nature, and I will therefore not suggest that his arrival may have been hastened by curiosity about the crime. Be that as it may, he did not come too soon, scarcely, indeed, soon enough, for Edward's extreme impatience; but their interview, so eagerly awaited, was also astonishingly short. They were shut up together less than ten minutes, and I imagine that Mr. Green himself was a little taken aback to find his business dispatched so very rapidly. If I say he had meant to stay to tea, my assumption is based on the fact that he did stay—lingering so long, in the first place, to chat with one or other of us, that it became necessary to give the invitation. Lawyers, however, cannot be supposed exempt from the weaknesses of other men; and if his persistence was ill-timed, his conversation was perfectly discreet and agreeable.

He did not appear to have made any second appointment with Edward, and nothing was said of the subject which had occupied them. Edward's spirits were not perceptibly relieved by what had passed; at teatime he sat, as always, near Miss Grant, and seemed to derive comfort from her proximity, but he rarely spoke, and his expression was as despondent as ever. In the slight bustle of Mr. Green's departure, I took him aside, and repeated, in an attempt to cheer him, Mr. Hatton's more hopeful remarks upon the case. He listened with a resigned and stubborn air, and made no answer.

"I fear", said I, "that Mr. Green's visit has done nothing to set your mind at ease. My dear Edward, if only——"

"Don't," he interrupted. "There's no use in talking about it. I am very grateful to Mr. Hatton, and to you, and I'm sorry the sight of me depresses you, but I can't help it, I'm afraid. I'd look cheerful and pretend to think there was hope if I could; as it is, you'd better give up bothering about me. My mind *is* more at ease, as you call it—I've made sure that Judith will be all right, and I can bear the rest. After all, it won't last for ever."

I would have renewed the conversation, expostulated, done whatever I could to melt his obstinacy and dispel his gloomy thoughts; but as I was begin-

ning to speak he turned from me and whispered to
Miss Grant. I could not immediately break in on
their confidences, and a moment later they quitted
the room.

"Well, Joseph," said Matthew at my elbow,
"snubbed again?"

I gave him a pained look, but said nothing.

"What an infernal busybody Green is!" was his
next remark. "I thought we'd have to ask him to
stay the night. Did Edward tell you what he wanted
him for?"

I hesitated a moment, for Mrs. Fairfax had joined
us, and was listening. Still, I reflected, there was
probably no secret about Edward's intentions, and if
there were, she was almost certain to be enlightened
by Mr. Hatton. I repeated, therefore, what the poor
young man had just said.

"Very touching," said Matthew. "I'm glad to find
him so amiably concerned for your feelings, Joseph.
And it's pleasant to think that if the worst happens
Judith won't be left destitute."

"You think", said Mrs. Fairfax, "that he's going to
make a will in her favour?"

After what they had heard, it seemed to me a needless question, and anyone else would probably have
received a sharp reply. But with Mrs. Fairfax my
old friend was never out of temper, and he said good-
humouredly:

"Yes, that's my theory; can you detect a flaw in
it?"

"He was in a great hurry to see Mr. Green, wasn't
he?" she asked.

"Yes," I replied, "he was very impatient to see him."

"But he can't want him again," said Mrs. Fairfax. "If Mr. Green had had any idea of coming back, he wouldn't have stayed so long this afternoon. The conclusion is that the will is made already."

"Very likely," returned Matthew. "I hadn't heard of it, but nothing would surprise me less. It's not the kind of thing he would take sane persons into his confidence about."

"He didn't confide in *you*, Mr. Colchester?" asked Mrs. Fairfax.

I shook my head.

"My dear Anne," said Matthew, "have you set up as an amateur? Have you begun detection on your own account?"

"Yes," she replied, "and I don't very much enjoy it."

"Have you any idea, then," I asked, "why Mr. Green was sent for, if it was not in order to prepare a will?"

Mrs. Fairfax looked very grave.

"Yes," she said again, "an idea *has* occurred to me."

We both fixed inquiring eyes upon her.

"I think", she said, "he wanted to make sure the will was valid if—if it should come into operation in these circumstances."

I uttered an exclamation of horror. Matthew said nothing, but when I looked at him I was really alarmed by his appearance; he had turned quite green.

"My dear Mrs. Fairfax," I said, almost shocked

that she should have hinted at that dreadful possibility, "what has led you to imagine——"

"I found", she replied, quietly interrupting me, "that I was in doubt on the same point myself."

"Well, well," Matthew jerked out, still very pale, and in his peculiar tone of bitterness, "I think I'll get back to the Greek drama."

When he had quitted us, it was somehow impossible to continue the subject. For a moment we stood awkwardly together without speaking; then Mrs. Fairfax said:

"Mr. Green hasn't gone *yet*, I believe!"

The engine of the car was, in fact, still audible. Mrs. Fairfax went to the window, and I followed her. Mr. Green, though, by his attitude, in the very act of driving off, was deep in conversation with Mr. Hatton, who stood on the footboard, leaning with both hands on the door. Every now and then a gesture or a motion of his head seemed to indicate that it was the car they were discussing, and the situation appeared likely to prolong itself; but just then, as it happened, Colonel Lawrence strolled up to them. Mr. Hatton stepped down instantly, and a moment later the car had moved off and passed out of view.

I had assumed that the Colonel's approach was the result merely of an idle desire to know what they were talking of; but the eagerness with which he at once fastened upon Mr. Hatton showed that he had himself something to say. He took him by the arm, and led him back into the drawing-room.

"Couldn't shake that fellow off," he was saying as they entered, "or I'd have mentioned it to you before tea. Duty is duty, of course, Hatton, but I won't stand impudence. 'Pon my soul, I'm surprised I didn't knock the fellow down!"

"Lockitt's not in my control, you know," replied Mr. Hatton composedly, "but I dare say he meant no harm."

"No harm! Why, sir, do you know what he had the impertinence to ask me?"

"I've no idea," said Mr. Hatton.

"Asked me if I'd been prying into those letters of Malvern's! He had the assurance to sit there and ask such a question to my face. Not in so many words, of course—he knew better. Knew I'd pitch him out of the window, I dare say. But that was what it worked out to—confound his impudence!"

"What *did* he ask exactly?" inquired Mrs. Fairfax.

"Wanted to know if I was quite sure Charles hadn't dropped a hint of what was in them—didn't I see the letters themselves at the time—did *I* put them in the covering envelope—was the envelope shut at the time —was I quite certain I'd locked the thing up straight away. *I* saw through the fellow's wriggling—told him what I thought of him, too. Do you think he had the grace to be ashamed of himself? Not he. Said it was his *duty* to ask me impertinent questions!"

"Too bad!" Mrs. Fairfax murmured sympathetically.

"Then he wanted to know where I kept the key of my suit-case—mightn't it have been *abstracted*, as he calls it—were there no signs of the case having been disturbed. He's a born idiot—what I've always said, you may remember. Knows nobody knew the things were there—and yet tries to make out that someone may have gone there and read them on the sly. No logic—that's the trouble with him. Can't use his head."

This reflection seemed to cheer him up, and restore his self-complacency. He enjoyed it in silence for a few seconds, and then began again:

"I tell you what, Hatton—I don't like the way this case is going."

"No?" said the young man, slightly raising his eyebrows.

"Don't like it at all, sir. It's not business-like. Too much suspicion going about."

"Surely", said Mrs. Fairfax, "that's the essence of a case."

"Yes, yes," returned the Colonel, "all very well in its own time, but there's a limit to it. Get your man and stick to him—that's what I say. Here they've got a clear case against this fellow Frampton, and yet they go on asking impertinent questions, and suspecting anyone who happens to have been in the house. The insolence of office—that's what it is, you know. Sound phrase of Shakespeare's—hits off that fellow to the life."

He brought out the quotation with some pomp, and Mrs. Fairfax could not restrain a smile.

"I feel for you, Colonel," she said pleasantly, "but then I'm a suspect myself, so I have cause."

"What!" he ejaculated in amazement. "Do you mean to say——? But of course you're joking, Anne. It's not possible."

"Not at all; I'm almost the favourite at the moment.

Miss Barry will tell you about it, if you like to ask her."

His curiosity was evidently intense, but he seemed ashamed to acknowledge it.

"Nonsense!" he said hastily. "Only a joke of yours —trying to pull my leg, I see. Though, upon my soul, I believe Lockitt would suspect anyone. Well, I mustn't stay chatting any longer—got a little commission from Miss Barry. Better make sure I know exactly what she wants. But as to your being a suspect—ha ha!"

With these words he left us—clearly unable to let another moment pass without satisfying himself as to this new development.

CHAPTER SIXTEEN

'Anon'

"You're springing the news, then?" said Mr. Hatton.

"As I can't help it," she replied indifferently. "You say it must come out."

"I hardly think", said I, "that Colonel Lawrence will be content with such information as Miss Barry is likely to give him. Are you anxious that nothing further should be known?"

"Ah," returned Mrs. Fairfax, "I suppose she won't make a good story of it—I hadn't thought of that. I referred him to her because she knew already. If he pumps either of you, elaborate it by all means."

"Not with Saturday night's incident?" asked Mr. Hatton.

"No, there's no need to harrow up his soul, though I dare say he would relish it intensely. A *little* diversion seems almost due to him after what he's been going through."

"You mean his last interview with the Inspector?" said the young man.

"Yes—I gather Frampton sticks to it that the last letter wasn't his. Has the Inspector come round to the idea of anonymous authorship?"

Mr. Hatton slightly shook his head.

"Not really; but he can't help looking into it."

"He *prefers* Frampton to have written it, I suppose," said Mrs. Fairfax. "He's clinging to Edward as the criminal, and doesn't want to embarrass himself with other suspects. You think if Frampton were cleared of that, he'd begin to see that Edward might be innocent?"

"It depends who did write it," said Mr. Hatton. "And don't forget that after all the probability is on Frampton's side."

Mrs. Fairfax was now reclining in the window-seat, with her hands clasped round her knees. At these words she looked up with a thoughtful wrinkling of the forehead, and said quickly:

"*Is* it on Frampton's side? I rather doubt that—even apart from the coolness of trying to blackmail Edward before Charles had left the house. Why was the letter destroyed so very promptly? If it wasn't Edward who destroyed it, there could be no reason—not if Frampton had written it, that is. It couldn't possibly do *Frampton* any good. Why should he have destroyed it before the murder? There were still plenty of blackmailing letters left as evidence against him, and if he'd grown shy of committing himself on paper, he could easily have tackled Edward by word of mouth in the first place. I think he would have—I think that's another argument as far as it goes. Even if he's innocent of the murder, he needn't have taken the trouble to pick Edward's pocket; if he's guilty, he'd actually have preferred the letter to be found."

"Surely not," I interrupted. "Would it not have exposed him to prosecution for blackmail?"

"He might have thought Edward was safe to hush it up; and, as I said, there were other letters liable to turn up at any moment. He wasn't risking a great deal by leaving that one. On the other hand, *if* he killed Charles, he must have known there was a possibility of his being suspected. That letter is the main part of the case against Edward—in fact the only solid part. Wasn't Frampton bound to realize the effect it would produce?"

"It may have been his artfulness," said Mr. Hatton. "Lockitt still believes it was Edward who destroyed it; it's the obvious thing to believe. That in itself would be suspicious, and Edward's denying it is worse. Frampton may have reckoned on all that."

"Rather subtle for Frampton," she replied, "and not very powerful against Edward. Even if he had destroyed it, it's just what an innocent man in a very natural panic *might* do. But now suppose Frampton *didn't* write the letter. In that case the motive for destroying it is as clear as daylight. It wasn't to be closely compared with the other letters—because Frampton didn't write it."

"Very true," admitted the young man laconically.

"Suppose", she went on, "that the person who wrote it also murdered Charles. Then there's no difficulty about the springs of action. He threw the guilt on Edward—or she did—by a letter which, if it were destroyed quick enough, would be attributed to Frampton, and he or she didn't appear at all."

"Very well," said Mr. Hatton, "we'll suppose it

for the sake of argument. The next question is, who *was* this anonymous letter-writer? Have you a theory on that?"

"I don't see why you should pump me," said Mrs. Fairfax. "Haven't *you* a theory?"

"Come," he replied, "the whole position is yours, don't forget. In any case, as a professional it doesn't become me to commit myself."

"What about your system of encouraging suspects to overreach themselves?"

"That's true," he replied calmly. "Well, tell me your own idea, and I may be provoked into contradicting you."

Mrs. Fairfax gave him a disturbed look.

"My dear Nicholas," she said, "you don't mean you think this is all wrong?"

Even at this interesting moment her use of the Christian name did not escape me. Clearly the two were approaching intimacy fast enough. On the other hand, Mr. Hatton seemed to me agreeably startled by it—I could have almost no doubt of his emotion. I concluded it, therefore, to be something new.

"Not at all," he replied, "I think it's worth considering. But have you made up your mind who wrote that letter?"

"Not yet," said Mrs. Fairfax. "Still, is it a point that eludes all speculation? Proving it may be difficult, but from a purely rational standpoint it seems to hang on opportunity. The writer must have been someone who knew all about the other letters. That narrows the field, surely?"

"And leaves—whom?" said the young man.

Mrs. Fairfax laughed.

"The Colonel, I'm afraid—which is certainly an anti-climax. He seems to have been Inspector Lockitt's happy thought. And as far as opportunity goes, there seems no getting away from him."

In Mr. Hatton her laughter awoke no response. When he spoke again, he looked much graver than usual.

"Anne," said he, "are you really prepared to discuss this in cold blood?"

"Of course," she replied, evidently startled by his manner. "Why not? What do you mean?"

"If we're going to reason it out, we must look facts in the face. It's nonsense to say that Colonel Lawrence had the best opportunity."

He paused. She said nothing, but kept her eyes fixed on him with an expression of bewilderment and some alarm.

"Does no one else occur to you?" asked Mr. Hatton.

Mrs. Fairfax shook her head.

"The person with the best opportunity was quite obviously *Charles*."

We were both struck dumb by this, as it almost seemed, impious suggestion. Mrs. Fairfax looked too completely staggered even to resent it, and before she could collect herself, he went on:

"Charles *certainly* knew about the other letters; there's no need to fall back on conjecture in his case. He had a unique hold on Frampton, and could therefore have blackmailed Edward without fear of competition. And besides that, he was notoriously hard up."

"But, my dear Mr. Hatton," I protested, "he was

to marry an heiress! That would surely have made such a crime unnecessary, even if we can imagine him capable of it."

"You believe he was marrying for money?"

"No," said Mrs. Fairfax with abrupt decision.

"Well, *I* believe he was getting tired of Jane."

"You're talking nonsense," Mrs. Fairfax said very coldly. "If he was prepared to get money by blackmail, he wasn't likely to jib at marriage, whatever his feelings for her may have been."

"That's not the point," said Mr. Hatton. "He was incapable of getting tired of her without showing it; she's exacting, and he'd begun to neglect her, or she was apt to think herself neglected. I think it's very probable that they had scenes. If it had gone on, she might easily have thrown him over. I don't say he wanted that; I'm supposing his difficulty to have been temperamental, not moral."

"Well," replied Mrs. Fairfax with great bitterness, "we'll suppose he wrote it. In that case, why was it destroyed? *Charles* didn't destroy it; he hadn't even the opportunity."

"Of course this theory of the murder isn't compatible with yours; I was taking that for granted. But it's compatible with the facts as we know them. There's nothing to prove that Edward didn't destroy the letter after all, except his own word, which in this case isn't evidence."

"Look here, Nicholas," said Mrs. Fairfax, "do *you* believe it possible that Charles wrote it?"

"Not for a moment," he replied promptly. "Not *morally* possible."

The colour returned to her face.

"All right," she said, "I apologize. But do you mean the Inspector thinks so? Of course he didn't know him."

"No," said Mr. Hatton, "it seems not to have occurred to him so far. But he's an intelligent man, and I think it's bound to."

"Intelligent, and suspects Colonel Lawrence!" she returned.

"Remember", I said, "that he does not know Colonel Lawrence either."

"That's true," admitted Mrs. Fairfax. "He may have an intuition that the Colonel is an honest man and think it more business-like to keep it under."

"Yes," said Mr. Hatton, "that's more or less his attitude; but he *doesn't* suspect Lawrence. In this case he doesn't want to suspect anyone; he prefers, as you say, that the letter should be Frampton's work. But the Colonel is not even his second choice."

"What!" exclaimed Mrs. Fairfax. "Has he thought of another possibility?"

"Unfortunately he has," said the young man. "He thinks you may have written it."

Mrs. Fairfax had already known herself to be suspected of murder, and had resigned herself to that with surprising calmness; but under this new and much slighter accusation her cheeks burned. She started from her reclining posture, and, sitting upright, returned with assumed carelessness:

"Well, well—and then the Colonel declares that the man's mind doesn't work. But of course you're in collaboration with him; did you undertake to surprise me with the guilty secret?"

"Anne," he remonstrated, "*please* don't be feminine at this juncture."

She appeared somewhat confused, but went on in the same tone:

"Or doesn't he like your communicative methods? Perhaps you thought it would be kinder to give me time to prepare my defence."

"My dear Anne," he replied, "feminine apprehension has run away with you. There's no question of defence, because there's no hope of proving that you wrote it; not without singular good luck, that is. *You* had no need to investigate the Colonel's suit-case. The whole ground of suspicion against you is that Charles may so easily have told you the whole story; and it's impossible to make sure whether he did or not. You *did* post some letters in the village on Friday afternoon; Lockitt's got that far, and he doesn't see his way to get beyond it."

"Lucky for me," she rejoined, this time with more convincing serenity. "Am I supposed to have indulged in blackmail as well as murder, or instead?"

I was shocked by her light manner, and was about to remonstrate when Mr. Hatton prevented me.

"Oh," he replied, "I don't see that you could have intended to do both, unless the murder of Charles was an afterthought. But if you *had* meant to kill him, and had seen the other letters, you might have written that one to incriminate Edward, like any other suspect. You couldn't safely have gone on to blackmail Edward afterwards, if he escaped; it would have given away the authorship of the first letter, and looked fishy."

"Would it?" said Mrs. Fairfax. "I don't really see that. Edward might have committed the murder just the same, and so might Frampton. The fishy thing would be for the unknown *not* to go on blackmailing; that would show that he had had other views."

"Really," said I, "it seems to me that you are confusing the facts here. How could anyone have continued to extort money from Edward, when Miss Grant's past had become generally known? And if the letter was designed to incriminate him, the guilty persons must have relied on their becoming known— on the first letters turning up, and the whole story being made public."

They both looked somewhat taken aback, and a little ashamed of their own blindness. Then Mr. Hatton laughed.

"Quite true," he said. "I did realize that in the first place, but exposition is very confusing to the head. However, we're left with a clear case. If you had been guilty of the murder, Anne, the letter could only have been a red herring. But now take the other case. You might have written it with no intention but blackmail, and Edward have been goaded into murder by it. Lockitt has really nothing against *that*."

"No?" said Mrs. Fairfax. "And who destroyed it, then? I had no opportunity; I was out with the others, and Edward says it wasn't there when we came back."

"He says so; but of course I'm assuming that he got rid of it himself."

"Surely", I protested, "my knowledge of poor

Edward ought to carry some weight on this point? I am convinced—sincerely and positively convinced —that he is speaking the truth."

"It may have weight with us," replied the young man, "but the Inspector sticks to his own view."

Mrs. Fairfax drew a long breath.

"Well," she said, "and so that's the situation. It was nice of you to let me know the worst."

"I thought we'd agreed to it," said Mr. Hatton. "I meant to be of use, as you're investigating on your own account; but I see you'd rather I had said nothing."

"No, no," replied Mrs. Fairfax, "you must allow for the influence of shock. I think I'll take a stroll and digest this."

"Would it put you out if I came with you?" he inquired.

"Yes—at the moment I feel a craving for solitude. But if I want to ask questions afterwards, you're still accessible?"

"At any time," said Mr. Hatton. "But don't let it get on your nerves; there's no possible danger, I assure you."

Without replying, Mrs. Fairfax left the room. A moment later I thought I heard her opening the side door into the garden.

"Really, Mr. Hatton," I said when we were alone together, "I cannot help thinking Colonel Lawrence is right. This affair seems to have become distressingly confused—and surely it has given birth to most dreadful and unwarrantable suspicions. I feel that each discovery is taking us farther from the truth. What is your own view of it—if I may ask the question? Have you any hope of a speedy end to all these difficulties?"

"There's plenty of time," said Mr. Hatton, "this is only Tuesday. And you must remember that anything which weakens the case against Edward is a good thing in its way."

His tone was less cheerful than his words; he was evidently thinking of Mrs. Fairfax. I caught at the last remark, however, and replied:

"That is true, of course—that, at least, is a consolation. You do not think he can possibly be convicted, or even arrested, in the present circumstances?"

"No," answered the young man, still rather absently, "not at this stage. Lockitt still believes he did it, but there's no solid case really. I thought him too hopeful from the first, and now even he can't help realizing that it won't do as it stands. He's yearning for an arrest, though; as I said, a very little might decide him."

"What steps has he taken about Mrs. Fairfax?" I ventured to ask.

Mr. Hatton started.

"Oh, there it's mainly a question of finances," he replied. "He's inquiring into her affairs, and of course into Charles's. There was no will, but it seems difficult to make out if there was any money or not; there may have been a little over, and of course she may have thought there would be more. It all depends on whether she was in straits enough to need a little."

"But surely", I said, "there is no reason to suppose her in financial difficulties?"

"None at all, so far," he replied. "Of course the whole thing is absurd—but it has to be gone into. If we could only be sure——"

He was interrupted by Phyllis Winter, who burst into the room with a white face, and an expression of horror and alarm.

"Oh, Mr. Hatton," she exclaimed, "what's wrong with Anne? They don't suspect *her*, do they? They *can't* think she did it!"

Mr. Hatton jumped up.

"What *is* wrong with her?" he asked. "What's the matter?"

"I went into the garden just now, and found her sitting on the pedestal of the sundial, looking so queer! I thought she was going to faint—I believe she did, nearly. She could hardly say anything at first. Then she seemed to get a bit better, and I wanted her to come in and lie down. But she said it was only the heat, and that she felt all right again—though she looked terribly queer even then. And she didn't seem to want to talk to me—after a minute she got up and walked away. Oh, Mr. Hatton, do *you* know what's the matter with her?"

Mr. Hatton did not stay to answer this question. I could not doubt that he had gone in search of Mrs. Fairfax, and I thought it more judicious not to offer to accompany him. Phyllis at once turned to me with the same appealing, yet despairing countenance.

"Oh, Mr. Colchester, it's too awful—it's all my fault! I *know* they suspect her, and it's all my doing."

After a pause, and with the air of one citing a damning circumstance, she added: "I suppose you know she was *married* to Lord Malvern."

I tranquillized her as well as I could, assuring her that the Inspector did not believe Mrs. Fairfax to be guilty, and that there was, indeed, no ground at all for such a charge. She drank in my words with an eager desire to receive comfort from them, but her self-reproach opposed itself to conviction; whatever I said, she recurred to the state in which she had just seen her friend, and was unable to view it otherwise than as the result of her own treachery. Even to me, the heat seemed inadequate to explain it; I could only suppose that the recent interview had been too severe a shock. She might have left us on purpose to conceal her agitation. Matthew, indeed, believed her incapable of needless tremors, but was not that too much to expect of any unprotected young woman under such a cloud?

She reappeared in the drawing-room before dinner, but neither in looks nor manner was she quite herself. She was still rather pale; I was more struck, however, by her peculiar constraint and uneasiness, which rather increased than diminished as the evening wore on. True, there was some cause for it, apart from what we had just heard. I could not doubt that her connection with the dead man had become public; no one spoke of it, but I saw the knowledge in every face, and was astonished at the rapidity with which it seemed to have passed through Colonel Lawrence to every other person present. This revelation, with the awkwardness of avoiding all allusion to it, would

242

have been enough to render the evening meal uncomfortable; but another little incident made matters worse. Just before dinner, when we were nearly all assembled, Miss Grant rushed in and flung herself, in tears, upon Edward's neck.

"Oh, Edward," she sobbed out, "*that* wasn't why you saw a lawyer? Oh, poor Edward! Oh, *what* shall I do?"

Her voice was lost in a violent outburst of affliction. Edward, with some difficulty, led her from the room, and neither appeared at the dinner table. I fear it was Matthew who had been unkind enough to hint at Edward's probable business with Mr. Green. Edward himself had obviously been at pains to spare her feelings by some harmless fiction—a proof of tenderness which, in his present state, almost surprised me; but Matthew, inclined as he was to blame her for all that had happened, was, I fear, only too eager that she should realize what she had done. The two empty places threw a gloom over the table, and even Colonel Lawrence was almost silent throughout the meal.

After dinner Mr. Hatton again borrowed Matthew's car, and went off on some unexplained errand of his own. At another time there would certainly have been talk of this in the drawing-room; but that night conjecture was dispirited, and his going was scarcely the object of a remark.

CHAPTER SEVENTEEN

Frampton's Next Move

The next morning I was rather later than usual in coming down to breakfast. All the others, except Phyllis and Miss Grant, were already at table, and, to my surprise, Miss Barry was presiding. Moreover, almost everyone wore an animated look which in itself would have convinced me that something new and startling had taken place. I had scarcely begun to ask myself what this could be, when my old friend turned to me and said:

"Well, Joseph, have you heard the news?"

"No," I replied. "Has anything occurred since yesterday?"

"Oh, yes; Frampton has been enlivening us again. The man has no off moments; he prepares his little surprises at the dead of night."

"What can you mean?" I asked in perplexity. "What has he done now?"

"He's taken himself off," replied Matthew.

"Gone!" I exclaimed.

"Clean gone," Matthew answered with a grin.

Just then the Colonel made a curious spluttering sound. Glancing at him, I saw that he was exceedingly red in the face, and had apparently just choked over his coffee. This accident brought the conversation momentarily to a standstill, and in the brief silence he met Miss Barry's eye, which was fixed on him with an expression of some disapproval. His confusion increased, and his efforts not to cough were so visibly painful that I hastened to cover them by returning to the subject.

"Frampton gone!" I repeated. "When did he leave here?"

"No one knows," said Mr. Hatton. "When the servants got up this morning he wasn't to be found."

"But surely", said I, "this is a very foolish step of his? Surely it must concentrate suspicion upon him?"

"Yes," agreed Mr. Hatton, "certainly."

"And a very good thing too," Miss Barry put in with her customary decision. "If the Inspector cannot see a pikestaff when it's held up before his eyes, it is quite time he was rapped over the knuckles with it."

"Has the Inspector heard yet?" I asked.

"Oh, yes," replied Miss Barry grimly, "he has heard. I am told that he expressed amazement."

"You think he should have expected it?" asked Mrs. Fairfax.

"On that subject", returned Miss Barry, "I am not competent to speak. If the majority of criminals wait patiently until he can make up his mind to arrest them, no doubt he had some ground for supposing that Frampton would do the same."

"But he's sure to be caught," said Mrs. Fairfax. "Isn't he, Nicholas?"

"Yes," replied Mr. Hatton, "with a much better chance he'd be caught, probably. As it is, he has no start to speak of, and I should think very little money

—he's even had to abandon his month's wages. It was a lunatic idea."

"I wish we could get him certified," said Matthew. "He must be very near the mark. And that would be pleasanter than leaving him in the Inspector's clutches."

"What on earth can he have done it for?" said Mrs. Fairfax. "He *can't* be such a fool! Does he never read detective novels?"

"Perhaps", Matthew suggested, "he's committed suicide, and buried himself in the garden."

My old friend's spirits appeared so much revived by this unlooked-for development that I began to feel what his previous anxiety must have been. I had known all along, of course, that he was greatly shaken; but I had supposed it to be more upon Lord Malvern's account than upon Edward's. Now it occurred to me that I had been doing him an injustice. True, he was seldom outwardly affectionate to the poor boy; but if he had not been feeling a great deal, he could scarcely display such intense relief at a diversion in his favour. In Edward's own looks, strangely enough, there was no similar improvement; he sat with his eyes fixed on his plate, harassed and despondent as ever, and seemed to take little or no interest in what was being said. Remembering Miss Grant's outburst of the night before, I thought it possible that she was the cause of his dejection, and at length ventured to ask if she were quite well.

"I am not aware", said Miss Barry, "that she has refused her breakfast."

This reply made me fear that we were again

verging on the servant problem. I should have been glad, I confess, to turn the subject, but no suitable remark occurred to me, and before I could think of one she spoke again.

"May I ask, Mr. Colchester, if you see no one else missing from the breakfast table?"

"Yes, yes—to be sure," I replied in some confusion. "Of course I observed that Phyllis was not here. I trust *she* is quite well?"

"Phyllis", said Miss Barry, "is not in the habit of giving unnecessary trouble. If she does not come down to breakfast, it follows that she is not in a condition to do so. No, Mr. Colchester—" interrupting me, "it is too late to express concern."

At this awkward moment Mrs. Fairfax came to my relief.

"Phyllis not well!" she said. "I'm so sorry—what's wrong with her?"

"Thank you," replied Miss Barry, "it is very good of you to ask. I am aware that no one but myself can be expected to think of her—she has no arts, poor child, and nothing to conceal, and therefore cannot be supposed to excite interest at such a moment."

As she said this, she gave Edward a look of reproach which suggested an entirely new idea to me. I thought, all at once, how probable it was that she had hoped for a match between her nephew and her young protégée. In that case, she might well view Miss Grant with more than ordinary disapproval, and be disposed to resent any mark of attention to her which even seemed to involve a slight on poor Phyllis.

"But what *is* wrong with her?" asked Matthew. "Is she absolutely bed-ridden?"

"She is in bed, Matthew, if that is what you mean."

"Dear me," said Colonel Lawrence, "bad luck—very bad luck, poor girl! Nothing serious, I hope? Quite well last night, wasn't she?"

"You, Colonel, would naturally think so. However, as I am responsible for the child, I cannot allow myself to give way even to your judgment in the matter; I must express my own opinion, however misguided it may appear to you. Phyllis's nerves have been shattered by what she has seen and heard in the last three days. She is quite unfit to stay here any longer. Now that the criminal has left the house, perhaps Inspector Lockitt will cease to consider it necessary for everyone else to remain in it; but in any case it is time Phyllis was sent home. I will not stand by and see her condition aggravated. Mr. Hatton, will you convey this to the Inspector, or shall I speak to him myself?"

"I'll tell him, if you like," said Mr. Hatton. "I should think there won't be any difficulty. Do you want her to leave the house to-day?"

"Certainly not," replied Miss Barry. "I should not dream of sending her on a journey in her present state. By *to-morrow*, if she is kept quiet in the meantime, she will perhaps be more herself."

Mr. Hatton, I thought, looked pleased that she was not to go at once.

"Very well," he said, "I'll speak to Lockitt; he won't make any objection, I dare say."

"I am delighted to hear it," replied Miss Barry,

though with the air of one to whom objections would have been rather stimulating than otherwise.

It was scarcely possible, at this time, to feel any great interest in Phyllis's departure, or even in her nervous state, which I was willing to hope Miss Barry had exaggerated—very naturally, and without the least intention to deceive. A few minutes afterwards she quitted the room, and Edward and Colonel Lawrence soon followed her. The conversation then reverted to Frampton's disappearance; we had all been thinking, I am sure, of little else, and my own amazement increased as I reflected on it.

"Do you think", I asked Mr. Hatton, "that we may take it as a confession of guilt on his part? Miss Barry, at least, has evidently that impression."

"Yes," replied the young man, "but I don't think I can agree with her. Of course he went off in a panic —he must have persuaded himself that it was his only hope; but innocent men have been known to lose their heads, unfortunately. What puzzles me is that even Frampton should have imagined he'd get clean away; only absolute desperation can account for it. He must have taken it as a mathematical certainty that he'd be convicted in the end."

"Just so," said Matthew. "If he did it, he had some excuse for thinking so."

"I don't know," replied Mr. Hatton. "It's a matter of temperament. He's behaved well in the last day or two, I must say, but not because he was inclined to look on the bright side of things; and his class-consciousness has been against him. He certainly had the idea that as the only working man involved he was

marked out as the scapegoat. And this kind of suspense is fatal to the nerves; he's had time to think
himself into a thorough panic."

"May I ask", said I, "if the Inspector takes your
view?"

"Not quite," said Mr. Hatton. "He hasn't, of
course, jumped to any conclusion about Frampton's
guilt, but he's more disposed to believe in it than he
has been. When the man's caught, he'll be rather
puzzled what to do. He doesn't want to arrest him
on suspicion, and he doesn't want, yet, to charge him
with blackmail."

"This has been going on too long," said Matthew
gloomily.

The young man did not answer; he himself had an
uneasy, almost a strained look, and it occurred to me
that he had begun to despair of a solution to the
problem. On second thoughts, I could not myself see
that Frampton's flight had really altered the position
of affairs, and yet it had raised a feeling of keen expectancy which made suspense harder to bear. I
invited Matthew to walk a little, hoping to distract
him; but he rejected the idea, and another quiet
morning with a book appeared inevitable. I established myself on the lawn, under my favourite tree,
and this time with a new novel, which might, I
thought, fix my attention at such a moment more
easily than a work requiring sustained thought. In
practice, however, I found it impossible even to grasp
the thread of the story. The heat was intense, even
in the shade—as great as it had been on Sunday; and
at a happier season I should probably have fallen

asleep. Now I could only sit meditating on Frampton's disappearance, in a confusion of mind which precluded any distinct train of reasoning, and added to my former disquiet a continuous painful impression of futility. I was glad to be roused by the approach of Mrs. Fairfax, who sat down near me with a writing-case, and begged me not to disturb myself on her account.

"Not at all," said I, "I cannot even say that I was reading—I have been trying to read, but with very little success, I am afraid."

"Yes," she replied, with an energy of feeling that surprised me, "it's too awful—it's *too* awful. I wish I had never come here."

This reminded me of her recent indisposition, and I asked her if she were quite recovered from it.

"Oh, yes," said Mrs. Fairfax, "I feel all right—but I'd almost prefer a breakdown; it would give one an excuse not to think about this any more. There's something to be said for Frampton, after all. Perhaps he ran away in the hope that when he came back it would be all over."

I made no reply to this fanciful suggestion, and after a moment she went on:

"By the way, I saw Milly Baker going up to the house just now. Surely she doesn't know where he is and mean to give him away."

"No, no," I replied, startled, "that cannot be possible! No doubt she has heard of his disappearance, and is anxious to learn the exact truth. In her situation, poor girl, this may well have been a blow to her—perhaps she fears never to see him again."

Death by Request

"It would be better if she didn't, probably," said Mrs. Fairfax. "Do you think he's really fond of her?"

"I cannot say. I feel sure there is a great deal of affection on her side."

"Poor girl!" she said. "Why did Miss Barry ever engage him? No doubt she had scores of applicants, and she chose *Frampton*!"

"My dear Mrs. Fairfax," I protested, "how could she possibly have known——"

"Of course not—but still it's been fatal to everyone connected with her. For whatever has happened and may be going to happen, Frampton was to blame in the first place."

"That may be true in a sense," I admitted, "yet it surely does not become us to lay it to his charge. If he is innocent of the murder, we ought rather to pity than accuse him. We have all enough to answer for in the *designed* consequences of our evil-doing."

"Yes, yes," she replied, "and besides, the same can be said of more than Frampton. *I* am responsible—more directly responsible than he is. When I dragged Charles into his own room that night, I was dragging him straight to his death; in a sense, *I* killed him. I can't forget it—I keep telling myself that I ought to have known."

Her face, as she said this, was almost haggard, and I could not doubt that it had really been preying on her mind. I expostulated with her, entreating her to dismiss these morbid fancies; I pointed out that such a way of thinking, carried to its logical extreme, would saddle each of us with a host of crimes, not only foreign to our intention, but outside our knowledge.

252

She was perfectly reasonable, and admitted the truth of what I said, but I could see that her nerves were not to be wholly mastered by her understanding; though she had more self-command than Phyllis Winter, she had, after all, passed through a trial incomparably more severe. Soon she began to speak of Lord Malvern himself, with more tenderness than I had yet observed in her—praising his charm, his courage, his high spirits, his serene temper, all in a softened and vaguely remorseful strain which at first took me by surprise. It was not long, however, before I began to suspect a new meaning in her attitude. I thought it possible that she secretly reproached herself for Mr. Hatton's influence upon her heart. True, she had long been separated from her young husband, and he had even engaged himself to another woman; yet so soon after his tragic death she might well feel it unkind, almost disloyal, to forsake his memory. This idea, once received, so readily passed into conviction that when, a few minutes later, Mr. Hatton himself joined us, his arrival seemed like a comment on what we had been saying.

"Well," he began, sitting down on the grass close by us, "there's already more news of a kind."

"Interesting news?" she asked, with an immediate return of her light manner. "Frampton can't have been recovered yet?"

"No, it's not that," said Mr. Hatton. "Milly Baker's come forward with another statement."

"What!" exclaimed Mrs. Fairfax. "She hasn't *really* given him away?"

"No, she's in a panic about him, and doesn't in the

least know where he's gone—at least she says she doesn't. She came up in a belated attempt to do him good. You remember those two hours unaccounted for on Friday afternoon?"

"When he was supposed to have posted the letter?" said Mrs. Fairfax, "the letter to Edward? Do you mean he was with her after all?"

"So it appears," said Mr. Hatton.

"But in that case," she exclaimed, "why on earth didn't he say so? He denied it, didn't he?"

"Yes," replied Mr. Hatton, "it's a queer thing. It seems he was afraid of getting her into a row. Her father and mother had been in a great state at all that business—they never thought much of Frampton as a suitor, and when it turned out that she was with child, and Frampton dismissed into the bargain, they actually wanted her to throw him over—which is surprising, though extremely sensible. They also led her rather a life, I'm afraid. They began to supervise her comings and goings, and insisted that she wasn't to meet Frampton in future without their knowledge."

"Shutting the stable door . . ." said Mrs. Fairfax.

"Yes, that was the idea. Of course she met him just the same, but precautions became necessary. Last Friday afternoon they had an appointment in the little wood beyond the paddock; Milly was to say she had work up at the house. But when the time came Mrs. Baker, who apparently does plain sewing for a good many people in the neighbourhood, was away on some job of her own, and the father was at his usual work of course, so Milly didn't find it necessary to admit that she had left home at all. She and Frampton were together quite long enough to make it impossible that he can have gone down to the village afterwards."

"Well, well," said Mrs. Fairfax. "It seems we haven't been doing justice to his sterling qualities. I shouldn't have credited him with enough of the martyr spirit to submit to false accusations for her sake."

"His motives were mixed, I dare say," replied the young man. "In the first place, I think he *is* fond of her; he may have been rather off-hand with her once, but now the tables are turned, you must remember. He's in a thoroughly unpleasant situation, and without a friend in the world, it seems, and he must know that her parents are determined she shall have no more to do with him. Whatever he may have felt at one time, I think now he's desperately anxious not to be cast off. For that reason, perhaps, he was afraid to say anything when she didn't. And by the way, there's no doubt she has a healthy regard for her own safety—quite as much as Frampton has. Then he may have realized, on second thoughts, that if he *were* supposed to have written to Edward he was no worse off. It doesn't make it more likely that he committed the murder, and as for blackmail——"

"That's true," said Mrs. Fairfax. "He'd written one blackmailing letter to Charles, and two to Judith, all unearthed and staring him in the face. One more could make very little difference."

"Yes," agreed Mr. Hatton, "and there's another thing. He may have thought that if he said he was with Milly no one would believe him. She might even have denied it herself—in fact she did till now—and if she'd admitted it, Lockitt might have assumed that she was lying to please Frampton. He couldn't produce any other evidence."

"But", said I, "is not that, perhaps, the real state of the case? May she not have invented this tale in her anxiety for him?"

"No," replied Mr. Hatton, "luckily she has a witness. Just after she had left him on Friday she ran into one of the village children, and gave him a penny to say nothing about it—with the promise of unspecified future bounties if he kept his word. That's all quite true; he was sick immediately afterwards on the sweets he bought."

"Well," said Mrs. Fairfax, with an air of lassitude, "is there nothing more?"

"No more news, do you mean?" asked Mr. Hatton. "I'm afraid not. You don't seem very much enlivened by this bit."

"No," she replied, "I was sure in any case that *Frampton* didn't write that letter to Edward—so my own ideas are exactly what they were before. As for the case in general, I suppose the Inspector has now quite made up his mind that *I* am the unknown blackmailer, and that I drove Edward to murder by it. So the cause of truth seems not to have advanced perceptibly."

"A fact's always a fact," Mr. Hatton rejoined, "and the mere professional is glad to have one. But I have also a theory. To be quite frank——" His face darkened, and he left the sentence incomplete.

"Yes?" prompted Mrs. Fairfax.

"I should like to know what yours is."

"That wasn't what you were going to say," she replied somewhat evasively.

"It wasn't; but at the same time I should like to know."

"Well," said Mrs. Fairfax, "I'm not anxious to monopolize it; but in the first place I think that *I*, as a suspect, ought to see a lawyer now."

"Waste of time," replied the young man steadily. "He wouldn't tell you what you want to know. I can."

She was about to speak when we heard a heavy foot upon the gravel. It was Colonel Lawrence, bearing straight down upon us.

The young people exchanged glances, and strolled off together.

CHAPTER EIGHTEEN

Financial Difficulties

At luncheon Miss Grant again made her appearance, but Phyllis was under Miss Barry's orders
to remain in bed. I could not believe that she was
really ill enough to require solitary confinement, and
very likely she would have been grateful for less solici-
tude on her friend's part; but no one could presume
to dispute with Miss Barry on such points, and the
Colonel, in particular, endeavoured to wipe out his
blunder of the morning by a show of great concern
for the poor invalid. I was anxious to know whether
any confidences had passed between Mr. Hatton and
Mrs. Fairfax after they had left me, and I observed
them as closely as possible throughout the meal. They
seldom looked at each other; both seemed out of
spirits, and Mrs. Fairfax was extremely silent.

Just as we left the table, a message was brought to
Mr. Hatton: the Inspector wished to see him immediately. I may here mention that despite the Inspector's forbidding manners, and the young man's somewhat invidious position in the house, there appeared
to be an excellent understanding between them. For
this Mr. Hatton's intelligence and tact were no doubt

258

chiefly responsible; but however that might be, the Inspector seemed completely open with him, evidently set a value upon his assistance, and was in the habit of using him as a kind of link with the family itself. In the drawing-room, over our coffee, we exchanged guesses on the new development which must have taken place—all of us, that is, except Edward and Miss Grant, who had already wandered off together. The general view was that something had been heard of Frampton; a whole morning might have been enough to bring some news of him, and when Mr. Hatton returned, not many minutes later, curiosity ran high.

"Well," he said, as he entered, "Frampton's escapade hasn't been a great success."

"Have they got him already?" inquired Mrs. Fairfax.

"Yes—he's back in the house now."

There were exclamations of astonishment.

"It was simple enough," said Mr. Hatton. "He did the most obvious thing: walked into Oxon and took the first train to town. They were on the look-out for him at Waterloo, and brought him straight here again."

"Too bad!" said Matthew sympathetically.

"He was relying partly on his disguise, I imagine. He'd shaved off those little side-whiskers of his—it looked very conspicuous, because of course the rest of his face was a different colour; and he was wearing spectacles. I don't know where he picked them up, but apparently he could hardly see out of them."

"Good Lord!" said Matthew, in a changed and un-

expectedly bitter voice, "is it *all* going to be turned
into low comedy? Was it really that clown who——"
He broke off, and then said with an attempt at his
usual manner: "Well, Hatton, what account does he
give of himself?"

"The curious thing", answered Mr. Hatton, "is
that he had more than a hundred pounds on him."

"Indeed!" I ejaculated in amazement. "But how
—— Surely he cannot have come honestly by such
a sum!"

"The police think he must have stolen it," said Mr.
Hatton. "If so, he must have thought it out beforehand; it's too much to get hold of at a moment's
notice. And the first thing, of course, is to know if he
did steal it from anyone in the house. Will anyone
who happened to have a large sum about make sure
it's safe?"

"I haven't," said Mrs. Fairfax, "I haven't very
much more than enough to travel with."

"All that I have in the house is on me," said
Matthew, taking out his notecase.

The Colonel clapped his hand vigorously to his
breast-pocket.

"Must have left mine upstairs," he said. "Better go
and have a look, I suppose."

"Yes, do," replied Mr. Hatton. "And if Miss
Barry——" He glanced inquiringly towards her.

"Oh, very well," said she. "I will go and look, as
you consider it necessary."

They both quitted the room. At the same moment,
Matthew returned the notecase to his pocket.

"Well," he said, "Frampton hasn't laid *me* under

contribution. Where does he say he got the money?"

"He says it was given to him."

"Who by?" asked Mrs. Fairfax.

"He hasn't gone as far as that yet; but of course he will. At present he bitterly invites the persons concerned to come forward and admit it; he wants to see some of the honourable dealing of the upper classes."

"Meaning that it'll be a new experience?" said Mrs. Fairfax.

"Yes," replied the young man, "and there's no doubt he's in earnest. He has an unshaken idea of himself as a victim of class tyranny; that's why he ran away. In his view of life the rich always get off, and this time they were clearly intended to get off at his expense; so he thought he might as well go, and risk being taken. At the worst it would come to the same thing."

"I see," said Mrs. Fairfax. " 'As good to die and go as die and stay'."

"Exactly."

"What about his blackmailing activities?" said Matthew. "Was he forced into them by the tyranny of the upper classes?"

"Oh, yes," replied Mr. Hatton, "it's all connected in his mind. The rich have fraudulently possessed themselves of what ought to be shared among the workers, and a sensible man will take every chance of getting some of it back from them. That's Frampton's view. He's not dishonest; he's merely a re-distributor of wealth. As for blackmail being illegal, the law was made by capitalists for their own advantage, and so it's a sound principle to flout it."

"Then", said Matthew, "he may have stolen this money with the same laudable intention."

"He may, but oddly enough he's very indignant at being accused of theft; it's a peculiar inconsistency."

"He drank my whisky none the less," said Matthew.

"There I can't blame him," answered Mr. Hatton. "It's extremely good. But I'm almost afraid he's telling the truth about the money."

"Really?" said I. "Why, who can possibly have given him such a large sum?"

Before he could answer, Mrs. Fairfax said:

"Of course, I see what *might* have happened—the money might have been a bribe to run away. If the criminal thought that would concentrate suspicion on Frampton, he—or she—might easily consider it worth a hundred pounds. The odd thing is that Frampton should have been fool enough to do it, but he *was*—and a sum like that would at any rate be an incentive."

Matthew's face darkened at this speech.

"Nonsense, Anne!" he said hastily. "Who would attempt to divert suspicion by a trick that was certain to come out? It would have been sheer idiocy; an infant in arms knows that bank-notes can be traced, and then the *criminal* would have been worse off than Frampton."

Mrs. Fairfax seemed about to answer; then she changed her mind and abruptly turned away towards the window. Mr. Hatton said:

"The notes may be traced, but will that prove whether Frampton stole them or was given them?"

This suggestion made me exceedingly uncomfortable, and indeed I think it brought home to us all, with a new and horrible distinctness, what a pit might at any moment gape before our feet. I could not but feel that Frampton had in a sense accused us justly: from the first he had been chosen as the scapegoat, he had been eagerly saddled with the iniquity which we must otherwise have looked for and acknowledged in our very midst. Through him it had been possible to maintain the attitude that Lord Malvern's death concerned us only as a misfortune. Now all at once we were confronted with the idea, almost the statement that among ourselves there was actually a murderer. One of the guests at Friars Cross, or —more likely and more horrible—one of the family, was supposed to have inveigled Frampton with money to his own destruction, and to be ready to complete the betrayal by denying his gift. How few there were of us, how frightful and immediate did this hint appear! I felt it not so much in my own person as in Matthew's, if I may so express myself; from his set and slightly distorted countenance I received an alarm not unlike that which I had felt for him on Sunday morning, when Lord Malvern's body was discovered. There was a long silence—long, at any rate, in our strained consciousness of it; for the two young people seemed to experience all the awkwardness they had created. Then just as Matthew, I could not doubt in anger, was about to break it, the door opened, and Miss Barry re-entered the room.

"Is it all right," asked Mr. Hatton, "or has anything been taken?"

"Not that I am aware," she replied frigidly. "I see

no sign that my own desk has been disturbed."

"The Colonel's a long time," said Mrs. Fairfax. "Perhaps *he's* missed something."

"I have just spoken with Colonel Lawrence," answered Miss Barry. "He appears to have no notion how much money he ought to have, and therefore I do not see that he can be of any use to you."

Though her manner was as decided as usual, something evasive in her actual reply struck us unpleasantly. Again Matthew was about to speak, and again he was forestalled.

"That's unfortunate," said Mr. Hatton. "But surely if a large sum had been taken the Colonel would be bound to notice it?"

"So I should imagine," answered Miss Barry. "However, it is not for me to give an opinion on the subject."

Mr. Hatton slightly shrugged his shoulders.

"Well," he said, "it can't be helped; perhaps on second thoughts he'll be more definite. In the meantime, there's Edward to consider; Frampton may have stolen the entire amount from *him*. Have you any idea where I shall find him?"

"No," replied Miss Barry; "I have not; but I can spare you the exertion. I happen to know that Edward has very little money in the house."

The promptness with which she brought out this statement, far from allaying our apprehensions, had an extremely sinister effect. It irresistibly suggested forethought, artifice, arrangement. Mr. Hatton looked grave as he replied:

"That's very odd; even Frampton doesn't deny

that the money came from this house, and now it appears none is missing."

"On that question," replied Miss Barry, "I have, of course, nothing to say. If you believe that Frampton's word is perfectly reliable, I cannot contradict you."

Matthew uttered something in a suppressed voice, and hurriedly quitted the room.

"Oh, well," said Mr. Hatton, "I can only try the man again. Perhaps by now he's ready to make his accusation more explicit."

With these words he also left us. I expected Miss Barry to follow him out, for she rarely sat downstairs in the afternoon; but she still lingered, busy, in appearance, about the room, rearranging and setting things to rights. After a brief period of silence, Mrs. Fairfax began to talk of Phyllis Winter. During the polite and rather stiff dialogue which ensued, I was surprised to observe Colonel Lawrence strolling jauntily past the front windows. Casual though his manner was, I could not but perceive that he directed a keen glance towards the drawing-room as he went by, and it occurred to me that he wished to make sure who was in it. When, almost immediately afterwards, he joined us, this idea gained strength; I felt almost convinced that he had been satisfying himself of Mr. Hatton's absence. Why he had come back at all was not so clear. He was very restless, and very ill at ease. He walked up and down incessantly ; he got in Miss Barry's way, and received more than one sharp reprimand; he hung over Mrs. Fairfax, who was now engaged on a piece of knitting, till she was obliged to ask him to go further off. Yet he remained with us, talking a great deal by fits and starts, and always in a jaunty strain peculiarly inappropriate to the situation. Stranger yet, Miss Barry, though she might have gone at any moment, and though he clearly irritated her almost to frenzy, seemed unable to tear herself away. I had the impression that we were all waiting for something, and, as it were, charmed to the spot. Even Mrs. Fairfax, knitting with a severe and absorbed face, appeared to me silenced by attention.

At last, however, Miss Barry suddenly broke through the fascination that imprisoned us.

"Colonel," she said in her sharpest manner, "I think you had better employ yourself, if possible. I am just about to do some gardening; perhaps you will not object to carry my basket for me."

"Not at all—certainly—very glad to be of use," the Colonel hastily replied.

In the doorway, however, Mr. Hatton intercepted them.

"Miss Barry," he said, "the Inspector would like to see you at once, if you're not doing anything."

The Colonel positively jumped, but not like a man taken unawares; on the contrary, it was impossible not to feel that the announcement startled him precisely because he had been expecting it.

"Nonsense!" he exclaimed in a loud voice. "Pestering Miss Barry in this way—I can't have it! No gentleman——" He choked a little, and then added with great violence: "I won't allow it to be done!"

"Really, Colonel," said Miss Barry, "I am not aware that it is any business of yours."

The Colonel hesitated, but only for a moment.

"Yes, yes," he burst out again, "it *is* my business—I can explain everything. I warned—that is, I thought from the first it was bound to come out. *I* gave the fellow that money, Hatton—thought it was time something was done to speed things up. Not the right thing, perhaps, but when Lockitt was so obstinate—— Can't always think for the best at a time like this, you know. Miss Barry had nothing to do with it. What I mean is," he added, as though recollecting himself, "I had to borrow some money from her—hadn't got enough myself. But she knew nothing about it. Didn't ask what it was for, and of course I didn't tell her—wouldn't have dreamt of such a thing."

"Oh!" said Mr. Hatton. "How much did you borrow, Colonel?"

"How much?" repeated the Colonel, evidently making a hurried calculation. "Let me see—I—oh, yes, to be sure. I——"

"Nonsense!" Miss Barry interrupted. "If you cannot hold your tongue, Colonel, you can at least refrain from making yourself ridiculous by transparent falsehoods." She turned away from him, and addressed Mr. Hatton. "It was I who told Frampton to leave the house. As the Inspector appears incapable of making up his mind, I thought it high time it was made up for him. Frampton refused to go without a hundred pounds, and so, of course, a hundred pounds had to be got together. The Colonel entirely disapproved of the whole scheme, but his opinion was not asked on it; I merely requested him to lend me the necessary sum, as I had not enough, and of course he

267

had no choice but to do so. It did not seem likely to me, I confess, that with a hundred pounds in his pocket Frampton would allow himself to be re-captured, and so far I was to blame; but do not imagine that the Colonel had any voice in the matter."

"But surely, Miss Barry," I could not help saying, "you would not have allowed us to believe that Frampton came *dishonestly* by that money?"

"And why not?" she replied unmoved. "I am not in the habit of being governed by sentimental con-siderations. As Frampton is guilty of murder, I see no reason for protecting him against a charge of theft."

For the moment we were all silenced by this.

"However," Miss Barry continued, "I suppose I must go to the Inspector and put matters right. It's the old story—no one in this house can even think without my help. As for you, Colonel—" turning abruptly on him as she left the room, "perhaps you had better not attempt it."

Nothing profounder than exasperation had been legible on her countenance, but, knowing her as I did, I thought it probable that she was seriously alarmed. Mrs. Fairfax laid down her knitting, and turned her eyes reproachfully on Colonel Lawrence.

"Colonel," she said, "why on *earth* did you do that?"

The Colonel blushed even more deeply.

"Really," he answered, "I'm extremely sorry—error of judgment on my part—no idea the fellow would be caught so soon." He appeared immediately afterwards to realize that this was scarcely a moral justification of his conduct, and went on with a con-

fused air: "After all, you know, he did it—that's as
clear as daylight. If he hadn't done it, why should he
have bolted, eh? No one forced him to go—an innocent man would have stayed where he was. And all
these suspicions going about—Miss Barry's quite right,
you know, perfectly right; this is no time for sentiment.
If a guilty man wants to give himself away, what
sense is there in making obstacles?"

"Oh, quite," said Mr. Hatton, "but that's not the
point. Didn't you see that when it came out
Frampton wouldn't be the only doubtful character?"

"Yes, yes," replied the Colonel, "it's an awkward
business, I quite see—damned awkward. But I'd no
idea the fellow would be caught so soon. Didn't know
how much money he had, either—thought he'd very
little more than what I gave him. How could I guess
Miss Barry had a sum like that about?"

"How much *did* you give him?" inquired Mr.
Hatton.

"Thirty-five pounds—that was nearly all I had.
Thought the fellow would most likely get rid of it
before they caught him—then who would have
believed any stories he chose to invent?"

The Colonel's manner suggested that he himself
would, in that case, have listened with incredulity to
the assertion that Frampton had received money to
go away.

"But, Colonel," I said, "if he had accused you, you
would not, surely, have persisted in denying the
truth?"

The Colonel appeared, for an instant, rather at a
loss. Then he replied with great energy:

"Certainly, Colchester—no use being sentimental at a time like this. Miss Barry's perfectly right— wonderful grasp of a situation. No use shutting one's eyes to the facts, you know."

"Well," rejoined Mr. Hatton sombrely, "I hope, at least, that Edward knew nothing about it."

"No, no," said the Colonel, evidently delighted to find himself on safe ground, "of course not—we took care of that, naturally. Wouldn't have done to get Edward mixed up in it. No, no."

He looked complacently aware of his own clearness of head, and seemed mildly to reprove the young man for having doubted it.

"That's lucky, at any rate," said Mr. Hatton. "Even then——"

Before he could finish his sentence the door opened, and Edward himself entered the room.

"Well, Hatton," he said, dropping into a chair, "I should think you can go now, if you like. It's all over with me."

He glanced from one to the other of us with dull eyes, which, however, as they rested on the Colonel, suddenly burned with an expression of acute resentment. Colonel Lawrence, as though in self-justification, instantly burst forth:

"Nonsense, Edward, nonsense—nothing of the kind. All this Frampton business—damned awkward, of course, but nothing to do with you. We took care to keep you out of it. Why, I was just saying to Hatton——"

"Never mind that now," Mr. Hatton interrupted. "What's wrong, Edward?"

"Oh, it makes no difference, after all," Edward replied, with something of the arrogant gloom I had before observed in him. "I know very well there was no hope for me. I suppose it's really a good thing to have it over."

"My dear Edward," I exclaimed, "what is the matter? The Inspector cannot imagine that you are involved in this last unfortunate affair?"

"On the contrary," replied Edward, "he's quite satisfied that it was my doing. He never had any doubt of it, of course, and now he's proved it."

"What!" said Mrs. Fairfax. "Do you mean to say——"

"Oh, it's not a question of what *I* say," returned Edward, interrupting her. "As I'm the murderer, what *I* say can't be expected to go for anything. I'm giving you Inspector Lockitt's account of the matter."

"Don't be absurd," said Mr. Hatton, looking irritated rather than compassionate. "What really happened? How have you got dragged into this?"

"As I told you, Inspector Lockitt has been quite sure all along that it was my doing. He asked me how much money I had in the house, and I told him about ten pounds. He rang up the bank and found that I had drawn twenty on Friday; then he wanted to know how I had spent the rest. As it happened, I couldn't prove that I *had* spent it."

"What became of it, then?" asked Mr. Hatton.

"My aunt borrowed it from me last night."

There was a general exclamation of dismay.

"To give to Frampton?" inquired Mrs. Fairfax.

"So it appears. She didn't tell me then what she

wanted it for. Now it seems that Frampton has accused *her* of bribing him to go away, and it's all come out, of course. I needn't say", he went on, with great bitterness, "that Aunt Susan did the whole thing for my sake. She didn't mean to bring me into it, but Frampton wouldn't go for less than a hundred pounds, and she and the Colonel couldn't make it up between them."

"Why didn't she ask Matthew, then?" said Mrs. Fairfax.

"I suppose she thought my father might ask questions, and put a stop to the whole thing. Anyhow, she came to my room last night and borrowed twelve pounds from me; Phyllis saw her going in, so our proceedings have come out in the most gratifying detail. Of course I am supposed to have suggested the whole scheme to my aunt; none of my own money was to have been used, in case something leaked out afterwards, and I was discovered to be short. That was my idea too, in the Inspector's opinion. But as Frampton's demand was so exorbitant, we couldn't help ourselves."

We were all silent, looking at each other with foreboding countenances.

"After all," Edward repeated, "a day more or less —what does it matter? I told my aunt so, but she won't listen to me—she's completely lost her head. First she abused the Inspector, which will no doubt induce him to look on me more favourably; and now she has rushed off to my father with the news. As though my arrest were an excuse for intruding on his literary work!"

"My dear boy," I exclaimed, "you do not mean you are *arrested*?"

"At this moment, no," replied Edward, "but I've probably spent my last night at Friars Cross."

The utterance of these last words seemed to break down all his false composure, and for a moment I thought he would burst into tears.

"In that case," said Mr. Hatton quickly, "hadn't you better explain to Miss Grant what the position is? From anyone else it would be more unpleasant."

I could not be sure whether he made this suggestion to get rid of Edward, or to put him in the way of consolation. Whatever its purpose, the hint met with a prompt response.

"Yes, yes," returned Edward, starting up. "I've no doubt my father or my aunt would be delighted to tell her; but as I'd rather they didn't, I'd better not lose time."

With these words he left the room, glad, I imagine, to conceal the weakness which was again threatening to overcome him. The Colonel, who had begun pacing up and down, came to a stop in front of Mr. Hatton, and said jerkily:

"This idea of his, Hatton—nothing in it, is there? This talk of arrest, I mean? Lockitt's not going to arrest him?"

"How can I say?" replied the young man. "It's quite possible."

"Good God!" exclaimed the Colonel, with a face of horror. "And it's Sus—— It's Miss Barry's doing! Good God, Colchester, how on earth will she stand up to it? Edward says she's lost her head—she must be ill, you know—the shock must have made her ill! And to think that I—— Excuse me, Hatton, I really——"

He got himself away, still muttering incoherent exclamations.

"I suppose he's gone to make sure she's not ill?" said Mrs. Fairfax.

"No doubt," I assented, "but I must confess my own fears are for poor Matthew. Miss Barry is exceedingly distressed, no doubt, but I have no apprehensions for her constitution. Matthew is far less able to bear such a shock; his heart is not sound, and the doctor has already warned him to avoid excitement."

"Rather an ironical warning in this case," said Mrs. Fairfax.

"Unfortunately, yes," I replied, "and that is why I cannot help being alarmed for him. I doubt if his health is equal to another experience like that of Sunday morning. He was frightfully shaken then—his look terrified me."

"Yes," said Mrs. Fairfax, without raising her eyes, "but then of course he was very fond of Charles. Do you think he's likely to feel quite as much for Edward?"

"My dear Mrs. Fairfax," said I, greatly shocked, "consider—only consider what you are suggesting! I entreat you not to speak with levity at such a time."

"No, no," she returned, "I'm quite serious. Of course I don't mean he's not uneasy; but then Charles's death was completely unexpected, whereas, now——"

"Ah," said I, "I sometimes think that expected

misfortunes are the more dreadful when they come. Even if Matthew bears up against the shock of Edward's arrest, I have more than once found myself doubting if he can live through the horrors of a trial. Mr. Hatton, is there *nothing* left for us to do—even now, at the eleventh hour? I understood that you had already formed a theory; surely now, if ever, is the time to bring it forward?"

"I intend to," said Mr. Hatton, "but one thing at a time. We're talking now of the case against Edward. Do you feel convinced that he had no idea Frampton was being bribed?"

"Certainly," I replied, "fully convinced—indeed it had not occurred to me to question it. You do not think it possible that he has deceived us—surely you cannot believe that?"

"On the whole, no," answered the young man, "but don't forget that his word is not reliable. We can't blame Lockitt for taking a different view. I told you another blunder might be the last straw, and here it is, whether Edward knew of it or not. Miss Barry couldn't have done a worse thing for him."

"But," said I, "after all, what *is* the case against the poor boy? Surely, even now, it is not really conclusive enough to justify arrest?"

"That's what I should have thought," agreed Mrs. Fairfax.

"Well," said Mr. Hatton, "let's run through it. In the first place, motive. He had very much the best motive, without doubt."

"Jealousy," I observed. "But Frampton also was jealous of Lord Malvern."

"Yes, but he frittered away the impressiveness of that by his blackmail. Edward received a letter accusing— as he thought—Charles, and on the night of the same day Charles was killed. Then opportunity: opportunity has been too general in this case, but even there Edward had distinct advantages. He could use his own pills to drug Charles without any risk of being detected stealing them; and he understood their operation—he would know how many to use. In the same way, he could turn the gas on from his own room without being observed—as anyone else might have been—where his presence needed explanation. In the Inspector's view he meant it to look like suicide, and hoped no one would notice about the drug. He turned the gas on when he went upstairs to fetch his tackle. On his return home, he tried Charles's door to make sure it was locked—he knew that Charles often locked it; it wasn't, so he rapidly took the key from the inside, and locked the door himself. When it was burst open in the morning, nobody was likely to ask straight away whether the key was duly in the lock. As soon as the tumult died down and the crowd dispersed, Edward slipped it back into its place, and it was assumed to have been there all along. There, again, he had a first-rate opportunity; his room was next door to Charles's, and he was almost sure of a moment to return the key. That's the substance of the case against him; but remember he has behaved rather oddly ever since—think of the remark that he smelt gas, for instance. He smelt gas at twelve o'clock, on his own showing, and yet took no steps about it. He lied about the drug; and now he's been taking part—

276

consciously or not—in this last idiotic enterprise. It's no use denying that it all looks pretty bad. Only a plurality of suspects has kept him from being arrested before now."

"But", said I in great distress, "when we last spoke of this, you appeared hopeful—you yourself said that the evidence was insufficient."

"Insufficient to convict him, I hope, but that's not what we're talking of. As to arrest, I share Edward's own view; I think he may be arrested at any moment."

Mrs. Fairfax jumped up with a flushed face.

"Not to-night!" she exclaimed. "You *must* get it put off, Nicholas! *To-morrow*, if nothing has happened, and there's no avoiding it—but you must at least leave me to-day. Promise to keep the Inspector quiet for this one night!"

CHAPTER NINETEEN

Coming Events

There was something startling, not so much in the appeal itself as in the sudden and desperate eagerness with which it was made. Mr. Hatton's surprise appeared almost equal to my own, though he betrayed it only by a look, and a slight alteration of countenance.

"You have an idea?" he inquired, eyeing her intently.

"I *think* I have an idea. It may be fantastic, but without *something* of the kind——" She checked herself, and then continued: "I depend entirely on the respite, though; can you compel your Spectre to obey?"

"Lockitt? Yes, I dare say, for as long as that; but you'd better be rather careful, Anne. Don't get yourself into more difficulties."

"That's all right," she replied. "I'll do nothing without your connivance—in fact, I couldn't. And, by the way, what's happened to the case against me? The Inspector seems to be letting it fall through."

"No, he's followed it up," said Mr. Hatton, "he's been inquiring into your affairs."

"Yes, I know that—but what conclusion has he come to?"

"None to divert him from Edward," replied Mr. Hatton. "You appear to live consistently within your means, and as far as it's possible to calculate you will make next to nothing. It looked sensational at first, but that's all."

"Yet he still credits me with blackmail," said Mrs. Fairfax, in a tone of sharper irony. "Or has he perhaps changed his mind?"

"I told you", replied the young man, "that he was bound to think of Charles sooner or later. Charles's financial situation was much worse than yours. But need we talk about that at the moment? If the letter to Edward wasn't genuine blackmail—if it was merely incidental to the crime itself, as you imagine——"

"As *I* imagine!" repeated Mrs. Fairfax. "Do you mean to say you've retracted your own view of it?" She gave him a look of sudden anxiety, as though ready all at once to doubt the inferences, whatever they might be, which a moment before had seemed to her finally established.

"I wasn't thinking of my own views," said Mr. Hatton. "I was considering your reputation, merely. If the letter was part of the crime, and you've really hit on a chance of solving that, you're cleared of blackmail as a by-product."

"Yes," agreed Mrs. Fairfax, "I suppose I am—though there's something peculiarly sordid in being *cleared* of blackmail. One couldn't believe much in the honesty of anyone who had gone through it. And if my idea's a failure—oh Lord, it *mustn't* be a failure, and yet——" She sat down again, adding with great fervour: "This is a horrible, *repellent* situation! Nicholas, are you sure he's going to arrest Edward?"

"I can't be," said Mr. Hatton. "He hasn't discussed it with me yet. But it's so likely that I can't promise you more than this one day."

"I wish I had longer," she replied gloomily. "I wish the criminal had escaped altogether. It seems almost fantastic to expect—and even if it works I'd rather put off the evil moment. But I suppose it's got to be done; if anyone's convicted, it *must* be the right person. I have one resource left—one forlorn hope of more substantial evidence. I'm going to do a little interviewing on my own account."

"Interviewing!" said I, more and more puzzled by her jerky and agitated speech. "But of whom, if I may ask the question? Surely the Inspector already knows all that can be learnt by that means? Or do you think that Frampton——"

"Not Frampton," she replied. "I'm going to speak to the maid who does the bedrooms."

"What!" I exclaimed. "In spite of all that has happened—in spite of so much terrible suspicion, you believe we are dealing with an accident after all?"

"Impossible," Mr. Hatton curtly put in. "Charles was drugged; they've already verified the fact."

"But in that case," said I, "what can be the object of troubling Violet again? Will it not distress the poor girl to no purpose?"

Mrs. Fairfax was about to reply; but at that moment Rhoda entered with the tea things. The conversation was necessarily suspended, and when we

were alone again, Mrs. Fairfax, now sunk in thought,
gave no sign of wishing to resume it. I feared to press
her with questions which in her eyes and her young
friend's might seem impertinently curious, and I was
driven back on silence and conjecture; my heart beat-
ing less evenly than usual, as though expectant of I
knew not what. Not that I felt much intellectual
confidence in these hints of a solution to the problem;
Mrs. Fairfax was an amateur and a young woman,
and her nerves, besides, were overwrought. But
crisis was in the very atmosphere; all agreed that we
were hastening towards some fatal change, some
movement which would define the future course of
things. It was impossible not to respond, emotionally
at least, to the idea that this change might be a startling one—not the mere arrest of Edward, but a turn
of fate utterly different, utterly unforeseen. I glanced
at Mr. Hatton, anxious to know how far he was in the
secret of his companion's thoughts; but from his reserved and calm expression it was difficult to tell. He
had been surprised at first; he might by now have
formed a guess at her real meaning. He it was who,
after a somewhat prolonged silence, turned to her and
said:

"You'll have to wait till after tea now, I suppose?"

"It looks like it," replied Mrs. Fairfax.

"You wouldn't prefer me to represent you? She
may say more to a person with official standing."

"Oh, I shan't need any standing," said Mrs. Fairfax. "If only she says the right thing——"

We were again interrupted; the other inmates
began to drop in for tea. Miss Barry herself appeared,

which was almost a surprise to me; she poured out as usual, and only her silence and extreme austerity betrayed that she was ill at ease. Of the agitation Edward had spoken of there was no sign at all. Matthew was also silent, his face gloomy with a conviction of disaster which reminded me of Edward's, though it had not Edward's peevishness and pathetic self-complacency. My old friend, I was aware, had little native self-command; he could obtain control of his nerves only by an afterthought, and at the price of a continuous effort, and I thought he avoided speaking for that reason—it was his safest course. It added, however, to the discomfort of the little gathering. Phyllis, Edward and Miss Grant were all absent, and the Colonel, desperately uneasy, never completed a remark without glancing at Miss Barry to make sure he had not blundered; when, as often as not, her stony disregard of the appeal routed his own notion of what he had been going to say. I did what I could to sustain a little conversation, and Mr. Hatton seconded the attempt; but it ended in our talking exclusively to each other, a proceeding almost more awkward than silence itself. Miss Barry, to the relief of all, soon broke up the party. Immediately on her withdrawal, Matthew said to me:

"I'm going into Oxon, Joseph; will you come?"

I was surprised by the announcement, and rather unwilling to leave the house at this moment of suspense. Suppressing the latter feeling, however, I ventured to ask what his business was.

"Oh, pure weakmindedness," he returned, "the natural instinct to foist one's troubles off on other people. I know Green can do no good, but I have an itch to consult him and be told that he'll see us through. Don't come, of course, if you don't want to."

This last remark made it impossible for me to refuse.

"Certainly I will come," I replied. "There can at least be no harm in taking Mr. Green's opinion, and who knows how the case may look from a lawyer's point of view? Very likely we are too apt to fear the worst; he may be able to give us positive reassurance."

"Yes, yes," put in the Colonel, "excellent idea—change of scene—what we all need, I dare say."

He said this in an off-hand manner, but with an expressive glance at my old friend. Matthew, however, received it very coolly, and had clearly no intention of asking him to join us. I thought for a moment that the Colonel would himself suggest it, but with unwonted diffidence he refrained, and instead turned to Mrs. Fairfax.

"Well, Anne," he said, "must do something to put in the time—what about a game of tennis? Exercise —must have exercise, after all."

"Not now, I'm afraid," said Mrs. Fairfax, "I have something to see to at the moment. But if you want exercise, Colonel, why not go for a ride? It's cooler now, and there's lots of time before dinner."

The Colonel seemed rather taken aback by this suggestion; he was not, I think, much in the habit of riding, except to hounds, and was not given to solitary amusement of any kind. But he evidently felt bound by his own statement that he needed exercise, and therefore limited his objections to a protesting remark upon the heat.

Death by Request

"It'll be no hotter than playing tennis," answered Mrs. Fairfax. "Do go, Colonel; I'm certain it will do you good. A ride will be change of scene, you know, as well as exercise—I only wish I could come too."

"Yes," put in Mr. Hatton, "it's a pity to mew oneself up in this weather. The country's looking very good just now; and there's no better way of seeing it than on a horse."

"Yes, yes—quite so," replied the Colonel with a bewildered expression, "wonderful country this—wonderful. Nothing like a cross-country run, Hatton, I agree. But really——"

"You're perfectly right, Colonel," interrupted Mrs. Fairfax, "I'm sure it'll cheer you up more than anything. But you'd better see about a horse at once, surely? It would be a pity not to have a good long ride when you *are* out."

"But really, you know, Anne——" the Colonel was beginning.

"That's quite all right," said Mrs. Fairfax, "I'll be delighted to excuse you—I'd be annoyed if you stayed at home on my account. Have a good ride!"

The Colonel, evidently in the last stage of confusion, but convinced that for some reason he ought to go, actually thanked her for her good wish, and went off to change. It was clear to me that Mrs. Fairfax's object had been simply to secure his absence, and a minute later she herself confirmed me in that view. Matthew had also left us, to ring up Mr. Green, and Mrs. Fairfax seemed to turn her thoughts once more to her intended interview. Before quitting the room, however, she said to Mr. Hatton in a low voice:

"Don't allow the Colonel to backslide, will you?"

"Oh, he won't now," returned Mr. Hatton. "Good luck, Anne."

Matthew returned presently with the news that Mr. Green, who had been just going home, would remain at his office on purpose to receive him; therefore it was incumbent on us to set off without delay. I went to prepare myself for the expedition, and was, in fact, ready before my old friend, who appeared to be in some slight difficulty with the car. He rejected my offer of help with an irritability which distressed, but in the circumstances did not surprise me, and as he seemed even to resent my looking on, I strolled away to wait for him in front of the house. Curiosity, I must admit, still ruled my inclinations; I still regretted that he had chosen this moment to take me away from Friars Cross, and as I sauntered to and fro my ears and my attention were very much on the alert. But no stir within the house was audible; almost the first sound was that of the car, which drove up to me some minutes later. As I was about to get in, Matthew observed:

"Better make sure there's some water in it. . . . Damn!"

He went off again to remedy this omission. Immediately afterwards I heard rapid steps within, and Mrs. Fairfax, in a voice of intense excitement, called out: "Nicholas!"

"Yes!" said Mr. Hatton, opening the drawing-room door.

As it chanced, I was then very near them, yet not

visible from where they stood. Their next words were spoken lower, but without special precaution, and I had no difficulty in hearing them.

"You *have* had luck, I gather," said Mr. Hatton.

"*Luck?*" she replied. "I wouldn't call it that exactly. But if you go to the housekeeper's room, and look in the shell box on the mantelpiece—it's entitled 'A Present from Margate'—you'll see something that will interest you very much."

The return of Matthew prevented me from hearing more. I now felt it doubly hard to resign myself to departure, and was almost on the point of making some excuse to stay behind; but the awkwardness of such a thing, besides the compassion I sincerely felt for my old friend, rendered it a practical impossibility. I was forced to go; and a moment later we were in parley with the constable at the gate. He made less difficulty than I had expected, though I think he went up to the house afterwards to report our going; but the encounter seemed to exasperate Matthew, whose driving, usually reliable, was now so careless that I could think of nothing but our personal safety all the way to Oxon. We escaped injury, however, and by the time we reached its outskirts he had grown somewhat more composed.

"Perhaps", I observed as we drove along, "it will be better if I am not present at your conversation with Mr. Green. I fear he might consider it irregular. There are a couple of books I should like to inquire about at Marton's, and no doubt I shall think of other things—I should probably not have long to wait for you."

"Just as you like," replied Matthew. "I'll drop you at Marton's, in that case."

He drew up, accordingly, outside the bookseller's, and I alighted.

"I know your habits, Joseph," he called back at parting. "If you don't turn up, I shall take it for granted you're still here."

Marton's bookshop, though an excellent one for a provincial town, had less interest for me at such a moment than his words implied. My own suspense, anxieties and conjectures fully occupied me, and I had wished for solitude only to indulge them in freedom—as for Mr. Green's view of the case, I was sure to learn it presently from my old friend, and I had no urgent curiosity about it. My thoughts turned unceasingly on what I had overheard before leaving Friars Cross: *what* could Mrs. Fairfax have discovered in the housekeeper's room, and why had she been so eager to get rid of Colonel Lawrence? Was it possible that she had really found out something—something that would alter the whole position of affairs? She clearly thought so; the unknown object appeared to have confirmed her theory, whatever that theory might be. I tried to recollect everything she had let fall at various times, but only one distinct idea emerged from the examination: she had been shocked, almost horrified by her own inferences. The more I thought of her manner within the last day or two, the more I was inclined to regard this as unmistakable. It gave me, in turn, a sensation of the keenest dread; but what further enlightenment could be derived from it? Which of the little group now at Friars Cross

would she not be horrified to detect in such a crime?
It was a frightful question—I attempted to dismiss it,
to assure myself that she was probably hunting a false
trail, under the influence of her own heated fancy.
But in that case, nothing stood between Edward and
arrest: was it possible, was it really possible that he
would be convicted? And in this torturing situation,
must I remain utterly inactive? Was there nothing I
could *do*? Such were the reflections that absorbed me as
I ranged among the book-shelves, now and then taking
down a volume and feigning to look into it, yet so fixed
in thought that more than once I came to myself with
a start to find that I had been, perhaps for several
minutes, rigid and unconscious, with my eyes immov-
ably bent on the same page. The people of the shop
were used to me, and left me in peace; but at last I
felt they were bound to observe my agitation. I
hastened, therefore, to complete my real business,
and walked on in the direction of Mr. Green's
office.

I had expected to wait at least another half-hour
for Matthew, and was astonished to meet him on the
way. At a glance I saw that his spirits were greatly
improved.

"Well," he said as I came up to him, "perhaps it's
a bugbear after all; Green seems to think so. He knew
the whole story, of course, only wrong, and he very
amiably says we're not to worry. Upon my soul,
Joseph, there are moments when I feel beyond worry-
ing—when I want nothing but to be left alone. If
only I could have the house to myself for a week—
one week of peace to finish my book and to think of

Charles a little—I'd be prepared to give the rest of my life for it."

"My dear Matthew," said I, "do not talk in that despairing strain. If, as Mr. Hatton thinks, and as you say Mr. Green thinks, the case against Edward is inadequate from a legal point of view, we need only a few weeks of hope and patience, and things will flow in their usual course again. This has been a heavy affliction, but it will not last for ever."

"Charles will still be dead, though," he replied, "and meanwhile we have to go back to that rabble, into that—that infernal whirlpool! Are you in a hurry, Joseph? Do you feel impelled to return to it this minute?"

I was so torn between curiosity and a vague dread that I would have found it difficult to answer truly. I gave, therefore, the answer he clearly desired.

"Very well," said he, "then for God's sake let's prolong the hour of respite; if we're there for dinner it will be time enough. Is there anything else you want to do here?"

On further consideration I could think of nothing.

"What about a glass of sherry, then? It's not bad at the Stag."

"My dear Matthew," I gently objected, "you know I am not in the habit of frequenting public houses. Not, of course, that I look on it as morally wrong; but in one of my profession——"

"Nonsense, Joseph," he replied. "I'm not asking you to *frequent* them, and we must do something."

"If we were to extend our drive——" I ventured to hint.

"And be trailed by a minion of the law. Besides, we should most probably have a smash; I feel quite in the mood for one. Come along, Joseph; there'll be no one in the private bar."

Impressed by this double argument, I gave way. The little room was in fact empty; nevertheless I declined to order anything for myself, for such things are invariably repeated, and I have often known them prove a stumbling-block to the light or maliciously disposed.

"Do you know", I said when we were alone together, "that Mrs. Fairfax believes herself to have solved this dreadful mystery?"

"Ah, yes," said Matthew, "she has a family interest in it, to be sure. And what *is* her solution?"

"Really, I have no idea; but if I understand her, she means to disclose it very shortly."

"Good God!" exclaimed Matthew, "they're all alike. I thought at least Anne had some intelligence."

"You think she is deluding herself?" I asked, rather taken aback.

Matthew did not appear to notice the question.

"But intelligent or not," he went on, "they're all the same. She's not even satisfied with plunging into a flirtation with the first young man she comes across; she must needs look on the whole affair as a potential triumph for her vanity, and prepare to startle us all with her detective genius. Well, well, it's true to type —there's no lunacy like regarding any woman as exceptional."

I could not help suspecting a twofold significance in this outburst. My old friend's affection for Lord

Malvern might naturally dispose him to resent the speed with which Mrs. Fairfax had, as it were, supplied his loss; while, on the other hand, his own liking for Mrs. Fairfax was particular enough to excuse a little harmless jealousy on the occasion. I thought it more tactful not to pursue the subject, and we talked instead of the recent interview with Mr. Green. This appeared to have been, if I may use the expression, rather in the air; but Mr. Green's attitude had been distinctly hopeful, almost confident. The facts were, in his eyes, too equivocal to secure a conviction against anyone.

"Do you know," said Matthew, "I'm sorry for Frampton, idiot though he is. We've all been wishing him hanged, not because we sincerely think him guilty —we don't care a straw about that—but simply as a convenience to the rest of us. He has some reason to complain of the upper classes. Look at the way Lawrence, for instance, goes about devoting him loudly to the gallows; do you think that's the effect of rational conviction? On the contrary, Lawrence hasn't given a serious thought to the subject—and we're all the same. I tell you, Joseph, it ought to call down a judgment on us all; if there were poetic justice in the world, one of *us* would be hanged as a convenience to the guilty person."

"God forbid!" I ejaculated in dismay.

"Oh, I don't say it'll happen—and after all, it would be unfair to hit on Edward; he's the least in fault. Well, well," rising to his feet, "I suppose we'd better go back now."

His driving on the way back was more cautious,

and I felt at liberty to look about me. It was an exquisite evening, warm and tranquil, permeated with that harmony of colour, that especial charm, which is only felt in autumn and towards the close of the day. Banks of white cloud were massing here and there on the horizon, and their full contours gave the landscape a richer, and as it were a final beauty. For Matthew, however, they had a more practical significance.

"The end of the heat wave," he observed as we drove along. "There'll be rain to-night, I dare say."

His words struck a curious chill into my heart; unreasonably enough, I felt them almost as an omen. We two were free as yet, still free, at large in a world immune from the spell that had ensnared our private lives: but second by second we drew nearer Friars Cross, and to what were we returning? What had been done there in our absence? What new horror was to meet us on the threshold?

CHAPTER TWENTY

The Final Blow

Yet I could perceive no visible change in the quiet house as we drew up before the door. All was silence and tranquillity; the noise of our arrival brought no one to greet us, and the pleasant building, more akin to earth than to the inhabitants of earth, seemed, like all around it, to be enjoying the leisurely close of a fine day. Matthew stepped out and glanced at his watch.

"Nearly dinner-time," he said. "I'd better put the car away afterwards."

His last remark had dismayed me without cause; from this, together with the peaceful aspect of the place, I derived a momentary reassurance equally independent of reason. Everything looked as usual, and daily life made its usual claims on us; Matthew himself, despite all that had happened, still thought it important to dress in good time for dinner, and to see that his car was put away at night. Since the normal had so firm a hold even on him, was it not bound very soon to re-establish itself altogether? For a moment the vague possibilities I had been dreading looked like a mere nightmare.

Death by Request

Nevertheless, when, after completing my own briefer toilet, I descended the staircase once more, a feeling of expectancy was strong within me. It seemed to me that on entering the drawing-room I should hear something—I should be confronted with some new development, startling at least, if not terrible; and I actually moved slower, and delayed my entrance, upon that account. It was in vain, however, to put off the evil moment, if I may describe it so; with an effort I overcame this natural shrinking, turned the door handle, and walked into the room.

Mrs. Fairfax was alone in it. She stood erect, looking towards the doorway in a manner which was sufficient evidence of her own nervous state; and her appearance, though more striking and attractive than usual, revived all my earlier foreboding. At first it seemed to me that she had put on mourning for her husband. She wore, in fact, an evening dress of black velvet, in which she looked unwontedly stately and tall; but though the dress itself was very simply cut, and with no touch of colour or ornament, it was relieved by an antique necklace whose red stones disputed my first notion, and showed the appropriate hue of the gown to be an accident. But in her face and manner I could not be similarly mistaken. She was pale with excitement, agitation, suspense, or whatever it might be; and her eyes glittered almost feverishly. Oddly enough, her look and manner suggested to me the phenomenon known as stage fright; I have more than once observed the same appearances, though less marked, in a young curate about to take his first service. The likeness recalled to

294

my mind Matthew's assertion that vanity was the secret spring of her activities; yet I could not look at her closely and believe it possible. She was not self-conscious, as mere stage fright or anxious vanity must have rendered her; the direct gaze she turned on me was so impersonal as to compel the recognition of a crisis in which mere social relations had lost all reality.

"I was expecting you, Mr. Colchester," she said at once. "I want your help."

"If there is anything I can do——" I replied in great and somewhat painful astonishment. "But, my dear Mrs. Fairfax, I entreat you not to keep me in suspense! Have you really made a discovery about this terrible affair? If the announcement of it is to be delayed for any reason, I will not repeat it; but this uncertainty is dreadful to me—I cannot describe to you how dreadful."

"I'm sorry," said Mrs. Fairfax, "I know it must be; but I daren't say anything until I've made a final test. I want——" she hesitated, and for a moment looked confused, "I want to re-create the situation of that night as far as possible—the night of the crime. No one else must know about it—I want everyone to be unconscious. But it can't be arranged without a little help from you, if you don't mind. When the rest of us went to bed that night, you and Matthew sat up playing chess, you remember."

"Of course I remember it," said I. "How can I forget any circumstance of that terrible night? But—excuse me—in what way can it be useful——"

"I can't explain," she interrupted, "but I want to

repeat the whole thing as far as possible. Will you, towards the end of the evening, ask Matthew to have another game of chess?"

"Without explaining my motive?" I said doubtfully.

"Yes, if you don't mind; I want nobody to suspect anything unusual. Of course, I can't go to bed myself, as I did then; but otherwise—— It ought to be before half-past ten that you secede to the library, but we're sure to break up earlier than that. Will you come to my help so far, Mr. Colchester? *I* could make the suggestion, of course, but it would look rather odd."

Her scheme had, to my imagination, something sinister about it; there was nothing I could less have relished than the idea of re-acting that fatal evening, for whatever purpose, and the worse notion that it was in some way a trap for someone made my blood run cold. I could not but hesitate, and at length said:

"Forgive the question—but does Mr. Hatton approve of what you have in mind?"

"Yes, he approves; he's partly responsible for it. Do be quick, Mr. Colchester—someone may interrupt us any minute. You'll propose the game of chess?"

I had no longer a sufficient pretext for refusing, and agreed, though still reluctantly, to do as she wished.

"Thank you," she said, "that's all right, then. But I must tell you—I'm afraid, Mr. Colchester, that when it all comes out you'll have rather a bad shock. I wish it could be avoided—but I'm afraid you must prepare for that. *I* got rather a jar when I first thought of it; Phyllis imagined I was in another fainting fit."

"Good God!" I exclaimed, the occasion she referred to flashing back into my mind, "was it at that time—I implore you, Mrs. Fairfax, in mere humanity——"

How she might have received my appeal I cannot say; for just then Mr. Hatton and Miss Barry, almost at the same moment, entered the room.

The dinner that followed stands out in my recollection with a frightful permanence: horrible to remember, it was almost cheerful. How often since have my very struggles for oblivion revived the image of that little group, serene and unconscious—so they now appear to me—on the brink of the abyss! For once, as though fate had arranged it, everyone was present—even Phyllis had obtained permission to come down; and the news of Mr. Green's hopeful observations had affected the mood of almost all. Colonel Lawrence especially, fresh from his ride, and, as Mrs. Fairfax had prophesied, the better for it, appeared absolutely in high spirits.

"Just what I thought," he remarked with perfect confidence, when Mr. Green's opinion was discussed. "Not the ghost of a case really—all Lockitt's nonsense from the first. Pity if Frampton's to get off scot free, though; a fellow like that oughtn't to be going about. Can't you rope him in somehow, Hatton, eh?"

"I'm afraid not," said Mr. Hatton.

"Let us hope", Matthew put in drily, "that his conscience will be a sufficient punishment."

"Nonsense, Barry," returned the Colonel, taking

this suggestion in good faith, "all nonsense—sounds well, but it's all sentiment, you know. Sort of thing parsons—I beg your pardon, Colchester—" (realizing his own blunder, he grew slightly discomposed) "very natural idea, of course, for an honest man to go about with, but if you'd known as many scoundrels as I have, you'd see that there was nothing in it. Stands to reason there can't be, after all—or what would we need jails for?"

"To terrorize the innocent," said Matthew. "People who've not yet experienced the pangs of conscience, and therefore have nothing but jails to deter them from plunging into crime."

"Nonsense," repeated the Colonel with a perplexed air. "It's not the innocent that commit crimes, you know."

"Very true," agreed Matthew, smiling ironically, "of course, I'd overlooked that fact."

"What do *you* think, Mr. Colchester?" asked Phyllis Winter, blushing, as usual, at the sound of her own voice. "Don't *you* think people suffer when they've done wrong?"

"Some people do, unquestionably," I answered, "though I fear it is also true that the conscience grows blunt with use. But really, Colonel, we are not justified in this assumption that Frampton is the guilty man. According to Mr. Green, there is not even a case against him; and if there were, we ought still to remember that the law supposes every man innocent until his guilt is proved."

"All jargon," replied the Colonel, unabashed. "Doesn't mean anything when you get down to it.

The police don't arrest a man because they suppose him to be innocent."

"Bravo, Lawrence," said Matthew. "You ought to make a practice of solitary rides—they do you good."

"No, no," returned the Colonel modestly. "I don't set up to be a thinker, but common sense—experience of life—that's all that's needed to get a sound view of most things. I said all along, you know——"

"Colonel," said Miss Barry in very distinct tones, "I hear you have been out for a ride. Where did you go?"

The interruption, though hardly a graceful turning of the subject, seemed to me particularly opportune. The Colonel's breezy manner jarred inexpressibly on my own mood of suspense, and to Mrs. Fairfax it was such an evident affliction that I wondered her countenance should escape remark. Mr. Hatton displayed more command of feature, but he joined in the new topic with all the promptness of relief. Indeed we all began to talk hard of local beauty spots, walks and rides in the neighbourhood, the picturesque merits of the county, its relative advantages and disadvantages; and when these subjects failed, Mr. Hatton immediately had recourse to a new safety valve. He introduced a discussion on motoring, at first from the tourist's point of view; this soon led us to cars and motoring in general, and no lack of innocent matter was felt or apprehended from that moment. I do not mean to imply that we were perfectly at ease. We talked with the assiduity and politeness of strangers afraid to let the conversation flag; yet I think most of those present were soothed in the end by their own platitudes, as I had been by Matthew's casual remark before dinner. For myself, I could no longer share this comfort; my fearful anticipations were not for an instant set at rest. I thought incessantly of what was to terminate this placid evening, and wondered, with a kind of incredulity, how we should meet at breakfast the next day—what faces we should show each other. Yet even to me the flow of conversation was not unacceptable; it eased the pangs of anxiety to some extent, and seemed to confer a decency on suspense and terror. The actor before his *début*, the criminal—horrid comparison!—before his trial, must, I thought, find a like half-unreal alleviation in continual talk.

When we returned to the drawing-room, the uncertainty became, not by degrees but all at once, harder to bear. So little now intervened between the present moment and the proposed scene of discovery —the *blow*, as Mrs. Fairfax had warned me it would be—that an hour, perhaps two hours of waiting seemed an age of torment. The company appeared to relax, as it were, and disintegrate with change of place: Edward and Miss Grant withdrew to the far end of the room, Miss Barry established herself at the table with the patchwork bed-cover she was just then engaged on, and Phyllis, sitting down by her, asked to be allowed to help. It formed in itself an agreeable home picture, but it tortured me with the idea that they might very well go on till midnight. The Colonel stood over them, coffee-cup in hand, chatting with Phyllis as a more amenable substitute for her companion. The rest of us, thrown upon each other, found little to say, and after a few minutes Mr. Hatton suggested turning on the wireless. It had not been touched since that night, the last night of his life, when Lord Malvern had obtained so much amusement from it; we all, I think, changed countenance at the recollection, and at first I thought Matthew would say no. He was startled and displeased, unquestionably; but after a second's hesitation he nodded his consent.

It struck me as odd that Mr. Hatton, usually so tactful, and perfectly acquainted with every detail of that fatal evening, should revive the memory of it in this way; and the surprise I felt at his behaviour led me to contemplate another possibility. Mrs. Fairfax had said that the whole evening was to be re-enacted: was this part of her scheme, and had the sinister rehearsal, if I may call it so, begun already? The idea cost me a painful heart-throb; but the more I thought of it, the less I understood how this particular evocation of the past could be of service. Nor did Mr. Hatton treat the machine as Lord Malvern had done. There was now no switching from one station to another; he settled down at once to a concert from Vienna, with at least an appearance of enjoyment, and with the plainest intention of hearing it right through. At the first sounds the Colonel had moved over to us; but finding that music, not mechanics, was in prospect, he sighed, hovered about for some time with a half-hearted show of listening, and at length subsided into *The Times*' crossword puzzle. Nor was it long before Matthew, for very different reasons, broke away. After sitting a few minutes lost in gloomy thought, he started up, and saying in a low voice to me: "I think perhaps it sounds better at a distance," walked out of the room.

"He's not gone to bed already?" inquired Mrs. Fairfax.

"Oh, no," I replied, "that is most unlikely. He has probably gone for a short stroll in the grounds; he often does so after dinner on fine evenings."

She said no more, and tried, I think, to fix her attention on the music; but it was more than either of us had the power to do just then. Presently the Colonel appealed to us, in an undertone, for a suggestion, and within five minutes we were drawn into the sphere of his activity. It was his habit, indeed, when thus occupied, to secure the assistance, if possible, of the whole room, and he himself often did little more than write down the words as he was given them—a share of the work which amused and satisfied him perfectly. On this occasion he had spread his paper on the table opposite Miss Barry, and we gathered round him by degrees, till only Edward and Judith on the one side, and Mr. Hatton on the other, were outside the circle. The business was soon going on briskly enough—always in undertones, in deference to the concert from Vienna. Even Miss Barry, who would never have dreamt of wasting her own time with a crossword puzzle, lent a remarkably attentive ear, and now and then rapped out a suggestion, invariably ingenious, and almost always right. So the minutes went by; the music went on and on; and we pursued our quiet, trivial occupation. The whole scene was domestic and ordinary to a degree that almost shook my faith in any unwonted conclusion of it.

I say *almost,* for one thing incessantly reminded me that my nightmare forebodings were after all closer to the truth. I could not so much as glance at Mrs. Fairfax without an instant revival of conviction, a horrible quickening of my former dread. Not that she behaved oddly, or even, to one not in the secret, looked particularly strange: the Colonel, it is true, rallied her once upon her desperate smoking—all the evening she continued to light one cigarette from another—but she replied without confusion that it stimulated the intelligence. To me, however, her appearance said enough. She was no longer pale, as she had been an hour or two before; her cheeks burned, and her eyes still glittered with painfully repressed anxiety. Again and again, as though by an irresistible attraction, and sometimes even in the act of speaking, she glanced with a casual air towards the clock.

Not very long after Matthew had left us, Edward and Miss Grant in their turn slipped away. Their departure hardly effected a difference in the scene, if not to settle it into a look of even greater permanence: Miss Barry, with her work-basket before her, and her eyes bent upon her task, still presided with dignity at our more frivolous amusement, and the dominant strains of the concert from Vienna appeared likely to go on for ever. But just as all change began to wear the aspect of impossibility, the clock struck ten.

Miss Barry at once took off her spectacles.

"Now, Phyllis," said she, "it's time for you to go to bed."

"Must I, Aunt?" replied Phyllis. "It's quite early."

"It's quite late enough for you. Now, my dear, help me to put these things away, if you please, and we will say good night."

Phyllis obediently gathered together the scraps of material and lozenges of cardboard, and replaced them in the work-basket, while Miss Barry neatly folded up the cover. It was a brief task, but to my feelings they seemed to linger strangely over it. Presently, however, all was done.

"Thank you, my dear," said Miss Barry. "Will you carry the basket upstairs for me?"

Phyllis picked it up, and then at length they bade us good night and left the room. Matters were at least so far advanced: but now what had become of Matthew? Until he appeared, we could only sit and wait for him.

From that moment every second was an age. The spirit had gone out of the crossword puzzle, and the music had become a terrible affliction to my nerves. I think, actually, not many minutes had passed in this way when Mrs. Fairfax turned abruptly upon the young man, and exclaimed in a strained voice:

"Do turn it off!"

He complied immediately, and, strolling over from the window, joined our diminished little group. The Colonel, still entirely absorbed, received him with enthusiasm, and Mr. Hatton himself made a show of entering into the pursuit. But he was clearly thinking only of Mrs. Fairfax, and I saw him give her hand a reassuring pressure when he imagined himself un-observed.

Almost immediately afterwards, as though he had only waited to convince himself that the music was really at an end, Matthew walked in.

"Ah," he observed, glancing at the Colonel's paper, "you're still intellectually employed?"

"Yes—oh, yes," replied the Colonel absently. "Caliban's dam's god?"

"Setebos," returned Matthew. "Joseph, you're not sleepy?"

"Setebos—how do you spell it?" asked the Colonel.

Matthew spelt it for him.

"If you're not," he added, "shall we have a game of chess?"

I positively jumped at these words. Matthew looked surprised.

"What's wrong?" he asked. "Don't you feel well?"

"Yes, yes—quite well," I replied hastily. "A slight twinge of rheumatism, that was all. I should like very much to have a game with you."

"Bad luck," said Matthew sympathetically. "I thought the weather was changing; that's responsible, I dare say. You're sure you wouldn't prefer to go to bed?"

"No," said I, with unspeakable reluctance, "I should never sleep so early—let us have a game, by all means."

The Colonel began to protest against our desertion of him.

"Too bad of you to go off like this," he complained.

"We're just getting to the difficult part. Must finish it to-night, you know."

"Never mind, Colonel," said Mrs. Fairfax, "Nicholas and I will stick to you, at any rate."

This remark puzzled me: surely, I thought, to suit her plan the Colonel, like everyone else, ought to have gone to bed—yet she seemed quite content for him to remain where he was. But I had little time to reflect on this anomaly; Matthew took me by the arm, and I was obliged to accompany him from the drawing-room.

My old friend had been curiously softened by his dark and lonely stroll. Instead of getting out the chess-board at once, he lingered some time at the window, talking of the beauty of the night; then, turning away, he added not uncheerfully:

"It's something to be in a place like this—in spite of what's happened in it. But I'm afraid you must be anxious to get back to your own house, Joseph. I like having you; but that's no reason why I should expect the sacrifice of your whole time."

"Not at all," I replied earnestly, "there are no urgent duties to call me away; and I am only too glad to be of any use or comfort to you."

"Thank you, Joseph; I admit I'd rather not lose you for a while, but I don't want to make myself a burden. After all, the worst of this business is over in a sense—I've no doubt I shall manage to live through it."

So saying, and with a return of his usual offhand manner, he unfolded the chess-board, and began to take the men out of their little box. As he was thus engaged, Mrs. Fairfax and the Colonel unexpectedly entered the room.

"We won't disturb you," said Mrs. Fairfax, "but we want to look up a quotation—I think I know where it's to be found."

"Go ahead," said Matthew. "Shall I get the book for you?"

"No need, thanks," she answered, taking down a volume of Shakespeare, "here it is."

"Turn on the fire if you're cold," said Matthew hospitably. "There are matches behind the clock."

"Thanks awfully—but I'm as warm as possible."

"Why," he observed, scanning her with more attention, "you actually look a bit feverish; how's that?"

"Perhaps *that's* the change of weather," replied Mrs. Fairfax, laughing rather shakily. "I feel quite well."

She sat down at Matthew's desk, and began running through the Shakespeare. Colonel Lawrence had already dropped into an armchair, where he sat motionless and silent, from time to time casting apprehensive and bewildered looks on one or other of us. Clearly the puzzle no longer interested him—he seemed to have forgotten it. What was *he* doing among us? And what did he know or suspect, to look like that?

"There," said Matthew, setting the last man on its place, "your move, Joseph."

Just then Mr. Hatton walked in.

"As everyone has deserted me," said he, "I thought I'd like to watch the game, if you don't mind."

"Oh, not at all," answered Matthew rather drily. "I begin to look upon this as a *salon*. Do you play chess?"

"Very badly," replied Mr. Hatton. "You're sure a spectator doesn't put you out?"

Matthew replied quite untruly in the negative, and again urged me to begin. Compliance was this time unavoidable; I repressed as well as I could all outward sign of discomposure, and did my best to apply some attention to the game. But it could not be; in the opening itself I made a blunder.

"My dear Joseph!" exclaimed Matthew, "are you aware what you're doing?"

"I thought", said Mrs. Fairfax, "that Mr. Colchester always drank milk with his chess. Perhaps he's confused now for the want of it."

"I'm so sorry," said Matthew, "I forgot the milk. Why didn't you remind me, Joseph?"

"Don't trouble," I replied hastily, "it is not that— I am absent-minded this evening, for some reason. If you will allow me to recall that move, I shall try to be more alert in future."

"Certainly," answered Matthew, "but you must have your usual stimulant in any case."

"Really——" I was beginning.

"Nonsense, Joseph; will you ring the bell?"

Thus urged, I stretched out my arm and pressed down the bell handle. The next moment a fierce roaring noise—so it appeared in that unnatural silence —filled the room.

The gas-fire had been suddenly turned on.

No one breathed, I think; we were all suspended in

a kind of horrible eternity. Yet it was only for a flash; an instant later—I must have heard the Colonel shout, and Mrs. Fairfax's book crash on the floor, for I can hear them now with frightful distinctness; but at the time I was aware only of a strange choking sound that came from the lips of my old friend. He had leapt up, and made that one effort to articulate: then all at once he fell forward across the table. Three or four chessmen, dislodged by the impact of his body, rolled upon the floor.

From that point I saw nothing clearly; the whole scene grew blurred, the room—crowded with people, as it dizzily appeared to me—swam before my eyes. Yet I was conscious that Inspector Lockitt had somehow appeared among us; he was leaning over Matthew, and his voice reached me, as from a great distance, and without conveying any precise idea, though I heard him perfectly.

"It's no use," he was saying, "he's quite dead."

CHAPTER TWENTY-ONE

Explanations

The rest of that terrible night is unreal, dreamlike in my memory. I was a witness of all that
was done—indeed none of us, except the Inspector,
went to bed that night, or thought of doing so; but I
was still dazed, and half unable to comprehend what
was passing around me. I think Mr. Hatton from the
first assumed control. It was he who suggested that
the other inmates should be left undisturbed, if possible, until the morning; and it was his presence of
mind which kept the house quiet enough to admit of
such a possibility. He sent Frampton for whisky, and
took it from him at the door of the room, explaining
that Mr. Barry was unwell; he obliged me to swallow
a little of it, and gave the Colonel, who was so
shaken as to seem physically changed, a stiffer dose.
Finally, he undertook to ring up the doctor on the
breakfast-room phone, which would be the least
likely to disturb the house.

Nothing else had been uttered all this time, save
broken phrases, unfinished questions, ejaculations of
horror and dismay. But at last, if my impression be
correct, the Colonel, somewhat revived, grew more

articulate; gripping the Inspector's arm, he urged, he adjured him to say what had happened—what all this could mean.

"I'm sorry, sir," said the Inspector, "I'm afraid it means it was Mr. Barry we've been looking for. It was the bell, you see—that's how he did it, just as you saw to-night. Mr. Hatton'll explain it later—or the lady, sir; I understand she was the first to get hold of the idea."

Colonel Lawrence collapsed into his armchair again without a word.

"You look bad, sir," said the Inspector, not unsympathetically, "and no wonder—it must have been a nasty shock. If I were you, I should have a little more of that whisky."

The Colonel made no answer. When Inspector Lockitt poured some more whisky into his glass, he gulped it down with a muttered word of thanks, and then sat silent, apparently half-stunned, the empty glass resting on his knee.

I pass over the blank interval which followed—it was probably little less than an hour, but it has no content, almost no existence in my recollection. At the end of it the doctor came; Mr. Hatton, I think, met him at the gate and walked up from there with him, lest anyone should hear the car. He had nothing to say which could be news to any of us; Matthew had died of heart failure consequent on shock.

"We can't leave him here," said Mrs. Fairfax suddenly.

I think we had almost all forgotten her. She had been inert, voiceless, in a corner of the room, and looking deathly enough, if my tenuous image is reliable. Now Mr. Hatton went quickly to her, and seemed to be asking how she felt.

"I'm all right," she said impatiently. "Won't you carry him upstairs?"

This was done. Inspector Lockitt, Mr. Hatton and the doctor, in their stocking feet and with infinite precaution, got him at length to his own room. In spite of Mr. Hatton's protests, I accompanied them; and in spite of his protests, I remained there when they went away. All three reasoned and remonstrated, I suppose in kindness; but at length the door quietly shut on them, and I was left alone with my old friend.

Through the dead hours of the night I sat there by his bedside, not knowing how the time passed, not caring what might be done elsewhere in the silent house—scarcely conscious, indeed, that it held any life besides. In the midst of my vigil I heard the rain begin; and I thought of Matthew's prophecy, and of his car standing in the downpour after all. But the deeper thoughts I had must be unwritten; there are some hours of midnight vision which cannot be dragged into the day. I will only say that that night was not long to me; when I perceived a faint lightening in the sky, I was astonished, half incredulous—it seemed time had shrunk, leaving far less than the wonted interspace between eve and morning.

Yet certainly day was at hand—the knowledge broke in upon my meditation, and I felt I could no longer shut out the living world. Going softly into my own room, I washed my face and hands, and made such improvement as I could in my appearance; then, after one last look at what had been my silent companion through the night, I passed slowly along the dark corridor, and descended the stairs again.

In the hall I encountered Mr. Hatton, no longer in evening dress, and looking, though somewhat heavy-eyed, amazingly composed and steady. He greeted me with an appearance of relief.

"We were all anxious about you," he said in a low voice, "and I should have come to *you* in another minute. You must have some coffee; I've just made some."

I followed him to the breakfast-room in silence. Mrs. Fairfax and the Colonel were already there, both, like Mr. Hatton, in morning dress, and seated at the table, which was spread with coffee-cups, bread and butter, and cold ham. Neither, however, appeared to have eaten anything, or to intend it; they looked haggard and weary, and the Colonel in particular had scarcely reacted, I thought, from the first shock. Mrs. Fairfax, in spite of the dark rings under her eyes, was more herself. The dark coat and skirt she was wearing suggested to me that she intended a journey; and immediately afterwards, to my surprise, I observed her hat and gloves lying on the sideboard.

"Yes," she said in answer to my look, "I'm going—almost at once." Then after a pause she added in a changed voice, "I—I'm so sorry, Mr. Colchester."

This was almost too much for my self-command.

"Indeed, Mrs. Fairfax," I just managed to articulate, "I do not blame you for what has happened—I——"

313

Utterance failed me. Mr. Hatton, however, came to my relief.

"Do have some coffee," he said, placing before me a cup he had just poured out. "After all this—Colonel, you must eat something. I'm afraid we haven't an easy day ahead of us, and unless you do——"

In another minute we were all seated at table with a forlorn appearance of composure. The Colonel, after great persuasion, ate a little, and Mr. Hatton made a reasonably good meal. Mrs. Fairfax and I could not attempt to imitate them, but the coffee really did me good, and Mrs. Fairfax, on being questioned, owned that she too felt the better for it.

"I couldn't have got all this without Frampton," said the young man. "He's behaved very well."

"But Miss Barry!" the Colonel burst out, as though he had thought of it for the first time. "What are we to tell Miss Barry when——"

"I'll tell her as little as I can," said Mr. Hatton, "and I think she ought to go home with Phyllis Winter, if it can be arranged. Do *you* think so, Mr. Colchester?"

"Yes, certainly," I replied. "If Miss Barry is willing—no doubt it would be best. But——" with a great effort I forced myself to utter this, "but you cannot leave *us* longer in this terrible uncertainty. How is it possible, conceivable—— Why, Lord Malvern's death ——"

"I can't believe it!" exclaimed the Colonel, striking the table with his fist. "By God, Hatton, I *don't* believe it! Why, we—we're eating his food at this moment!" He pushed back his chair abruptly.

Explanations

"Mrs. Fairfax," said I, "if it is true, as Inspector Lockitt declares, that you first thought of it—will you tell us *why?*"

There was a silence, broken only by the steady plashing of the rain upon the gravel. Then Mrs. Fairfax too pushed back her chair, and said in a low but composed voice:

"Yes, I'll tell you if you like—it's all I can do now to justify myself. At first I was merely puzzled; puzzled by things that didn't seem to worry anyone else. I was puzzled about your geyser, Colonel."

"*Eh?*" said the Colonel with a horrified look.

"Yes—you remember how it exploded that morning. Well, geysers don't explode for no reason, after all. Of course the reason might have been quite unconnected with the crime; but then—a murder by gas, and that explosion, happening almost together. It felt as if they *couldn't* be quite separate things. I found myself trying to work out how the one could possibly involve the other, and the answer when I did get it seemed absurd. It occurred to me—not for ages, I was completely befogged for a long time— that the gas might have been turned on from the *cellar*; from the main tap, that is, which would affect the geyser as well."

"But how——" I was beginning.

"This was it. Suppose someone had turned *off* the main tap earlier in the evening—before dinner—and turned *on* the gas in Charles's room at the same time. Of course there would be no escape of gas there, as the current was off; but the flame of the geyser would go out. Then, if the cellar tap were turned on

315

again at night, Charles's room would fill with gas, and meanwhile the *geyser* would be doing the same. No one re-lit it; it was quietly filling with gas all through the night, and in the morning, when you put a match to it, Colonel, of course it exploded."

"Good God!" said Colonel Lawrence.

"That idea, when it *had* occurred to me, was fearfully convincing—and yet it appeared ridiculous at the same time. *Why* take all that extra trouble? And then the evidence that the gas had been turned on through the wall, from Edward's room; you remember the gap in the bricks between the two fireplaces, and the plaster that had been removed. If the cellar theory was right, that must all have been faked deliberately—why? To incriminate Edward? But Edward had been out for hours that night, and anyone could have gone into his bedroom. Again a lot of apparently quite futile trouble. And yet there *had* been a design of throwing the guilt on Edward; the letter to him about Judith's past proved that. I was *sure* Frampton hadn't written it—I was *sure* it had been destroyed for that reason, to avoid closer scrutiny. How could Frampton have had the folly to write such a letter with Charles still in the house, and threatening to prosecute him for blackmail? What was to prevent him from holding on till Edward and Judith were married, when there would have been some sense in it? But if that letter had been written by the *criminal*, it was easy enough to see why. He was providing Edward with an immediate motive for the crime."

"My God!" I exclaimed, "but have you thought

what that implies? You are suggesting that *Matthew*
——"

With a grave look Mrs. Fairfax interrupted me.

"I told you", she said, "to expect something pretty
awful—and I'm afraid you haven't heard the worst
yet. From that moment I assumed that Edward was
meant to be suspected. But I was still worried about
the locked door. The key might have been taken
before dinner, when Charles's gas was turned on—
always keeping, that is, to my cellar theory. But the
criminal must have gone specially to Charles's room,
some time in the middle of the night; he must have
locked the door then, and after *that* the key had to be
put back in the morning. Why all that risk and
trouble, unless the locked door was *highly* important?
And yet was it? Was it actually done to give a feeble
colour of suicide to the affair? Was it meant against
Edward, to prove that the gas must have been turned
on through the wall? There was no force in that when
anyone could have gone into Edward's room. The
more I thought about all these futilities, the more I
was convinced that something had gone wrong—that
the crime had not been according to plan, somehow.
And then it suddenly occurred to me—what had been
wrong was *Edward's moth-hunt*."

"You mean", I said slowly, "that otherwise——"

"Otherwise he would have been in his room all
night—and Charles's door locked. That was to be
the evidence. We were to think the gas *must* have
been turned on through the wall, and if Edward was
in his bedroom, who else could possibly have done it?
There was no escape for him. And when the crime

was planned, he was *expected* to be in his room. The moth-hunt was a surprise to everyone; he hadn't gone out in the evening since Judith had come. But Charles was leaving the next day, and the murder had to be that night if at all. So the criminal banked on the evidence of motive—he should have trusted it entirely, and not locked the door, but then he had very little time to change his plans."

"The *criminal!*" repeated Colonel Lawrence, in a stupefied voice. "But—but you're talking about *Matthew!*"

"Yes," replied Mrs. Fairfax, "and I have something worse to say. My next idea flashed on me all at once—whoever planned the crime, it was of course not Edward, and it wasn't Frampton; for the criminal wrote that letter to Edward, and Frampton *didn't* write it. Yet Frampton and Edward were the only two people involved who had any motive at all for killing Charles."

"But that is nonsense!" I exclaimed. "It is not possible——"

"Yes," said Mrs. Fairfax. "The real murderer had *no* motive for it—no direct motive. He had no grudge against Charles whatever. It was *Edward* the real murderer was aiming at."

Colonel Lawrence sprang to his feet.

"I won't listen to this!" he exclaimed. "It's lunacy —it's monstrous—I——"

"Sit down, Colonel," Mr. Hatton quietly put in. "You'll disturb the house."

The Colonel dropped on to his chair again heavily, without a word.

Explanations

"I don't know how I first came to suspect— Matthew," resumed Mrs. Fairfax, sighing, and half turning her face from us. "It was against my will— one thing after another came into my mind, all pointing the same way, and I tried to prove to myself that he *couldn't* have done it, and every time—— The first hint of all, I think—the first thing that looked queer to me was a mere trifle—scarcely that, indeed. Do you remember what he said that morning, just after the body had been found?—'And when we have our naked frailties hid'. It startled me at the time, but it was only afterwards—— Why should he have quoted from *that* scene of *Macbeth* just then? Charles's death was supposed to be an accident; no one had thought of anything else. Why did *he* think at once of the finding of Duncan? I told myself it was all nonsense —but then I remembered his remark the night before, about how helpless he was over anything mechanical. He said that *à propos* of the wireless; and I noticed it because it wasn't true. I knew he was quite good about that kind of thing. Could he have had any reason for *wishing* to be thought incompetent?"

"But surely," said I, "it was not on such evidence as that——"

"No, no—that was only the beginning. Afterwards I tried to convince myself that he couldn't have written that letter; that he couldn't have known what was in the blackmailing letters to Judith, or even what they looked like, so that it was impossible for him to write one to Edward in the same strain. But when I came to look into it, he was always the first down in the morning; he was alone in the breakfast-room for hours sometimes. And those letters were conspicuous enough. Everyone noticed them. He'd already seen one addressed to Charles; when the first one came for Judith, wasn't it easy enough to suspect blackmail? They *looked* like it—and he'd heard the stories about Charles and Judith. If he wanted to make sure, there was nothing to prevent him from steaming Judith's letters open; it was safe enough, and he had the spirit lamp at hand. Judith would never notice anything. So far it wasn't impossible to believe him guilty."

"But why should he have done it?" Colonel Lawrence insisted. "Why in God's name should he have done it?"

"Oh, he had motive enough," said Mrs. Fairfax heavily, "or at any rate he thought so. Edward had just inherited a fortune."

"But surely," I exclaimed, "you said he had made a will in Miss Grant's favour! You were convinced of it; and I had some reason for believing the same thing."

"Yes," she replied, "he'd left nearly everything to Judith; but when it came out, it was evident that Matthew had known nothing about it. But there was an earlier will, made almost as soon as he—Edward —was twenty-one. By that Matthew would have got three-quarters of the inheritance—and he *had* heard of that will."

"How do you know?" asked Colonel Lawrence.

"Mr. Green told us—or rather he told Nicholas. Nicholas went to see him one evening after dinner."

"Good God!" said the Colonel, "were you *both* in it all along?"

"Not all along," she replied, "but we found out at last that we were on the same track. Matthew believed he would come into that money on the death of Edward—but what chance was there of Edward dying before him? In any case, the will had been made before Edward's engagement—before he had met Judith; and it was natural he should alter it in her favour. Matthew expected that, though he had no idea it had been done. His only chance of inheriting at all was for Edward to die *very soon after his twenty-fifth birthday*, and, if possible, seriously estranged from Judith Grant. Charles's murder was intended to have both those consequences; the blackmailing letter was to incriminate Edward and to estrange him from Judith at the same time."

"But it's all guesswork!" protested Colonel Lawrence. "It's pure guesswork, Anne—how do you *know*—— Why, good God, you must *prove* a thing like that!"

"There's no alternative," said Mrs. Fairfax. "Judith, who would actually have profited most, is out of the question; she wouldn't have chosen *that* method, even if she had the brains to think it out. And then—if Matthew wrote the letter to Edward, there's no difficulty about how or when it was destroyed. You might have *written* it, Colonel—no, no, I never thought you had, but the others were in your possession, after all. You couldn't have destroyed it that afternoon while Edward was out, for you were out with him; no one was left in the house except Matthew and Miss Barry."

"Look here, Anne," stammered out the Colonel

with a fiery face, "what the devil are you getting at? I hope you're not hinting that *Miss Barry*——"

"No, no—good heavens, no! I meant that precisely because she was out of it, there was only one thing to believe. But the crime itself—I mean the way he turned the gas on—I was in the dark about that still. He *must* have done it while he was sitting in the library with Mr. Colchester—and then I realized why the cellar tap had to be used, and why he had said he didn't understand machinery. Of course he had some mechanical device connecting the main tap with something in the library—a device that could be unobtrusively worked as he sat there. I made sure of his position; I went over all that had happened towards the beginning of the game. And suddenly I thought—of course, *the bell*."

"So that, after all," I said, "it was my hand—— But did this wild—this apparently wild guess really affect you like a piece of solid evidence?"

"Yes," she replied gravely, "as soon as I had worked it out I was convinced by it; that idea cleared up the whole problem. The crime had been prepared on Saturday afternoon, when we were all out, and there was no chance of interruption—for of course Miss Barry sits upstairs. It was then he turned off the cellar tap, and connected the bell with it—that was done with a piece of strong cord. He tied the ends together, weighted the tied end of the loop, and let it down through the bell handle; then in the cellar he slipped one end through the main tap, and re-knotted it. He got hold of some of Edward's pills, and dissolved them in the whisky. Very likely he turned on

Charles's fire at the same time; but about the window I'm not certain. It would be safer not to shut that until Charles had gone down to dinner. And the whole thing was elaborately planned; I think he had even prepared against someone thinking of the cellar tap. You remember how he sent Edward down for wine that evening, and how Edward was longer than usual because he said he'd looked in the wrong place? That would have been suspicious enough, if anyone *had* thought of the cellar; and it left no doubt that Edward had a key. He could very well have gone down again later in the evening, to turn *on* the main tap—he did go down for his lantern, as it happened. Even that stroll in the grounds after dinner may have been premeditated. Charles might have noticed that his window was shut, after all. It was moonlight: if Matthew had glanced up and seen that window open—— It's *possible* that he meant it for a final test—that he might not have ventured to go on. That, of course, *is* only guesswork; but I couldn't hope all the rest was a delusion. And yet God knows I wouldn't have said anything—God knows I didn't want Charles to be *avenged!* Why, that very night he said——" She paused, and then went on more collectedly: "Edward couldn't be allowed to suffer, though. I made up my mind that if Edward was arrested I'd speak out; and to-day—yesterday—I heard he was going to be arrested. I felt I couldn't hang back any longer—in fact, Nicholas would have gone to the Inspector if I hadn't."

"Yes," said Mr. Hatton. "There was nothing else to do."

x*

"But when it came to the point," went on Mrs. Fairfax, "what evidence had I to convince him? There *was* no tangible evidence—except the string. It had been removed from the bell handle; I supposed he'd simply cut it at that end, and pulled it out. And it was natural to think he must have done it at the earliest opportunity: that is, on Sunday evening, when the Inspector had gone. But what had become of the string afterwards? Could he simply have put it in his pocket? It seemed a forlorn hope—but I made up my mind to try what could be done I went to Violet and said I wanted a long piece of cord—that Mr. Barry had had just the thing not long ago, an unusually strong piece, which was what I needed, but he wasn't sure what had become of it; it might have got turned out of his pocket, or perhaps he'd thrown it into the waste-paper basket in his little study. Had Violet come across it by any chance? To my astonishment she remembered it immediately: she'd found a lovely bit of cord on his bedroom mantelpiece a day or two before, and she didn't think he'd want it, so she gave it to Cook, who had a whole box full of string. She described the box to me—I looked in, and *there it was*."

"But—but—" objected the Colonel, "how the devil could you tell——?"

"It was just the right length; and it was knotted in the middle. I thought even the Inspector would take that as proof, and it did startle him; but he'd so made up his mind to Edward that he refused to be convinced. He said the string was our only piece of evidence, and that might be faked, or even accidental.

So I had to try the experiment after all."

"The experiment!" said I. "You mean——"

"I mean the second game of chess," said Mrs. Fairfax. "I'd thought of it as a last chance if no other evidence was forthcoming; he might be surprised into giving himself away. Oh, I know it was horrible; but he *was* guilty—I knew he was guilty—and if Edward —— But it's no good trying to justify myself; it's done now."

"It was as much my doing," said Mr. Hatton.

"Yes, but you didn't know Matthew; and I—— However, it's childish to go back on it; I killed him, and that's that—it seems to make very little difference why. Nicholas and I fixed up the string while you were in Oxon, Mr. Colchester, and the Colonel was out riding. You both saw the rest."

She rose, took her hat from the sideboard, and began to put it on. For a moment there was a dead silence.

"But the Inspector——" I asked at length. "Did he agree to—— Did he know what you intended?"

"Not in detail," replied Mr. Hatton. "He had no responsibility; but I shouldn't think he was really in the dark. He was there, of course; he came in when I did."

"Good God!" I exclaimed, "the folding screen!"

"Yes," said Mrs. Fairfax with great bitterness, "a pleasant detail. Well, I think I may go now. Nicholas is staying to face the situation."

She turned off the electric light and the strange dusk of early morning filled the room. It was still raining in torrents. Through the window, the leaden sky, the sad-looking trees were now quite visible, and there were dimpling pools of water on the gravel sweep.

"Are you going up to town?" I asked—conscious, at the same time, how feeble my question was at such a moment.

"This afternoon; but I have to meet Jane Elliston in the first place. She came down here last night— that is, to Oxon; and I've undertaken to cure her injured vanity, and to show that Charles's deceit was the effect of love. Let me get out of this with one thing to my credit."

She gave a last look at the dreary scene outside, and then turned to Colonel Lawrence.

"Will you drive me in, Colonel?" she asked. "Nicholas may be wanted, and—I'd rather use your car, if you don't mind."

"I doubt if you could start the other," observed Mr. Hatton. "It's been standing outside in all this."

EPILOGUE

A week later Friars Cross was empty. Its shuttered windows looked blankly out over the lawn; its locked gates silently testified that all was over.

Edward had been the last to go. Throughout the intervening days I had seen little of him; but he came down to the Vicarage to say good-bye.

His manner was strange: it made an instantaneous impression on me, and yet I hardly know whether I understood it. He sat three or four minutes in my study, not looking at me, scarcely opening his lips, and my own attempted commonplaces died away unspoken. Then, as I took leave of him at the front door, he averted his eyes and said abruptly:

"Mr. Colchester—I misled you about the sum that was left you in my will."

"Edward!——"

"I meant to change it," he went on, interrupting me. "I always meant to change it, after what I promised you. But the real sum was three hundred pounds—to extend your library."

Not giving me time to answer, he walked off. From the doorway I saw him step into his car.—I saw it in motion.—I watched it turn into the main road and disappear. That was my last glimpse of Edward; the last, as I have no doubt, in this world.

Death by Request

He alone, strange as I feel it, has the least suspicion.
Did Mrs. Fairfax, in her pursuit of Matthew, never
glance for a moment at another possibility? Are Mr.
and Mrs. Hatton, when they look back on the case,
never visited by any doubts? It seems almost incredible to me; but perhaps they, like the Inspector, received Matthew's death as conclusive evidence
against him.

And, indeed, if I were to confess the truth, who, except Edward, would believe me? Since these events I
have lived a solitary life, and my health is, as they
say, quite broken: it is notorious that I have never recovered from the loss of my old friend. If I were now
to relate the whole story, I should no doubt be pitied,
even esteemed the more for a delusion grounded in
moral sensitiveness and extreme tenderness of heart.
For I have always been well thought of by my neigh-
bours, and, I trust, have in some degree earned their
regard. I have spent a lifetime in conscientious labour:
a fixed portion of my stipend has been yearly devoted
to charitable objects: I have heard myself cited as the
type of a mild, benevolent, selfless parish priest. Nor
was I insincere in all this: but how easily we learn to
accept the selflessness of others! Did it occur to no
one that there might be an alloy of human pride in
my almsgiving and my voluntary celibacy, or that I
might sometimes regret both the one and the other? I
lived for a quarter of a century in the same village as
my old friend Matthew Barry, whose tastes and pur-
suits were identical with my own, and whose abilities
were, I may say, not superior: yet no one dreamed of
my contrasting my narrow circumstances with his

wealth and leisure—wealth that seemed to him so little and leisure he had done nothing to deserve. Matthew himself, though greatly attached to me, had no idea of it. Our relative situations were, to him, quite natural: he would have been amazed to learn that they were an exasperation, a constant injury to me. Yet they had long been so by the time Edward Barry came of age.

Mrs. Fairfax must have believed Matthew not attached to Edward, and the idea was natural enough in one so little acquainted with my friend. It was an error; but, on the other hand, Matthew was certainly disappointed in Edward, and too apt to show it. His father's irony and his own rather poor health had had, I think, a depressing effect upon the young man's character; he was awkward in society, and indeed showed on all occasions a sad lack of confidence in his own powers. But the thought of his inheritance was a great comfort to him. Not that he was avaricious, or expensive in his tastes, but in the prospect of independent fortune he felt himself less insignificant: he pleased himself in advance with the good use he would make of it, and with the gratitude of some who had previously undervalued him. As soon as he came of age, he made a will. He was still four years from the enjoyment of his property; this premature disposal of it was therefore absurd enough in itself—a boyish act; and the nature of his bequests was still more laughable. It showed, no doubt, much amiable feeling: but he need scarcely have forestalled his inheritance in order to secure it to a father and aunt who were, in the course of nature, unlikely to profit by his liberality. He dropped a hint of this will before Matthew, but the effect was not what he had doubtless hoped for; Matthew treated the whole subject as a joke, and made it clear that he thought the young man a pretentious simpleton. Then it was that Edward began to insinuate—not directly to Matthew, but through me—his conviction that he would not live to enjoy the inheritance for long.

This idea, even if just, would have been no reason for making a will at twenty-one; he would have nothing to bequeath till four years later. Nor did I believe Edward at all likely to die young. His state of health, though far from satisfactory, was no longer alarming; it seemed to me that with care—and he was very careful—he might well outlive robuster men. But Edward, having once conceived the notion, was extremely loth to let it go. He talked of his own demise with assumed carelessness, and a delightful sense of the pathetic. He cannot, I think, have been perfectly sincere; but I do believe that, in imagination, the prospect of dying young and bequeathing a fortune to cold-hearted relatives had a stronger appeal for him than any prosaic idea of living agreeably upon his money. I pitied him at first; but soon he merely irritated me. Young, independent, certain to be rich, he was for ever calling on me for sympathy, inviting me to compassionate his unhappy lot. He would never allow me to forget the difference in our prospects. Yet for some time I still believed that I was fond of him.

It was his second will which undeceived me on this point. He said nothing of that will to his father; I suppose he was ashamed to, after having made so great a merit of his original bequests. He may have thought, too, that it would aggravate Matthew's strong prejudice against Miss Grant. To me, however, he did hint at it in confidence. I made no attempt to reason with him; he would not have listened, and it was, after all, his own concern. He rewarded my secrecy and apparent acquiescence with obscure promises of advantage to me also from his early death. At first this new intention of his was a mere hint in passing; but before long he was making it a frequent theme. Perhaps he thought I had begun to feel for him too little; he may have designed to revive my flagging sympathy, and to heap coals of fire on my head. Soon he mentioned the precise number of thousands which were to be mine; and when I spoke of the difference in our time of life, a look of great expression was his only answer.

Edward's demands for pity had been provoking enough in the first place; I felt it intolerable that he should, in addition, pose as my benefactor. For it was, I had no doubt, a mere pose; he believed in his own melancholy forebodings less than he had ever done. His engagement had inspired him with new life and hope, but he could not bring himself to renounce the sad dignity of his former attitude. And I was obliged to lend myself to this farce; I was to profess gratitude for a constant reminder of my narrow circumstances and advanced age.

The very fact that I could not hope to profit by his legacy turned my thoughts upon it more and more. I teased myself with reflecting what it would have meant to me: how it would have enabled me to enjoy, at any rate, some years of freedom after a whole life of obscure toil. Next I found myself, to my horror, actually wishing for the death of Edward; until that moment I had continued to imagine that I had a rooted affection for him still. I told myself that he deserved to die young, that it was even his duty to die young: within a week I had begun, and by this time with very little self-reproach, to speculate how his death might be effected.

In short, I was planning Edward's *murder*: but, I thought, as a mere exercise of ingenuity. The idea of gas occurred to me at once; an escape of gas in my own house a week or two before suggested how easily such a thing might be given the appearance of an accident. The obviousness of the *motive* was what staggered me: supposing Edward to perish in that manner *very soon after his twenty-fifth birthday*, might not suspicions arise which in another case would never have presented themselves? Then, when his will came to be examined—— It was not merely that I feared detection: the slightest suspicion was more than I could bear to face. My character in Wampish was the breath of life to me; I could not bear it to suffer after all these years. Yet how could that be avoided, when I should so obviously be a gainer by the death of Edward?

For some time this objection appeared final: I had no doubt that the fact of the legacy would turn all eyes on me. Oddly enough, from first to last I never questioned the *amount* of it; I knew how often vanity or weakness led the young man to pervert the truth, yet I received his word on this point without scrutiny. I had a motive for the crime, and to avoid suspicion I ought to have no motive: was there any means by which these contradictories could be reconciled?

The answer I reached at length shocked me exceedingly—for the first time I viewed myself with loathing. I resolved to banish the whole subject from my mind. Not that, even then, I looked on it as more than a fantastic speculation; but how cold-blooded, how monstrous a speculation I now fully realized. For a long time I maintained this attitude, I kept my vow; for a long time—or was it, in fact, no more than a day or two? At any rate, the result was the same. The new idea, though not dwelt on, grew familiar; its horror insensibly diminished, and I found myself reflecting, as it were in my own justification, that it was not practicable: for how could Edward ever be supposed guilty of another's murder? He had no enemies, his temper was mild, his principles were excellent.

Then I heard of Lord Malvern—and it seemed like a fatality. My idlest theories had become *actual*; I grew disturbed, eager, agitated, as though I had learnt something which concerned me deeply. Yet I had formed no distinct plan, nor even thought of doing so, when one afternoon Milly Baker came to see me.

How can anyone have believed her not in the secret of her lover's attempts at blackmail? It amazes me; and I am scarcely less amazed that no one should have thought of her confiding in me. Mr. Hatton repeatedly remarked on the number of things I *did* hear, yet the possibility of this seems not once to have occurred to him. Milly happened to have brought me a note from Matthew; but she had a more serious errand of her own. She told me the whole story: how Frampton had tried to blackmail Lord Malvern, how he was now trying to blackmail Miss Grant instead. She had known it from the first, and at first, I suspect, she had no strong objections. Frampton had said that, now he had lost his place, he could not afford to marry her without more money: that Lord Malvern deserved to suffer for the attentions he had paid her, and that if she thought otherwise it showed whom she really loved. Milly was eager to escape from the restraint of home—to be married and go off to London, of which she had romantic expectations; she agreed therefore, and, I gathered, willingly enough. But Lord Malvern's rebuff changed her views; she became alarmed, and the attempt on Miss Grant frightened her still more. When Frampton wrote to Miss Grant a second time, she made up her mind to seek counsel on the subject.

Her terrors were my greatest help in all that followed. She made me promise not to repeat what she had told me—not even to Frampton, who was sure to take it very ill. Our interview was to remain a profound secret, and I was never to betray her complicity in Frampton's guilt, if it should come out after all. I agreed to this, but in exchange for a solemn promise on her side: namely, that she would at once put a stop to the whole business. She had only, I pointed out, to threaten her lover with exposure, and he must necessarily give way; and I urged the dangers of his course with so much vigour that she gave the required pledge in tears of fright.

Thus my whole course was, as it were, planned out for me. Milly had actually shown me a rejected version of the second letter to Miss Grant; and she had left an urgent appeal from my old friend to come up to Friars Cross as soon as I was well enough. "We'll have a game of chess," Matthew had written.

I had never yet—not for a moment—abandoned the idea that my schemes for Edward's death were purely speculative, yet I set to work on this one instantly. And all was done as Mrs. Fairfax later reasoned out.

So acute, yet so fatally deceived—so fatally misled by her own acuteness! How could she attach meaning to a chance boast of incompetence—that strange kind of boasting we are all prone to? And the quotation which evidently meant so much to her—how often, during those days, the words of Macbeth himself were in my mind!

> *Had I but died an hour before this chance*
> *I had lived a blessed time—*

If I had uttered them, would the course of her suspicions have been altered? She did not even inquire into the hour of my arrival at Friars Cross; she assumed I had walked up in time for dinner. Yet I had had the afternoon at my disposal—Matthew, of course, was in his study, and Miss Barry always kept to her own room. I knew where to find the cellar key, and it was deliberately that I returned it, not to the same place, but to Edward's pocket—Mrs. Fairfax guessed the reason why. But that Edward should have been still further

335

delayed was a mere accident; I had no idea which wine
Matthew would select, and so, of course, could not
have moved it. I took the key from Lord Malvern's
door at the same time, for fear of having to enter a gas-
filled bedroom for that purpose, and I replaced it the
next morning, when Phyllis Winter's hysteria had
called attention from the immediate scene of the crime.
I knew exactly where Edward kept his morphine pills
—I was not obliged to search his room for them at the
risk of detection, as his father would have been. Moreover, I was precisely informed as to their strength, and
I knew that Edward had just bought a fresh supply.
Every valetudinarian, I suppose, must have a confi-
dant, and I had been Edward's for years past; while
Matthew knew little of his ailments, and nothing at all
of his *régime*. Mrs. Fairfax, I cannot help thinking,
might have guessed as much; but of course it was a
minor point. On the other hand, Matthew's acquaintance with the first blackmailing letters was essential to
her theory, and it amazes me that she should have been
so easily satisfied on that head. How can she have
imagined him steaming them open at the breakfast-
table, on the mere chance of being interested by their
contents? The simplicity of the idea is in strange contrast with her usual readiness of mind.

I must confess that in my calculations I utterly forgot the geyser bathroom; but this omission alone
would scarcely have been fatal. I was wrecked by two
unpredictable accidents—Edward's moth-hunt and
Lord Malvern's visit to his wife. The proposed moth-
hunt was a frightful shock to me. For the time all my
faculties were paralysed; I felt incapable of recon-

sidering my plans. Was it still best to lock the door? Ought that part of the scheme to be given up? Ought the scheme to be abandoned altogether? All I could be sure of was that I was not in a fit state to decide; nay, I could not even concentrate my mind upon the problem. How was I to avoid ringing the library bell that night, or how be sure Matthew would not ring it? Almost in desperation I resolved to rely on Edward's supposed motive, and ignore the change of circumstance.

In the days which followed I scarcely suffered from remorse; but I suffered, none the less, acutely. I had lost all anxiety for the death of Edward, the sole object of my crime: I felt bewildered and dismayed, as though I had committed some fantastic blunder. Matthew's grief and suspense were exquisitely painful to me—I had formed no idea of them beforehand. Moreover, it began to seem as though he could not escape the slow torture of a murder trial, and this, at any rate, I had never meant. I had been sure that Edward, when all hope was lost, would commit suicide; he had the means, he was only too prone to despair, and there seemed to me a kind of justice in it. Too late I saw that this calculation was a blunder; indeed, I now question whether he would have taken his own life in any circumstances.

I had envisaged my own role after the deed as an entirely passive one; but in fact I was harassed continually on every side; fresh decisions were continually demanded of me. My chief anxiety throughout was Milly Baker. I was horribly startled when Mr. Hatton joined me on my way to visit and, if necessary, reassure her; when I look back on that interview, I am terrified by my own boldness. I was bent on obviating in advance any suspicion that I had an understanding with her, but it could be done only by placing myself entirely in her hands. At the time I was on thorns lest she should blurt out the truth to Mr. Hatton: afterwards I lived in dread of her drawing her own conclusions from my strange behaviour. When the letter to Edward began to be understood in its true light, my fears redoubled; but I suppose Milly never heard of its significance, and drew no inferences. One frightful moment she caused me—when I heard that she had come up to the house to make another statement I felt all was lost. I do not believe that she ever suspected me, even at last: whether or not, however, I have long been safe from her. Five months after these events, she died in childbirth.

The confidences I received from all concerned were very awkward; but I attempted to treat them exactly as I should have done had I been innocent. Even Phyllis Winter's revelation, though it shook me horribly, did not, I think, impair my self-command. On a later occasion, indeed, I made a slip which might well have had worse consequences: I was asked if Edward had told me of his second will, and in a moment of panic answered in the negative. I perceived the blunder almost before I had committed it: the lie seemed to me transparent, and it certainly escaped detection by the merest chance.

I grow cold still at the thought of that last evening —it appears incredible that I should have lived through such torture of suspense. And if I had known what was to be the outcome of it—what should I have done? On one point only I cannot forbear to justify myself: when I left the string on my friend's mantelpiece, it was simply to get rid of it—how could I dream of its incriminating Matthew, whom I knew to be almost heartbroken at the young man's death? The bitter irony of his fate haunts me continually: to be supposed guilty of *that* crime, and by Mrs. Fairfax! —and, by his death, to turn suspicion into certainty! Did no one but myself see his last look?

Miss Barry entrusted me with the manuscript of *Theology and Morals in the Greek Drama*; it wanted very little of completion, and I saw it through the press. Its success is known to all educated readers: and I have heard its author compared to Eugène Aram.

Matthew bequeathed Friars Cross to his sister, along with a sum of money sufficient for its upkeep. Edward, being already possessed of a fortune, was passed over, and almost everything else left to me—a legacy much more considerable than I had been brought to expect on Edward's death. I bestowed it all on a hospital in Oxon.

Edward married Miss Grant three days after his parting from me; but they have never returned to Friars Cross. Nor does Miss Barry now live there; except for a week or two in the summer, when a sense of duty, I think, brings her back, the house is shut. I have had full opportunity to realize how much of my own life centred in it, how entirely I depended on it and on its owner for the best pleasures of existence: and, as my renunciation of the legacy has made it impossible for me to try new scenes or make new friends, the change is not likely to grow more bearable with time.

I stand, indeed, higher than ever in the estimation of my little world: I am pitied everywhere for the effect Matthew's death has had upon me, and almost venerated for the use I made of his bequest. I now know the exact measure of happiness to be derived from such regard; yet I must carry the burden to the grave with me. Can I undo my life's work, such as it is? If I were to confess, and be believed, what good would come of it?—my own soul might be at peace, but those around me would set me down simply as a hypocrite, and distrust all religion thenceforward for my sake. It seems part of my punishment to conceal the truth for ever; and yet even here I may be self-deceived. What if this shrinking, in the garb of conscience, is the tempter's doing after all? What if this is the trial which is to decide my fate eternally? I have nothing to do but think of it; and every morning I rise with the decision still unmade.